This book is dedicated to my husband, Chris, who knew I wanted to write it before I did, and who didn't stop asking me, "Did you work on your book today?" until I was hooked on it—even though his preferred recommendation for sections he didn't like was to "nuke it from space."

CHAPTER 1

JEN ADJUSTED THE SCOPE AND peered through the long-range lens, once more searching the sea of faces. Her attention landed on a couple at the center of the action: a brunette in a skin-tight emerald dress stood facing a handsome man in a dark suit. As he leaned toward her, speaking into her ear, a woman with disheveled red hair and smudged eye makeup jabbed him in the shoulder from behind. He straightened and turned, startled, as she flung the contents of her drink in his face and disappeared back into the crowd. While the brunette tore into the dripping-wet man, Jen tilted her head a few degrees, frowning in curiosity before letting her attention wander.

Across the room, her eyes were drawn to another couple. A tall man stood close to a woman in a black cocktail dress, his fingers tangled in her shoulder-length chestnut hair and his face inches from hers. Her back was pressed against the window, accentuating the plunging back of the dress; it dipped lower than any Jen had ever seen. She rolled her eyes. *Definitely designed by a man.* When the man's hand came into view, blatantly groping at the woman's bottom, Jen scanned onward.

It's way too crowded in there. And there's so much touching. A shiver threatened to throw the rifle off balance, but she regained control. While the party was full of interesting characters, the entire thing made her uncomfortable.

Her mark was easy to locate. Fish Lips, as she thought of him, looked exactly like the pictures in his dossier, only slightly less gangster in real life. Maybe a tad chubbier, too.

She checked her watch. Midnight. It was time.

Rolling her shoulders, Jen settled into the stock of the rifle. She took a deep breath and cleared her mind. For a second everything was perfectly still.

Click.

Shattered glass rained down on the partygoers, reflecting flashes of the strobe light all the way to the top of the cathedral ceiling. Murmurs of awe rolled through the crowd, some guests assuming they'd witnessed the release of sparkling confetti or fairy dust, not the splintering of a floor-to-ceiling window. Almost immediately, amazement turned to shrieks of terror.

Panic spread like wildfire through the room, and people surged away from the void where the window had been. The only one in the room not moving was a well-dressed man in an armchair with his back to what was now the open air, the ends of his long, slicked-back hair dancing in the wind. He slumped forward as blood gushed from a bullet hole in the back of his head and his newly disfigured face.

The rhythmic strobe lights flashed and the bass pounded as the crush of terrified guests scrambled toward the only exit, colliding, frantic to escape. With blood running down their glass-peppered faces and arms, some guests looked like they'd been attacked by a wild creature.

Jen gazed across the street at the chaos, imagining the underground tunnels of an ant colony after their anthill had been stepped on: from calm to frantic in seconds flat. So many jobs ended like this.

By the time distraught socialites began streaming out of the tall glass building's street-level doors a minute later, her equipment was already packed. She climbed down the fire escape at the opposite end of the abandoned structure. Releasing her grip on the ladder, she landed safely on the ground several feet below and strode away from the confusion she'd caused.

This had been an average night's work; everything went exactly as planned. Glancing at her digital watch, she noted the date for the first time—two years to the day she'd met up with Brett by the Reflecting Pool in the center of Washington, DC. She'd been numb and desperate that day, and their conversation had altered the course of her life.

"You look like something ran you over. You okay?"

Brett had always been blunt. For over a year he'd been her commanding officer, watching her back but giving her hell. After her mom, he was the person she trusted most. That bond was the only reason she'd agreed to meet him that day, even though she was still reeling from her mother's news.

"Thanks. That's exactly the look I was going for." The words came out more harshly than she'd intended.

He stared at her hard and then used that voice that told her there was no use giving him anything but the truth. "You going to tell me what's wrong?"

She nodded, staring at the ground and numbly reciting the words she still couldn't believe. "My mom has cancer. Stage four. She's been doing chemo and radiation for a year and she never told me. Said she didn't want to worry me while I was out of the country. I found out the day I got back. Last week." Her voice broke at the end, and she bit her lip so hard she wondered if she'd drawn blood.

"Shit. I'm sorry." Normally, his expression gave nothing away, but this time the concern on his face made her look away before she fell apart again.

"Yeah. Now her insurance company says she's almost reached her lifetime maximum coverage. They're not going to pay any more bills." She tried not to glance at him, not wanting him to see that her eyes were glassy with tears. "I can't let her die. I need to find a way to pay for her treatments."

"I don't know much about chemo, but I'm assuming you're talking about a hell of a lot of money."

"Yeah. So far I've struck out."

He nodded sympathetically. "I might know of a job you'd be interested in. You have the right skills. It's why I called you, actually. I wondered if you were looking for work."

"Seriously? What is it? Because I'm interested. My resume isn't getting me anywhere."

There weren't many tourists around at that early hour, but he moved closer to her and lowered his voice to avoid being overheard anyway. "I started a business when I got back. In our first six months, we made three million dollars."

"What kind of business?"

Brett had always been unapologetically loud, and her forehead creased at his sudden show of discretion.

"You and I know all too well . . . too many monsters just roam free out there. Terrorists. Traffickers. Scum of the earth. So I thought, what if we could do something about them?"

"Wasn't that what we were doing in Germany?"

"It was. I guess you could say this is a different way of serving your country."

Her eyes narrowed. "Different how?"

Her father figure and mentor had always been skilled in the art of persuasion, but she saw through the positive spin he gave his business. Yes, the odds were against her, but Jen knew one thing for certain: her mother hadn't raised a vigilante. She knew right from wrong, and what Brett was doing was wrong.

The more thought she'd given his offer that night, the sicker to her stomach she became. He'd been one of the good guys, but now . . .

I was so naïve back then, before I let him pull me down that same path.

In the days following her talk with Brett, she'd found out more about her mother's aggressive and rare form of cancer. The more

Jen learned, the more desperate she became. Her limited options dwindled to nothing. She needed the money for her mom's ongoing treatments, and needed it fast. She had no other option.

Lying in bed two nights after Brett made his pitch, she'd stared at the ceiling, wide awake. A particularly vivid memory of herself at age five sprang to life, as real as if it were happening in front of her.

The thought of monsters hiding in the dark corners of their apartment had terrified her ever since her dad had walked out two months before. Every night before she could go to sleep, she made her mother check every inch of every room, ending with her closet. Her mother went along with it, putting on her purple "monster-hunting hat" and spritzing the darkness randomly from a spray bottle of "monster repellent." Afterwards, she would sit with Jen on her bed and hug her tight, exclaiming, "The only monster here is this cute little one!" Jen would collapse in giggles, satisfied that she was safe.

Smiling in the darkness that night, still reeling from both her mother's admission and Brett's offer, the next memory hit her hard. She'd been six years old when she announced to her mother that from then on, *she* would take over the monster patrols. "I promise to keep us safe, Mommy!" she'd proclaimed. Twenty-eight years later, she still hadn't forgotten that promise. In a way, it was part of the reason she ended up in the Army.

Mom would've slayed monsters for me, and she made sure I always knew it. How can I not do the same for her? She tossed and turned for hours before getting out of bed. Sitting with a pad of paper at her kitchen table, she made a pros and cons list, as she so often did when she was struggling with a decision. Not long before the sun came up, with one short line of text circled in heavy black marker, she crawled back into bed with an aching heart. *Save Mom.* When it came down to it, nothing was more important. That new experimental treatment they'd given her cost a fortune, but for the moment it was working.

The next morning, she called Brett.

"So, did you change your mind?" he asked, skipping past "hello."

"Yeah." She had never hated herself more than she did in that moment, but it had to be done.

Jen pushed the memory of two years ago away. Working for Brett was a necessary evil for which she would never fully forgive herself, even though she'd kept her mother alive. She forced herself to focus on the only thing that mattered—the fact that the job had let her catch up on her mom's medical bills and even put a little aside for the bills yet to come. That was what was important. And her targets were legitimately bad people. Her research had proven it time and time again.

She pulled the elastic out of her hair, releasing the tension in her scalp. Settling the strap of her bag casually over her left shoulder, she melted into the masses who were out and about and enjoying this unseasonably mild early June evening. Her fingers flew across the screen of her burner phone as she walked.

Project completed. Ready for another. She hit *Send* and stuffed the phone in her pocket.

Her stomach rumbled as she approached a street vendor's cart. Smiling sweetly at the tired-looking man inside the tiny window, she paid cash for a bag of potato chips and a diet soda.

It wasn't the life she'd wanted for herself, but it was the one she'd ended up with. She didn't envy the groups of friends or the couples around her as she darted between them, down a side street and then around the next corner, ostensibly stopping to adjust her bag so she could check that she hadn't been followed. At least, she told herself she didn't envy them. Her life was complicated enough as it was.

Despite what seemed like a clean getaway, Jen took the long way back to her hotel, as always. She couldn't be too careful.

CHAPTER 2

JEN SAT FORWARD IN HER chair, her eyes glued to the computer screen even though she knew exactly what would happen next. This episode was her favorite so far, and the comforting background noise of the coffee shop around her melted away.

The small, green numbers of the digital display ticked down without mercy. In only eighty-seven seconds, Agents Cleary and Greene would be out of time.

Sweeping the building had turned up nothing at first, and for a while it appeared that the tip from their reliable source was wrong. But then they'd reached the spacious conference room at the south end of the third floor, where they found enough explosives to bring down a much larger structure and a display informing them that seventeen minutes remained until detonation. While the rest of the team continued clearing the building, the two agents stayed behind to deal with this new problem.

That was now almost sixteen minutes ago.

"How's it going, Mel?"

Agent Melissa Cleary kept her hazel eyes on the task at hand and didn't let the tension in her partner's voice break her concentration.

He always got fidgety as the time ran low. She didn't have to see his expression to know what face he was making—that vein on his forehead would be throbbing in annoyance, his scowl partially hidden behind the dark stubble that matched his brown hair. Adorably annoying.

"You're cutting it too close." His brown eyes bored into her back as if doing so could speed her up. "Come on. Stu and I have basketball tickets for tomorrow night. I'd like to live that long."

When she didn't budge, he tried again. "Don't make me drag you out of here, kicking and screaming. You know I'll do it. I don't care how stubborn you are; we're not going to die here."

"I get the point." She gritted her teeth, making one last, futile attempt to stop the countdown. "And we don't want to disappoint Stu." With an exasperated sigh, she turned away from the complex grid of electronics, rushing for the door as if she'd been the one waiting for him and not the other way around. "Let's go!" He was only one pace behind her as they dashed for the stairwell.

A handful of seconds later, they flew through the emergency exit on the ground level, temporarily blinded by the sunshine. But they weren't safe yet, and they tore across the wide concrete plaza, diving behind a car parked at the curb.

For half a second as they fell toward the ground, the world was silent. Everything moved in slow motion, trapping them in an endless freefall.

The moment Matt and Mel hit the pavement, debris erupted from a fireball that climbed high into the sky. Shards of glass and metal showered the two agents. All they could do was lie motionless and wait for it to stop, pressing closer together. Agent Greene had thrown his arm over his partner's back to shield her from the fallout of the blast, and he left it there even after the air was still once again.

Thick smoke billowed around them, stinging their lungs, and visibility was limited to a few inches. Matt lifted his arm from Mel's back, carefully releasing her. He coughed, cursing under his breath. "How much do you want to bet this is going to end up on the news?"

Her only reply was a loud groan, which made him pause his own self-evaluation and twist around to face her.

"You okay, Mel? You never stay still this long. Or quiet, for that matter."

Groaning again, she shifted before answering. "Shut up. I'm okay." She was already halfway to a sitting position. "I mean, I— OW!" She winced, cradling her right arm.

"What's wrong? Your arm?" He leaned closer.

"Yeah. God, that hurts. Otherwise I'm fine. What about you?" She grimaced as she attempted to sit up the rest of the way without moving her arm.

A gentle breeze was already clearing the air, and the hazy shapes of cars and buildings loomed in the distance. "Diving onto pavement isn't my favorite way to take cover, but I guess it beats getting blown up."

They sat catching their breath, still coughing, taking turns on their radios to try to reach the rest of the team. Their calls yielded nothing but static.

"I'm going to check out the damage. Don't move."

A sudden gust of wind pushed more smoke out of the way, revealing a scene that resembled a postapocalyptic movie. Mel's voice came out as a raspy whisper beside him. "Damn."

"Seriously, sit down for a second."

Agent Cleary scoffed at her partner, already on her feet. "You know me better than that."

Where the building had been, now there was only a mountain of smoking rubble. The cars parked along the curb were burnt-out shells, everything but the frames having melted away like wax.

"If we'd been a little closer . . ." Matt couldn't finish his thought.

Neither of them could tear their eyes away from the remains of the building. "Matthew, tell me they finished evacuating." Mel's ordinarily confident voice trembled, and her attention shifted to him, as if enough intensity would produce the answer she wanted.

"I hope so." He shook his head as he surveyed the damage.

They both heard the sound at the same time—a faint cry in the distance. "Hey, was that . . . ?" He stood straighter.

She squinted hard, moving though she saw no one. "Yeah, I think so." Before he could react, she took off sprinting toward the voice. Any caution she should have shown in the aftermath of an explosion, or even her own injury, had been forgotten.

"For God's sake, woman!" Matt launched himself into the smoke after her, calling as he went. "Mel! Slow the hell down!"

He followed the sound of her coughing. The faint voice was still pleading for help, and it was louder than before. He'd almost caught up with her when—

Jen was yanked out of Matt and Mel's fictional world by a hand on her shoulder. She jumped several inches in her chair, gasping loudly. It was hard to resist her instincts, the urge to grab the hand along with the person it belonged to and flip them to the ground, but she did. She wasn't in danger here, at her favorite café that doubled as her second home, watching last night's episode of *Gemini Divided* for the fifth time.

She swung around in her chair. Her noise-cancelling earbuds helped her concentrate no matter how chatty people around her got, but this time they'd allowed an excited young woman to sneak up on her. This was why Jen sat in or near the corner whenever possible, but those seats had been taken when she arrived.

Tucking her hair behind her ears self-consciously, she removed the tiny but powerful earbuds. The brunette who'd appeared over her shoulder was Layla, one of the waitresses and a fellow fan of *Gemini Divided*.

"Sorry to surprise you. Was that last night's episode?"

"Yeah." Jen's heart rate slowly returned to normal.

"I haven't seen it yet—I had to work late last night. Was it amazing?"

"The best one so far this season."

"That's what everyone's been saying!" The girl bounced on her heels with an elated grin. "Okay, I've got to run. I'm working on Friday, so we can discuss it then. You'll be here, right?"

"I should be," Jen said. With a wave and a swish of her long ponytail, the younger girl was gone.

For a second, Jen stared after her through the glass door, at the lettering that spelled out *Jane's* in black script. Below it, an artistic swirl of lines formed a steaming mug. The café was tucked in the middle of an average city block, between a Chinese restaurant and a dry cleaner, in northwest Washington, DC. It was her happy place.

Her earbuds in place, she was sucked back into her favorite fictional world. When the episode ended, she pulled up the video clip of an interview with the male lead that had aired the evening before. A perky blonde entertainment reporter in a tight blue dress filled the screen.

"I'm here with Will Bryant, star of *Gemini Divided*." As she turned, the camera panned toward a handsome man in a dark-gray hoodie, dark jeans, and a fitted white T-shirt seated beside her. "Will, it's so good to see you again."

"Thanks, Brooke. I'm happy to be back."

"So, what scoop can you give us about the new episode of *Gemini Divided* that your fans will be watching in another few hours?"

His relaxed demeanor said he was at home in front of the camera, and he took his time before answering. The camera now centered on his face, which broke into his trademark boyish grin.

"Well, I can tell you that Agents Greene and Cleary get themselves into a bit of a tight spot tonight, and they make some decisions they may regret."

The woman beamed at him with perfect white teeth, shaking her head and chiding him good-naturedly. "Will, that's not exactly news. I could say that about every single episode."

Will's laugh was infectious, and Jen couldn't keep a straight face. She'd already watched this interview multiple times, but it didn't matter.

"Well, alright, you have a point there. But tonight's episode is going to be even more explosive than usual." He raised his eyebrows and grinned harder.

"In other words, someone's going to try to blow you up again?"

"I'm sorry, that's really all they'll let me say. Except, of course, that I hope you'll watch tonight at ten."

"Wouldn't miss it, Will. Anything else we should know? Where are you and the cast volunteering this month?"

"Thanks for asking. Some of the cast and crew, myself included, will be volunteering and taking donations at the West LA Animal Shelter this Saturday from nine to two. We'd love to see everyone come out."

Brooke turned to the camera, fanning herself with her note cards. "How can you not love this guy?" She shifted her attention back to Will. "Thanks so much for stopping by to tease us and tell us absolutely nothing about what's going to happen on the show tonight."

Will's face lit up once more as he laughed. "My pleasure."

Again smiling into the camera, Brooke said, "Make sure to catch *Gemini Divided* tonight at ten o'clock, right here. In fact, don't change the channel between now and then. Just leave your TV on. Right, Will?" She batted her eyelashes at him as he smiled back at her.

"Absolutely." Shifting his attention to the camera for a final second, he held still until the clip ended.

As the video ended, freezing on his face, the rest of the world reformed around her, and her own grin melted away.

"I brought you more coffee." A waitress set a large mug down and picked up the empty one. When Jen, baffled by her astuteness, opened her mouth to ask how she'd guessed, the young woman added, "You're yawning more than usual today, so I guessed you were up late last night."

The mention of her late night made her yawn again, and she nodded. "Thanks. You know me so well." Jen gave the waitress a grateful smile, shaking off a memory triggered by the observation. It nagged at her from a faraway time and place: *"You look like something ran you over. You okay?"*

She avoided thinking about Brett Kingston whenever possible, and especially about those days when she'd looked up to him. By offering her the job that saved her mother, he had condemned Jen to a life of guilt from which there was no escape.

As the memory faded, she stared into Will Bryant's handsome face on her laptop's background image. Pushing the past back into the box in the corner of her mind, she smiled at him before opening a document she'd been working on earlier.

She'd tuned out the world around her for quite some time when a tingling sensation told her she was being watched. Not wanting to make it obvious that she'd noticed, she glanced toward the door. In her peripheral vision, three young waitresses peered at her, with a young man she'd never seen before standing awkwardly between them. Embarrassed, she did her best to pretend to focus on her laptop.

They were doing it again. Jen loosened one of her earbuds so she could catch what they were saying about her. The young woman spoke softly, but between lipreading and having heard the speech many times before, Jen could fill in what she couldn't quite hear.

"That girl over there by the door—the blonde?"

The new server wore a bewildered expression.

"Her name is Janine Calley, but call her Jen. She's one of our most loyal regulars. Seriously, she's here more than some of the staff, and she's always either writing or watching *Gemini Divided*. She's going to be a famous author one of these days."

Jen's face turned pink. She hated to be the center of attention.

She'd only just recovered from her embarrassment and gotten back to writing when her phone vibrated against the table, and she tensed when she eyed the caller ID. "Hi, Mom. Did you get your test results?" As usual when her mother called, she braced herself for the worst.

"Yes, sweetheart. The tests were negative."

Jen let herself breathe again. There would be more tests, of course, but at least they could rule out the worst for now. As usual, the topic then turned to money.

"Mom, I told you. Don't worry about it. I'll make sure it's paid. You just relax. Remember what your doctor said about stress?"

When her mother tried to press her further, she took proactive measures. "I hate to cut this short, but I have to go. Don't worry about anything. I promise I'll come and visit as soon as I can." That did the trick, as it usually did. "Yes, maybe next weekend." If another job didn't come up before then. "Alright, bye, Mom. I love you." Setting her phone back on the table, she exhaled long and slow. *She's going to be okay.* It was more a pledge to herself than a fact, but it helped.

"So, what are you writing?"

Jen's head jerked up to find that the new server, whose name tag proclaimed him to be *Carter*, had appeared behind her. She shifted in her chair. *Too bad they didn't include that information in their "All About Jen" session and save me the trouble. Maybe I should suggest that for their next one.*

Meeting Carter's curious gaze, she steeled herself. She was almost halfway through her thirties, but answering this particular question transported her back to her awkward middle-school self.

"According to those three, you're here writing all the time. Are you in grad school or something? Are you writing a thesis?"

It would be so easy to say, "Yes, I'm writing a thesis." But it's a stupid thing to lie about.

"No. Actually, there's this TV show—"

Carter didn't wait for her to finish. "No way! You write for a TV show? That's so cool!"

For a second she was thrown off by his interruption. "What? No. I only wish." She took a deep breath. "Actually, I'm a big fan of a TV show called *Gemini Divided,* and I . . ." She winced, forcing the words out. "I make up stories about the characters. It's like writing my own version of the show, I guess. Except . . . for fun. I post it online."

"Oh, you're writing fanfic?" He pronounced the word as if it tasted bad and he was trying not to spread it around in his mouth. His expression had gone from impressed to something more like scorn.

Her cheeks burned, and she wished this conversation could be over. "Yeah."

Carter was solemn. "Jen, no offense, but you're kind of . . . old. I mean, don't you have a job?"

The three waitresses materialized on either side of Carter, glaring at him in unison.

This was one of the reasons she didn't tell anyone what she was writing if it could be avoided. Most people just didn't get it. And she couldn't exactly say, "So, I'm an assassin and I work mostly at night, which is perfect because it leaves my days free to write."

Six eyes blazed at him in indignation on Jen's behalf. Carter turned, understanding only now that he'd made a grave mistake.

Jen couldn't decide if she was more embarrassed or insulted. "Actually, I do have a job. I work from home, and it's flexible. My roommate is annoying, so I like to get out of my apartment, and I end up here." She glanced at each of the waitresses, then back to Carter.

His attention flipped between Jen and the three women whose red aprons matched his own.

"Well, I think it's cool," said one of the waitresses, the flash in her eyes daring Carter to disagree. "Everyone should be lucky enough to have something they love to do, and enough time to do it. I wish I had a hobby I loved that much."

"Sorry," Carter mumbled, ducking his head as he made quick strides on the way to the kitchen.

"So, when are you finally going to write a book?" another waitress asked.

It was the other question she dreaded most, even more than "What are you writing?"

"What? Oh, I mean . . ." Jen paused. "I'd like to, but I haven't come up with an original idea yet."

A family with two small children walked in from the street, the kids barreling ahead of the parents. This was the cue for the three waitresses to get back to work.

"Sorry about Carter. Don't worry. We got your back," one of them said over her shoulder.

"Thanks." Jen ignored a twinge of discomfort. She had their misplaced loyalty because they didn't really know her.

Before she could compose herself, an email notification popped up at the bottom of her screen. The sending account was a random string of numbers and letters ending with *@mail.com*. Anyone else would assume that the email was spam, but that was the point.

A switch flipped inside her, taking her from awkward fangirl to unemotional and all-business in under a second. Jumping from one to the other was second nature.

Another one already, Brett? I haven't even been home twenty-four hours.

The sender had intentionally left the body of the email blank. This was their protocol. Only the timing ever changed.

Checking the numbers in the email address and then her watch, Jen calculated how much time she had. It was time to leave. As she packed up her things, she was already mapping out the route she would take to the drop point, making sure it differed from her last few trips.

"See you later!" she called to the waitresses.

"Leaving already? You'll be here tomorrow, right?" one of them asked.

"That's the plan." With one more "Goodbye," Jen was out the door.

CHAPTER 3

THE DAY HAD STARTED OUT with a perfect blue sky, the temperature hovering around seventy degrees, and the gentlest of breezes. It was the kind of day that made her miss living in the suburbs, back when the most stressful thing she had to worry about was being late for her job as a paralegal. While the job hadn't been right for her, she'd loved the commute—winding along the back roads with the windows open, her hair blowing in the breeze. She tried not to think too much about her old life, before she'd enlisted in the Army and seen so much death, before she'd taken this job that had her eliminating targets. Once upon a time, she'd been a regular person. Looking back now, she cursed the part of her that had insisted she go out and look for something more, something to give her life meaning. That had backfired spectacularly.

The day, like her life, had taken an unexpected turn, and was now unseasonably chilly, with dark clouds hanging heavily in the sky above her. She pulled on her sweatshirt before climbing into her car. She could get to the drop point in under twenty minutes if she had to, but for security, she would take an out-of-the-way route that took at least twice as long.

She arrived one minute early, pulling her black VW Jetta into the parking lot of a run-down shopping center and choosing a space off to the far side, as she did every time—not so far away that she was removed from all other cars, but also not so close as to have an overwhelming number of witnesses, should anything go wrong. As always, Jen remained in her car, rolling down her window a third of the way. The air was still, as if it were holding its breath. She scanned her surroundings, ever watchful for anything or anyone out of place.

Not sixty seconds later, a teenage boy approached her car from the front, his eyes darting nervously to the surrounding cars. It was always a different teenager who brought her a large shipping envelope, the kind used by overnight delivery services. Their words were the same each time, as if someone had provided them the same script to memorize.

"Excuse me, miss? I think you dropped this on the sidewalk back there." He gestured back to the storefronts as she rolled down her window the rest of the way to take the envelope. There were no identifying marks, just plain white cardboard, sealed shut. The protocol for these drops was old fashioned, but it worked—even if it wasn't as glamorous as the movies.

"Thank you."

"You're welcome, miss." His task completed, the boy jogged away.

On her way home via a different but equally indirect route, she pulled into a parking garage attached to a medium-sized office building. Only when she had parked on a deserted floor near the top did she retrieve the envelope from under her seat.

Usually at least a few weeks or more passed in between these jobs. Twenty-four hours was unheard of. As she pulled the single sheet out of the envelope, the air was sucked out of her lungs, and her mouth went dry.

No. Squeezing her eyes shut so hard she saw stars, she counted to ten. *It wasn't him.* But when she opened them and checked again, the same warm, familiar smile and face full of laughter stared back at her.

Will Bryant was her target.

But how?

She didn't like to admit how much time she'd spent reading about him online, rewatching *Gemini Divided*, and imagining what it would be like to be friends with him. Jen knew Will's opinions on the environment (he was passionate about protecting it), education (he'd marched with the teachers in their last strike), and gun control (he was for it), among many other topics. He didn't know she existed, but she knew him better than she knew her own cousins, who she only saw every few years at family reunions. His show had been her escape from the hellish two years of her mom's cancer and the deal with the devil she'd made to pay for the treatments. And now because of that job, she was supposed to kill the man who was the heart of it all.

Outside of work, she was just Jen, a shy, dorky fangirl who'd arranged her nonworking hours around a TV show she loved. Writing fanfiction about the two main characters was her favorite hobby, and because of the nature of her job, she often had days or even weeks off at a time when she could immerse herself in that fictional world. She'd much rather have been a writer than an assassin. If only life had worked out differently.

How could Brett do this to me?

It would be so much easier to blame him, but the truth wormed its way into her thoughts and demanded to be heard. *You have no one to blame for this but yourself.* After all, Brett hadn't forced her to do anything.

Resting her forehead against the steering wheel, Jen could not catch her breath. Her military training meant that normally she could be perfectly objective, logical, and unemotional. It was what allowed her to do her job. But not this time. In that second, the two halves of her double life collided, and she had no idea what to do next.

Her eyes prickled with tears, and it was only with a great deal of effort that her voice finally escaped in a whisper. "Dammit, Will. What the hell did you do?"

CHAPTER 4

JEN DROVE HOME AS IF on autopilot, and when she finally parked near her apartment building, she had no memory of the route she'd taken to get there. Given that she was normally hyper-aware of her surroundings, this was concerning.

After shutting off the engine, she sat perfectly still, holding her keys in her lap with every intention of getting out of the car. Instead, still numb with shock, she listened as the silence roared.

Fumbling with her phone, she typed a message to Brett. She wasn't allowed to text him about work, but what she needed to know required no elaboration.

Why me?

She tapped her fingers against the wheel a few times, taking deep breaths until a text from a new number popped up on her screen. *New burner*, the message read.

Of course he wouldn't reply on his own line.

As for why you—you're the most qualified. You know everything about him. You talked my ear off about Bryant and the show last year, remember?

She did remember. He'd called and interrupted her while she'd been engrossed in writing, and he convinced her to tell him why she was so frantic to hang up. Though she'd felt silly, she trusted him enough to tell him everything.

Yeah. I remember.

That's why I chose you. You got this, kid.

His confidence that she'd be fine with taking the life of an actor she so admired made her nauseous. *What happened to him? And for that matter, what happened to me?* She shoved her phone back in her pocket.

She had two choices. Kill her favorite actor, or refuse her assignment and lose the money that kept her mom alive. *Who knows if he would keep me on after that?*

The voice in her head that made it possible to do her job was calm. *Oh, come on. It's not such a big deal.*

Not a big deal? This is a very big deal!

Don't be so dramatic. He's not a friend of yours. You're just one of his crazy fangirls.

She thought of that pragmatic side of her as Stephanie, the name of her favorite cover identity, which came complete with the highest-quality forged documents: driver's license, credit cards, etc. Stephanie wasn't technically a separate voice in her head—more a way to talk herself into doing what she had to do, a coping mechanism developed since working for Brett. Giving that part of herself a separate name was a way to convince herself that the assassin wasn't the real Jen, even though she knew better.

She'd cried herself to sleep after her first assignment but the next morning gave herself a stern talking-to. Falling apart was no longer an option. The world around her was spinning out of control, and the only thing she could do was decide how to deal with it. She needed the money, so she didn't have the luxury of guilt—she simply turned it off. Yes, it was just as unhealthy as when she'd turned off her feelings years before, after her boyfriend dumped her and confessed that he'd been sleeping with her best friend. She would have to deal with those traumas later. Saving her mother was her only goal now.

It went without saying that she didn't want Will Bryant dead. Having collected every scrap of information about him and his career for several years, Jen was as certain as she could be that Will was a good person; this made him her first target who wasn't some kind of monster. Could Brett have it wrong? He usually sent her criminals, drug-traffickers, the worst of the worst. How could Will possibly be on the list? Surely it was a mistake. She couldn't imagine him getting anything worse than a parking ticket.

Unless everything I know about him is wrong.

As the world faded back in, her focus returned to the envelope on the seat beside her, which she glared at in frustration.

Stephanie's voice was relentless. *So he's not the squeaky-clean TV star you thought he was—so what? Do you have a little crush on him? He is hot, I'll give him that. But neither of those is an excuse not to do your job. You're not paid to judge them. You're paid to follow orders.*

Angry at her own logic, Jen snatched the offending envelope from the seat beside her, folded it, and shoved it into her purse before getting out of the car. Her head pounded as she approached her apartment building. Since she couldn't talk to anyone about her dilemma, she tried to imagine what advice her mother would give her. She came up empty and clasped her hands into fists in frustration.

In her apartment, she locked the door to her room behind her, gritting her teeth as the voice of her ditzy roommate, Summer, and her not officially live-in boyfriend drifted through the paper-thin wall.

Jen sometimes daydreamed about telling Summer to move out. Summer was unreliable and had some truly revolting habits, and Jen hated having to tiptoe around her own home. But splitting the rent left more money available to pay off her mom's bills. For now, at least, having her own space was a luxury she couldn't afford.

Eyeing her purse with hostility, she retrieved the envelope and perched on the edge of her bed. Unfolding it and taking a deep breath, she pulled out the single sheet of paper again. She willed the image to be of anyone else, but there he was again—the handsome face she'd recognize anywhere. It was no mistake. Will was now her target.

I think I'm going to throw up.

The paper fluttered to the ground as her hands flew up to cover her face.

Having TV characters in her life instead of real people was so much less complicated, in the same way that surveilling the party the other night was better than being there. She could observe everyone without running the risk of being the one idiot standing by herself—or worse, having some stranger's hands all over her. TV characters had never taken advantage of her naivety, spread ugly rumors about her, and then lied about it all; only people in her real life had betrayed her that way—specifically Sarah, the woman she'd thought was her friend until Sarah humiliated her. Jen didn't even flinch when she thought back to the night everything had come out in the middle of a crowded bar. No, she was done with real people. Fiction was definitely the better choice. *Gemini Divided* was her escape from reality, and the characters were better friends to her than real people had ever been.

She retrieved the paper from the floor, bile rising in her throat. Looking at the text below the picture for the first time, she found his name and personal information.

William Scott Bryant
Age: 38, Height: 6' 0"
Current Location: Los Angeles, CA.
Occupation: Actor, Gemini Divided.

At the bottom of the page was additional text: *Must appear accidental.*

Being shot by a long-range, high-powered carbine rifle, her favored tool, would never appear accidental. They would expect her to find another way to do it. Something up close. That made it personal, which was even worse.

I can't do this.

Of course you can. It's your job. Enough whining. Shut up and be objective. You've done this plenty of times.

Unable to stare at Will's photo any longer, she folded the paper in half—and then in half two more times for good measure—and placed it deep inside her purse, beneath a hidden flap in the bottom lining. She zipped her purse and hurled it at the empty wall, but it didn't help. All at once her small room threatened to suffocate her. She needed air. Never mind that night was falling—she needed to get out of her apartment. Now.

CHAPTER 5

JEN FLEW BACK AND FORTH on the swing in the tiny playground a few blocks from her apartment, trying to talk herself down. She found swings oddly comforting, maybe because when she was growing up, she and her mom often sat side by side on adjacent swings in their neighborhood playground to talk about everything and nothing.

Start with the basics. What you already know about him.

She began every job this way. As the chilly air rushed past her, the adherence to her usual routine helped her relax, at least a little.

He's one of the lead actors on Gemini Divided. *He's thirty-eight, single, and six feet tall with brown hair and brown eyes. He's originally from Maryland, and he pops up there randomly to visit family when they're not filming. He uses social media a lot, so he's easy to track. Years ago, before he became an actor, he wanted to be a doctor because he wanted to help people.*

But he's an actor. That whole friendly, down-to-earth persona could be a lie. Maybe he never wanted to be a doctor. Maybe he thought it would be good for his image to pretend. If he's as good an actor as you believe he is, you would have no idea.

No. It couldn't all be an act.

Of course it could. Easily. That's his job. He's good at it, isn't he?

She stabbed her shoes into the soft sand, jerking the swing to a stop. Everything he'd said in interviews, everything she knew about him . . . it could all be lies, despite how honest he came across.

But he's not like the rest of them. He's not a monster.

The seed had been planted, and now Jen doubted all her previous assignments as well, even though she'd done her own research on her other marks and confirmed they were monsters. Some had been terrorists. But what if . . . ?

How can I ever be sure about anyone?

She couldn't, of course. She knew that all too well. Though she desperately wanted to believe he was better than that, what she believed wouldn't change anything. The truth was the truth, no matter what.

Frustrated, she walked the swing back and jumped back and up once more, pumping her legs harder and faster than she had in a long time. She needed to get some perspective and stop making it so personal. He was a guy she'd never met. There were two possibilities: either he had a horrible secret, or he was a good person mixed up in something he shouldn't be.

That only happens in movies. The simplest answer is usually the right one.

Unfortunately, what seemed like the simplest answer was the one she didn't want to believe. From now on, he could not be Will Bryant, her celebrity crush—he had to be her mark. Her assignment. Her target. Killing him was her job.

Jen shivered, but not from the wind, dragging her feet to stop the swing. Glancing around, she noted that the sun had set. Only the dim glow of the streetlamps around the park perimeter remained. A sign by the entrance stated that it was closed after dark. Given her job, she avoided law enforcement at all costs, so she stood and walked across the grass.

Lying in bed later that night, her thoughts remained a cyclone of activity.

If I do this, what kind of person will I be?

You've been that person for two years already. Get over it.

If she refused a job, she was just one more person who had more information than they needed. On TV, at least, the people who "knew too much" were always the first ones to die.

It occurred to her then that even if she declined the job, they would send someone else. He was going to die either way.

But that doesn't make it okay for me to do it. Can't I stop it?

No. She had to stop whining about the life she had chosen and do her job. The only alternatives were to let her mom die or let herself drown in medical bills. Neither of those were acceptable.

She finally dropped off for a fitful few hours of confused, blurry dreams, in which she found herself forced to make impossible choice after impossible choice with the sound of her mother's screams featured prominently in the background. It wasn't quite six o'clock yet when she woke up, and for a while she just lay still, catching her breath as she stared at the ceiling. She was disappointed that the answers hadn't come to her in her sleep. Her favorite actor from her favorite TV show was still her target, and she still didn't have any idea what to do about that.

It's my job. It's who I am.

Now fully awake, she showered and got dressed. The apartment was blissfully silent, with no sign of life from behind Summer's bedroom door as she passed. Jen could tell Summer had been cooking again because the kitchen was a disaster zone. The pile of dirty dishes in the sink was tall enough to block the faucet and leaned precariously to one side, each piece encrusted with chunks of leftover food. At least four flies buzzed happily around the pile, and Jen's face twitched in disgust. If she'd had an appetite, she would've lost it.

She backtracked down the hall, collected her purse and laptop from her room, and left her apartment as quickly as possible. She couldn't deal with her roommate's mess—a glaring reminder of the state of her life—on top of everything else.

Five minutes later she pushed open the door to Jane's. Moving straight to her favorite table in the corner, she pretended everything was the same as the last time she'd been there. *If only wanting something badly enough could make it true.*

A waitress arrived with her favorite coffee without her having to ask. She was thankful when the young woman disappeared again without stopping to chat, since she didn't have the energy to pretend she was fine.

For a few seconds, she ignored the world and inhaled the aroma wafting out of the mug, its warmth comforting in her hands. Her muscles relaxed, and the past eighteen hours melted away. It was a temporary fix, however, and all too soon loud laughter from across the room snapped her out of her reverie. She had work to do.

Top-of-the-line security protocols and her own Wi-Fi hotspot made her laptop secure enough that she could browse work-related sites from anywhere. Her only worry was passersby who might happen to look over her shoulder, which was why she preferred the corner table.

She opened a new tab in her computer's web browser, and for the next few hours she did the same research she would've done on any other assignment. The search results numbered far more than usual, thanks to Will's celebrity. Of course, almost none of what Jen found was news to her, so the whole exercise was pointless. More than two hours later, she'd accomplished nothing but making herself sick to her stomach. She was staring at her screen without focusing when an email alert popped up at the bottom. Like the one directing her to the drop point, the sender's email address was a random combination of letters and numbers ending in *@mail.com*. But this email had a subject line—unhelpful though it was. It was simply *FYI*.

The email contained no text, but three PDF documents were attached. As soon as she read the first sentence of the first one, her jaw dropped. Reminding herself she was in public and didn't want to answer nosy questions, she quickly closed her mouth and read from the beginning.

The first PDF was of an email addressed to Stephanie Murray—except she'd never received it. She reread the first few lines, unable to process the words.

Dear Ms. Murray,

Thank you for your interest in working with us here at Gemini Divided.

WHAT?

The fangirl she'd been yesterday would've killed for this job, figuratively speaking. But this was in no way figurative. With a sense of foreboding, she read further.

I enjoyed speaking with you yesterday. Based on a high-level recommendation, we are happy to offer you the position of Personal Assistant to Will Bryant, which will be based here at the studio in Los Angeles. Travel to domestic and international filming locations will also be required.

Please let us know at your earliest convenience if you will be accepting this position. We look forward to meeting you in person.

Sincerely,
Curtis Brown
Staffing, Gemini Divided

Rereading the email twice more, she had more difficulty getting air into her lungs each time. Her wildest dream and her worst nightmare had merged into one.

So this is how I get close to him. They've already set it up. But who did they talk to who pretended to be me?

She clicked the next file with a sense of foreboding and watched the tiny circle in the center of her screen spin as it loaded.

The second document was a reply to the email that had offered her the position, but she hadn't written it. She clicked back to the sent mail folder of her Stephanie Murray email account to be sure. It wasn't there, of course. Someone had spoofed her email address. The sender, whoever they were, had written a short, polite reply accepting the job offer.

She clicked on the third file, which opened a form letter from someone in Staffing, giving details about when and where to report to work. Most notably, the "when" was the following Monday, which left her four days to get to California.

Her phone buzzed in her pocket, and she dug for it, stiffening when she saw the number on the display. She'd gotten enough distressing calls from that area code in recent years to recognize it, so she took a deep breath and answered.

"Ms. Calley, this is Dr.—" The line crackled, and the name was swallowed as the female voice continued. "I'm here with your mother. She asked me to call and explain what's going on. She came in today with a high fever, and given her history . . ."

Jen couldn't process the doctor's words. Her mother had just had a perfectly clean scan. *Please don't let her be sick again.*

Her teeth clenched so hard her jaw ached, and she got off the phone with the doctor without any real answers. Never mind any doubts about her assignment. She had to do this.

Her head hurt.

Two different paths opened in her mind. At the end of the first, she saw herself leaning over Will's unmoving body to check his pulse, then darting away. At the end of the second, she saw the two of them being chased by a group of men wearing black and carrying heavy guns with silencers. She pushed Will roughly around a corner in front of her, then turned to take a stand as more and more well-armed men converged on her. It was bad enough that she saw herself falling to the ground, but then a flash of her mother in a hospital bed appeared, her eyes closed and a solid line on her heart monitor, one never-ending note droning louder and louder.

Sacrificing Will was unavoidable.

With shaking fingers Jen exited all the tabs on her browser, her eyes widening in alarm when Will Bryant stared back at her from the laptop wallpaper. She opened a blank Word document to block out the image. Only then could she breathe normally.

I guess I need to make a list, because I need to be in California by Monday morning.

Stephanie nodded approvingly. *Good girl. I knew you'd come around.*

CHAPTER 6

OVER THE NEXT FEW DAYS, Jen quieted her inner turmoil. Her mom depended on her, and nothing else mattered.

Sunday morning came far too soon, and she squinted against the bright sunshine on her way to the airport. She never walked into assignments blind, and yet that was exactly what she was doing. A voice whispered to her to question her actions. She ignored it.

Past the TSA checkpoint, she stood before the departures board, coffee in hand. The rote actions helped her forget what she was doing. Almost.

At her gate's waiting area, she pretended her layover destination of Chicago was her final destination, and that she had an exciting reason for going there. *A black-tie event. A reunion with an old friend. A book tour. A romantic weekend.* It was fun to dream.

Glancing around at her fellow passengers, Jen passed the time with a game she'd created long ago, in which she guessed the backstory of those around her. Part of her job was looking for tells—the tiny ways people gave away information about themselves. Even when she didn't need to, she was in the habit of reading people. Halfway through her game, a man raised his head and met her eyes. He was about ten years her senior, with shaggy hair somewhere between brown and blond and a tan that said he spent time outdoors. She kept her expression blank even as he smiled at her, her eyes darting to the man beside him.

Time passed at a crawl, but finally the shrill sound of a microphone being turned on drew her attention. At the podium, a tall woman with dark curly hair was making announcements about the flight. Jen stood along with the first boarding group, her legs itching to move.

While she waited, she ran through what few details of the job she already had. She was due to report to the studio tomorrow morning at nine. Her contact was Curtis Brown. Hours for the job varied depending on filming schedules, so her exact hours weren't set. She hadn't bothered to read the information about salary more than once, pathetic as it was. It was unlikely she'd be there long enough to draw a paycheck, anyway. In preparation for this assignment, she'd found out as much about Castor & Pollux (C&P) Studios as she could. She'd have liked to pull up building blueprints, but not surprisingly, that information wasn't posted online.

Jen moved to the now half-empty seating area by the window, her eyes darting from the plane to the horizon and then settling on a bird gliding across a cloudless blue sky.

The microphone crackled again, the gate agent called the final boarding group, and the remaining passengers surged forward en masse. Jen joined without pressing, trying to be an unremarkable part of the crowd without giving up more of her personal space than necessary.

Near the back of the plane, she paused beside a teenager in an aisle seat, his earbuds firmly embedded. He stood silently when she pointed to the window, letting her slide past him.

Jen had just buckled her seatbelt when the casually dressed man with shaggy blond-brown hair who'd caught her studying him appeared in the aisle. She turned and pretended to look out the window, hoping he wasn't coming for the empty seat beside her.

No such luck. He addressed the teenager with a hint of a Southern accent. "Excuse me. I have the middle seat."

There was movement to her left as he settled in. She had planned to keep to herself, but in direct violation of her instructions, her head pivoted and her eyes darted up.

Get it together. This assignment has you rattled, but you know how to do this.

As her seatmate beamed at her, the mask of Stephanie Murray smiled back at him. From what little she'd observed about him so far, Jen guessed that this guy was used to getting what he wanted because he was charming—but two could play that game.

Most of the time, being herself was hard. She could never quite shake the feeling she was doing it wrong. Being Stephanie, on the other hand, was a relief. For example, Stephanie could not only talk to people without blushing or being awkward, she could also lie to a complete stranger without a second thought. Jen only wished she could be so confident.

"What a perfect day to fly, isn't it?" He sounded like one of those annoyingly confident guys.

"It is. I hope I get this lucky with this weather for my whole trip."

"Where are you headed?"

"LA."

"What a coincidence. I'm headed there myself. But where are my manners? I'm Adam."

"Stephanie." Jen examined him with a critical eye as she shook the hand he offered.

"Nice to meet you." His attention did not leave her, even after he finished speaking.

"You too."

Adam's exaggerated charm reminded her of something her mom used to tell her when she was a teenager: *"Look out for the boy with the perfect smile. You're not the first girl he's used it on. He thinks it gives him permission to do whatever he wants, and he'll try to get away with a lot. Be smarter than he is."*

Jen held back a wince at the thought of her mother, turning her dismay to a smile. She plucked her water bottle out of the seat pocket in front of her. *If he's one of those guys, then I have a surprise for him. I'm not exactly harmless.*

She purposely ignored him for a few more seconds as he continued watching her. To Jen, this would have been unnerving, but Stephanie turned and stared back at him without blinking, as if a challenge had been issued.

"So, what do you do for a living?"

She had a sudden urge to be brutally honest with him. *I don't do small talk, and I kill people for a living. If you don't want to be next, shut up.*

"Personal assistant. A little bit of everything. What about you?" She tilted her head slightly to show interest, even though she wasn't the least bit curious.

"I'm a personal trainer. It's a good gig. And the best part is, after work, I don't have to go to the gym . . . 'cause I'm already there!" He chuckled while Jen fought the urge to roll her eyes. "So, what's taking you out West? Business or pleasure?"

Again, the brutally honest answer ran through her head.

"Both. I'm meeting a friend to do all the touristy LA stuff, but I also have a new job lined up."

"Nice. Have you been there before?"

Adam had checked his phone a few times since he'd sat down, and had sent at least one text. Ever attentive to details, Jen tried to read it in a nonchalant downward tilt of her head but couldn't get the right angle without being obvious. Now he put his phone away.

"No, it's my first time. I've been reading all about the things to do there. I like research."

As the two-hour flight wore on, Jen tried to deflect his attention, asking Adam all sorts of questions about himself and doing her best to act interested in his responses while keeping her own answers short.

See? This is who you are. Her alter ego's voice stung, and she ignored the shudder in the back of her mind. It hadn't always been who she was, but it was too late to take back the things she'd done.

While it wasn't surprising that they ended up on the same flight from Chicago to LA, Jen was unsettled when they changed planes yet ended up seated next to each other again. *Such a strange coincidence.* She'd reached her limit of Adam's charm. Shortly after they were back in the air, she mumbled something about being tired and leaned against the hard, curved wall beside the window, closing her eyes and pretending to sleep.

They made small talk as they deplaned at LAX, Adam beside her on the jetway, his charming smile wearing on her more and more. She was relieved to continue on without him when he fell behind her at the bottom of the ramp, but it didn't last. He was beside her once again by the time she was halfway up the passage to the terminal.

"Sorry. Work was texting me," he said. "They can't stand to be out of touch for even a few hours." He grinned at his phone as it illuminated again, and they continued into the terminal.

What kind of workout-related emergency requires an immediate call to your personal trainer?

Past the sunny boarding zone and another eager group of travelers waiting to board, they joined the throng in the wide hallway.

"Are you headed to baggage claim?"

She shook her head. "Nope, rental cars. I travel light." She patted the duffle bag hanging from her shoulder as evidence. "I don't like checking bags. Mine always get lost."

"Well, I'm heading to baggage claim, but rental cars are this way, too."

They entered the stream of other travelers, following the overhead signs through the airport until they reached the first giant rotating carousel.

"Well, this is my stop." Adam was as smooth and confident as he'd been since the first word he'd spoken to her. "It's been nice talking to you today."

"Thanks for keeping me company. It was nice to meet you."

He dug his hand into his jacket pocket and pulled out a white business card that was bent at the corners. "If you need anything, give me a call. I'll be here for a few weeks visiting family." He handed her the card, on which stood only his name—Adam Lewis—and below that, a phone number.

"Thanks so much." She had no intention of calling him, but she could be polite.

"I'm serious. If you need anything, don't be shy." Leaning closer, he put one hand lightly on her back in a gesture that resembled a half hug, and kissed her on the cheek.

She stepped back from the unexpected gesture as he straightened. Bidding him goodbye, she strode away, glad to be rid of Adam Lewis. As soon as she turned the next corner, she took off her sweater to check that he hadn't planted a spy device on her back, then laughed at herself when there was nothing there.

With her purse and duffle bag stowed on the passenger seat of her rental car, she sat and drank in the silence of the compact white sedan for a count of five. So far, everything had gone as planned. Even so, the hairs on the back of Jen's neck stood up; she felt like she was being watched, though no one was nearby. Her eyes darted to the rearview mirror, and she gasped to find Stephanie, not Jen, scowling back at her. The difference resided in her cold and menacing stare. Never before had she been afraid of herself, and she forced her eyes away from the mirror with a shiver.

Hey, dream big. Maybe you'll uncover a giant conspiracy, solve the mystery, and the contract on Will's life will be cancelled. You could end up a hero.

But experience had taught her time and time again that assuming the best of people made her naïve at best, and at worst, stupid.

She clenched her fingers around the steering wheel, started the car, and headed out of the parking lot, annoyed at herself. This assignment was already getting to her.

My targets are always bad people. Therefore, Will must be a bad person, too. He hides it better than the others because he's an actor. I need this job too much to start being nosy. Even if I didn't, if I backed out now, I'd be putting myself in danger.

Sighing heavily, she joined the trail of red taillights illuminating the road ahead of her, making her way to her hotel. It was all so simple—as long as she didn't let her mind stray to anything other than her objective.

She was there to kill Will Bryant.

CHAPTER 7

THE SUN WAS MOVING LOWER in the cloudless cerulean sky when Jen pulled into the hotel parking lot. Her seventh-floor room was like any other at a midrange hotel, with one exception. As usual on her jobs, a loaded Glock 17—all black with squared-off sides and the serial number conveniently filed off—had been tucked under the right side of the mattress. A supply of extra ammunition was there, too. How Brett always made it happen was a mystery to her.

This time, beside the gun she found a small, rectangular box with three black prongs sticking off one end, each slightly longer than the last. It was a jammer to block electronic signals—specifically for this job, signals from security cameras.

Holding the gun in front of her, she inspected every inch of the space: opening the closet doors, checking under the bed and in every corner, even pushing back the shower curtain. Satisfied that she was safe, she set the weapon on the nightstand and peeled back the thin bedspread with the tacky floral pattern, tossing it to the floor. She settled under the covers and tried to tune out all the noise in her head.

More than six hours after she'd fallen asleep—though she would've sworn only a few minutes had passed—she sat upright in bed.

What? Where? How?

As the details came back to her, her heart rate slowed. Her limbs, tingling from the leftover adrenaline of momentary panic, were lead weights as she fell back onto the pillow. The only thing left of her dreams was an overwhelming sense of dread. Glancing at the clock beside her bed, she groaned—it was 3:29 a.m. She turned over, hoping to fall back to sleep.

Her thoughts strayed from Will, her target, to *Gemini Divided* as a whole. She knew the main characters better than most people she knew in real life. Matt and Mel led the shadowy Team X, which did not officially exist. Their characters' work relationship was complicated by the fact that they'd been married to each other and then divorced. In their fictional timeline, they'd parted ways six months before they were thrown back together as the pilot episode began.

They immediately regretted the decision to work together. Still, only days into the job, the two learned more about each other than they had in several years of a marriage that had been too full of secrets to work. Little by little, they began to trust each other, admitting that they made a good team. They also discovered that their feelings for each other weren't completely gone, and eventually they fought over who would charge into danger so the other didn't have to.

"You are two of the best," their boss had said in the pilot episode. "And we have a hunch that your history will be a strength, not a weakness."

Two and a half seasons later, Jen had written over a million words of fanfic for the two, putting them in every kind of hazardous situation imaginable. It only made them stronger.

What would they do in my place?

After hours of tossing and turning, the alarm on her phone blared beside her. It was finally 6:30. She was as rested as she was going to get.

She wasn't due at the studio until nine, but in under an hour she was ready to go, and her nerves made her restless. Before she left, she returned her gun to the spot under the mattress. There was no way to know what sort of screening she'd have to go through that day, after all. She grabbed her car keys, her burner phone, and her purse, hanging the do-not-disturb sign to keep the maids out and making sure the door latched securely behind her.

Though this was her first time there, she was too deep in work mode to appreciate her introduction to LA in the daytime. She'd traveled to so many different places while working for Brett that being in a new city had lost its novelty anyway. All that mattered was that according to the GPS, the direct route to the studio would take eighteen minutes with traffic. Needing to kill time, Jen purposely chose a longer and far more congested route.

As she sat in bumper-to-bumper traffic, her mind wandered. Though fuzzy at first, the scene quickly came into focus—she was in the middle of a storm at sea, torrential rain falling on rough, choppy water. The image was so vivid she could smell the salt from the spray, and she shivered from the chill of a blustering wind. A sailboat appeared between the waves, its bright-green sail a lonely spot of color against the dark ocean. It grew nearer, the current pulling it directly toward a wall of jagged rocks. If the boat continued on its current course, it would be smashed to pieces.

As suddenly as it had appeared, the image dissolved before her eyes, leaving her unsettled as she stared into the traffic ahead of her. The symbolism wasn't hard to figure out. She was the boat about to smash into the rocks.

Think of it this way: If Will was the nice guy he wants everyone to believe he is, you wouldn't be here. Either he slept with the wrong person, he stole from the wrong person, he betrayed the wrong person, or he owes money to the wrong person. Basically, he pissed someone off.

The timid fangirl voice spoke up. *Maybe he was just in the wrong place at the wrong time.*

Don't be stupid. He's guilty of something. They're always guilty.

She tried not to let the image of a smiling Will dance before her.

They're always guilty. The sinking feeling eased just as traffic began to move.

At the entrance to C&P Studios, Jen handed the guard Stephanie Murray's ID.

"Good morning." Her expression was the picture of innocence.

The young man in the kiosk consulted a clipboard, compared her face to the picture on her license, and handed it back. "Welcome to C&P Studios. First time here?"

"Yes."

The guard handed her a lanyard with a badge depicting the studio's logo, which prominently featured a sailboat that bore a striking similarity to the one that had popped into her head earlier. On the sail was a drawing of a horse, and above the horse, a field of stars. She slipped the lanyard over her head.

"I just need to search your car. Standard procedures."

"Of course."

"If you could open the doors, the trunk, and the hood for me, please."

She did as he asked and then stood to one side, out of his way. Luckily, she'd been smart enough not to bring anything compromising on her first day.

"How often do you search people's cars?"

"Only for visitors. With an employee badge, it's not necessary." That was exactly the information she needed.

"You're all set," he said as she climbed back in her car. "Now you just go straight back through here to the first stop sign, turn right, and it will be the third building on your left. Number ten. They'll buzz you in and tell you where to go from there."

"Okay, great. Thanks." The long metal arm blocking the road creaked open, and just like that, she drove onto the lot.

A shiny silver sign bearing a large, black *10* stood by the road in front of a nondescript office building that rose five stories. An identical but smaller sign was posted beside the front door. A security guard in the lobby buzzed her in, took her name, and after a short phone call directed her toward the elevator. "Go on up to the fifth floor, and Curtis Brown will meet you there."

As she made her way across the lobby, her fingers clamped around the shoulder strap of her purse. The large metal doors of the elevator heaved apart in slow motion. The moment they closed again, her face relaxed into a blank stare as a faint, petrified voice in the back of her head shrieked, *What are you doing?*

Relax. This job is no different than the others.

The elevator's *ding* brought her back to reality. When the doors parted, they revealed a wide hallway with white walls stretching to her right and left. While to most people it wouldn't have been noteworthy, this was a magical place as far as the fangirl in her was concerned.

Muffled voices echoed from both directions, and a few people walked past her with purpose as she stepped out of the elevator. She made a mental note of the wireless cameras mounted at regular intervals where the walls met the ceiling.

Good. Those will be easy to scramble.

Though her feet were on the floor, she felt like she was floating. A shiny metal sign on the wall in front of her grabbed her attention: *Gemini Divided* was written in the same font as the show credits. Below the show name, arrows pointed the way to various departments and offices.

The comforting numbness that had so far prevented strong emotional response evaporated. Somewhere in the time it had taken her to exit the elevator, an unconscious struggle between Stephanie the assassin and Jen the fangirl had taken place. To the disbelief of both sides, the fangirl seized control without warning and wasn't letting go.

"Stephanie?"

Jen turned at the sound of her name, finding a man with tightly cropped, tight blond curls studying her expectantly. She guessed he wasn't too much older than she was—maybe forty.

"Yes, hi. I'm looking for Curtis Brown."

"That's me. Nice to meet you." She shook the hand he extended. "I'm in charge of your orientation. We have you and one other staff member starting today. She should be here any minute, and then I'll give you both the tour."

"Okay, great."

"You know what? I left something in my office. Hang tight here; I'll be right back." Before she could respond, she was watching him walk away.

Her attention was pulled with magnetic force to the posters on the walls that prominently featured Will Bryant and his co-stars. Any remaining notions of surveillance systems and finding systemic weaknesses that would help her mission flew right out of her head. A thousand-watt grin lit up her whole face, replacing Stephanie's practiced but dead-eyed simper.

Each poster was better than the last. Before she knew it, she'd moved halfway down the hall, in complete sensory overload. She registered the sound of soft laughter, and suddenly Curtis stood nearby, obviously amused. Her face burned, and sweat dripped down her back.

"So, I take it you're a fan of the show?"

"Since the beginning." She turned from red to a deep shade of pink.

"In that case, you're going to enjoy this job." He handed her a folder with the *Gemini Divided* logo on the front. "There you go— our new-employee welcome packet. You're official now. You've got all the basics in there, including your first travel itinerary. The only thing missing is the filming schedule, which is being revised. The new ones will be ready soon. I hope your passport is in order, because you're in the group going to Dublin next week."

"Oh, wow." Jen clenched the folder in her hands as if he'd handed her a winning lottery ticket. In addition to the travel itinerary for the flight to Dublin, the folder contained standard material: information about C&P Studios, several facility maps with varying degrees of detail, a few HR forms to fill out, and *Gemini Divided* promotional materials.

Curtis regarded her with interest. "It seems you come highly recommended by one of our executives."

And just like that, she was no longer conscious of the welcome packet she was holding. She stood perfectly still. Was her cover already blown? An awkward smile froze on her lips. Stephanie's calm was still notably absent—another obstacle she'd never encountered on previous jobs.

"Oh, well, I . . ." A few things clicked into place at that moment. *Someone here got me this job, which means someone here is in on it. Chances are those cameras I want to scramble are already watching me.*

Curtis patted his pockets, at last pulling out his cell phone. "Excuse me, I'm sorry." He lifted the phone to his ear and walked away, giving no indication he'd noticed Jen's sudden awkwardness. "Hey, Shawn." The call lasted only a few seconds before his attention was once again on her. "Our other new employee will be arriving momentarily."

"Great." Jen was relieved that the interruption had changed the subject.

They returned to the elevators just as one of them dinged loudly, and Jen moved back to be out of the way. The petite redhead who emerged would've been at least six inches shorter than Jen if not for the sky-high heels on her strappy sandals, which made up more than half the difference.

Curtis greeted the young woman, who approached him with the confidence of someone who owned the building. The newcomer bothered Jen, but she couldn't place why. Not a hair on the younger woman's head was out of place, but it wasn't her perfect appearance that captured Jen's attention. Not exactly.

Jen's eyes widened in recognition and she shuddered. The cute little redhead would've fit in well at the party where Jen had shot Fish Lips. She could easily imagine this life-sized Barbie hanging out with any of the sleazy guys there.

Just like that, Jen was back on the dark and silent rooftop. In her head, she studied the glass as it shattered into a million pieces in slow motion, shards of the floor-to-ceiling window flying everywhere. Even though she'd been out of earshot that night, the sound thundered in her ears.

Get a grip.

Distracted, she took a step back and bumped into someone behind her. She lost her balance and made a clumsy attempt to catch herself but found nothing to grab.

The only reason she did not end up on the floor was because the person she'd bumped into managed to catch her. She became conscious of hands gripping her arms just below her shoulders—a sensation that made her stiffen. She didn't like anyone inside her personal space.

"Excuse me. Are you alright?"

Though she turned around fully prepared to insist that the person let go of her, she stood frozen in shock. Jen stood face-to-face with none other than the dark-haired, scruffy-faced actor whose career she'd followed with such interest for the past few years: her target, Will Bryant.

CHAPTER 8

WILL GAZED DOWN AT HER with concern, but Jen could only blink. She'd rehearsed this moment but underestimated how intense it would be. Backing into him had not helped. Standing in front of him now, she was zero percent calm, one hundred percent awkward and embarrassed.

"What?" Her mind couldn't process what was happening fast enough. "I'm so sorry. I didn't even . . . That was my fault." Her normally sharp powers of observation were proving useless here, which was a setback she would have to deal with immediately.

His grip loosened; then all at once he let go. "Let me get that for you." He bent down to the floor by their feet, and Jen recognized the papers around her as the scattered contents of her welcome packet. Though she wanted to tell him not to bother, she couldn't form the words fast enough to stop him.

Will stood and handed her the packet. "Here you go. Are you sure you're okay?"

She could only nod in reply. The fangirl grin that she tried not to show in public now spread from ear to ear. Seeing him on TV was one thing, but standing in front of Will Bryant himself was infinitely more powerful.

"Oh, uh, thanks," she said, blushing.

At the same time, he blurted out, "Sorry, I—"

They both stopped, waiting for the other to go on. Will finally spoke. "Okay, let me try again. I'm sorry. I swear I don't usually go around grabbing on to women I've never met." A look of horror came over him. "Uh, or anyone else, for that matter."

The fact that he was embarrassed put her at ease. Not waiting for her to reply, he put out his right hand. "I'm Will."

"Oh, I know who you are." Jen flushed again as she shook his hand. *Did I just say that?* It didn't occur to her that she hadn't introduced herself until he raised his eyebrows at her. "Oh, right, sorry. I'm Stephanie."

As their hands released, alarm spread across his face again. "Please tell me you're not Stephanie Murray, my new assistant."

"I am, actually."

His hand shot to his forehead, and he dragged it down over his face before letting it fall to his side. "And I'm even sorrier now. I mean, I didn't— Not that it would've— I should stop talking now. I'm sorry."

The more uncomfortable he became, the more she relaxed. "Well, in your defense, I was literally falling over, so your reaction was appropriate."

"Will! Stephanie! I see you two have already met." Curtis approached them, grinning broadly.

"Oh, yeah, we just ran into each other." Will delivered this line with a straight face while Jen sputtered with laughter. She bit her lip to hold herself together.

Curtis stepped aside, motioning to the young redhead to join them. "I'd like you both to meet Liz Crenshaw. She'll be working in Hair and Makeup. Liz, this is Stephanie Murray and Will Bryant. Stephanie is Will's new assistant. Today is her first day, too."

Without any acknowledgment of Jen whatsoever, the younger woman walked right up to Will, not stopping until she was inches away from pressing against him.

Meanwhile, Will smiled at Liz as if nothing were amiss.

I'll bet he's used to girls launching themselves at him. Probably happens to him all the time. Though more like the way Little Barbie did it—not so much the way you did.

Jen's face heated up all over again in renewed embarrassment.

Meanwhile, Liz grabbed Will's right hand to shake it before he could offer it to her, the intensity of her gaze bordering on unsettling. He must not have expected that, or the firmness of her handshake, because he glanced down at their hands and raised his eyebrows.

"Mr. Bryant, it's such an honor to meet you. I'm a huge fan of all your work, especially on *Gemini Divided,* and I'm so excited to be here."

A few feet away, Jen's stomach churned. *I'm sure I made an even bigger fool of myself, but this is painful to watch.* She scanned the area, but Curtis was nowhere to be seen. Meanwhile, Liz assaulted Will with compliments.

Is it part of my job as his assistant to protect him from . . . whatever it is she's doing?

She's just hitting on him. It's not as though she's dangerous. Please tell me you do not seriously have the urge to protect him. This chick just wants to . . . well, I'm sure you can use your imagination.

Jen did her best not to use her imagination.

Liz seemed to notice Jen for the first time, sneering at her as if she'd interrupted a private interlude. Icy blue eyes slid from the top of Jen's head all the way down to her shoes and back up, ending with a smirk. Jen's focus darted to Will, who was watching her. By his raised eyebrows, she assumed that he'd observed Liz's silent evaluation of her. Even after Liz reattached herself to him, he watched Jen for several heartbeats before he had no choice but to acknowledge the other woman who was once again in his personal space, peppering him with questions.

"How much of the stunt work do you have to do? Or can you let your double do it all? How many hours a day do you usually film? How many days do you work on an episode before you can let the others finish it up? Do you get days off in between? Is there anyone from the cast that you just don't like? I would never tell anyone, I swear. Do you like Rachel in real life as much as Matt likes Mel on the show? What's she really like?"

With each new question, Jen felt more offended on Will's behalf. *Who does she think she is?* She could only hope that Curtis would be back soon.

For a painfully long time, Jen stood and suffered through the awkwardness. Will, meanwhile, kept his answers brief, stepping back slowly each time Liz stepped forward. For a petite girl, she had a surprisingly large personality.

By the time Curtis finally reappeared, Will had backed up against a wall.

"Alright, sorry about that. I had to take a call."

When Liz ignored Curtis's return in favor of ogling Will, Curtis cleared his throat loudly, and she grudgingly faced him with a pout. From the men's amused reactions, Jen guessed this wasn't the first time an introduction had gone this way.

Oblivious to the friction between the two women, Curtis continued. "I need to take care of a few things that have come up, so, new plan. I'm going to walk Liz down to Hair and Makeup, introduce her to everyone and let her settle in." To Liz, he said, "And if one of them can't give you a tour, we'll do it later today."

"Oh, okay." Liz didn't attempt to hide her disappointment. A vicious glare at Jen made it obvious who she blamed for the situation.

Curtis turned to Will. "Are you on your way to anything right now?"

After checking his watch, Will shook his head. "I'm free for another hour at least, more if they're running late. I'd be happy to show Stephanie around."

"Great. You can orient her better than I can, since she's your assistant. Thanks, Will. Stephanie, it was great to meet you. If you need anything, let me know. My office is just down there, the last door on the right. Oh, and I'm sorry our hallway is so distracting." He winked at her, and she once again turned a dark shade of pink.

"Yes. Thank you so much. It was nice to meet you, too."

"Ready?" Will grinned at her, and she nonchalantly pinched her wrist to prove to herself that this was real. Her reason for being there was all but forgotten.

"Absolutely. Lead the way."

They hadn't gone far before she got the feeling she was being watched. Sure enough, when she turned back over her shoulder, there was Liz, scowling directly at her, ignoring Curtis's attempts to engage her as they waited for the elevator. Jen presented her broadest smirk in return.

Liz is jealous of me. She glanced at Will, ready to pinch herself again.

That's not some kind of personal victory. Don't forget why you're here.

They rounded a corner, and after a quick check behind them, he leaned toward her and spoke in a low voice. "So, Liz is probably around twenty, right? At the risk of sounding like a jerk, between you and me, it's creepy when twenty-year-olds act like that. I could be her father."

Jen couldn't help but smile; Will's unsolicited opinion was a lot like hers.

"Would you say that happens a lot? Twenty-year-olds throwing themselves at you?" She was genuinely curious, but it was also fun to tease him about it.

"Um, if I say yes, and that a lot of them are younger than twenty, do I sound horrible?"

She shook her head at him in pretend disappointment. "It does sound bad."

It should've been hard to know how much to tease him, but not only did she feel like she already knew him, but the glint in his eyes said he had a sense of humor about it. When he stopped and hung his head in pretend shame, raising his eyes slowly with his trademark mischievous grin, she burst out laughing.

Stop it! You're not here to flirt with him.

I . . . wasn't. Was I? I don't think so.

The familiar cool, detached sensation of Stephanie's influence descended upon her once again, displacing the pleasant buzz in her head.

Enough of this nonsense.

Jen swallowed hard and recalibrated her thoughts. Even though she was now looking at Will through the filter of Stephanie, she still didn't see a target. She saw a person—and that was a big problem.

"So, first lesson of the day: no thank you on the aggressive twenty-year-olds. Should I be taking notes?"

Will's mouth opened, but at first no sound came out. He shook his head in disbelief, his eyes dancing with laughter. "Well, that wasn't an official rule or anything, just an observation."

She couldn't help laughing again.

"You're enjoying torturing me, aren't you?" His pretend indignation just made the whole thing better.

"Me?" Jen held her breath in an attempt to stop laughing. "Of course not."

The corners of his mouth turned up, and he stopped in front of a door at the end of the hall on the left, pulling it open and motioning for her to go in ahead of him. "I thought we'd start the tour with something important, like the kitchen. Are you hungry? They've got a ton of snacks in here, and the coffee's good, too."

"This is a tour I already like."

The fact that this job might not be straightforward was unimportant just then, as she beamed back at him, then walked past him into the sunlit kitchen.

CHAPTER 9

JEN AND WILL SAT ACROSS from each other at a square white table, their hands wrapped around oversized mugs of coffee. The window beside them overlooked the rest of the studio lot, a view that would normally have fascinated her, but her attention was fixed on the man in front of her.

"I have to apologize now, before we go any further," he said. "You should know that I've never had an assistant before. No offense, but I've never wanted one. I'm not some diva who needs things done for them. But I was informed that I didn't have a choice anymore, so here we are."

He sipped his coffee, tilting his head to one side as he studied her reaction. Even though she was aware she was being disarmed by his smile, she couldn't stop it—nor did she want to. He was even more charming in person than she'd imagined.

Not sure of the proper response to such a confession, she said simply, "Okay."

"I'm just not sure what I'm supposed to have you do. But don't worry, I'll pick Rachel's brain about what her assistant does. I'm sure you don't want to sit around while I run lines or film or— What?"

"I might as well confess something." Her jaw clenched. This was even harder than telling strangers about writing fanfic, but it was better to infuse truth into her cover where she could. And it wasn't as though she could pretend not to love *Gemini Divided*. "I'm . . . kind of an obsessive fan of the show."

She stared into her coffee and forced herself to continue as her cheeks burned. "And 'obsessive fan' may not be strong enough to describe me. For example, I made books of notes and observations about each episode, one book for each season, complete with transcripts, pictures, and color-coded highlighting. I've seen all the episodes more times than I can count, and I can recite a lot of the dialogue from memory. So you don't have to worry about me being bored, because being here is basically my dream come true. Whatever you need, I'm on it."

Finally tilting her head back up, she braced herself for him to back away from her slowly, as he had from Liz. When she found him still sipping his coffee as if this were all perfectly normal, his eyes sparkling in amusement, she relaxed slightly.

He shrugged. "I'm glad you enjoy it."

"Oh, okay. Good." Of course, Will had no idea that she was far worse than any of the other fans. Even the worst ones only wanted to sleep with him. Guilt gnawed at her, but she forced it into the box in her mind with the rest of the things she couldn't deal with.

Desperate for something else—anything else—to talk about, she wracked her brain.

"Anyway, you must need help with something."

He regarded her hesitantly, as though arguing with himself. "There is one thing that I do need help with, but it's not within an assistant's job description. HR would be furious with me for even bringing it up. And then there's the fact that I just met you. So never mind."

When Will was the awkward one, she could forget her own discomfort. She studied him.

"You're kidding, right?"

"No, I shouldn't even have brought it up." He shook his head. "Forget it."

"Oh no, no way." Her own self-consciousness had been forgotten. "No way are you allowed to build it up like that, whatever it is, and then not tell me. Now spill it." Stephanie's intensity proved to be a major advantage for Jen as she stared him down.

Even when Will finally glanced up at her and his hesitant smile widened, she remained as still as a statue. After half a minute of this, he chuckled quietly and shook his head.

"Okay, okay. You win. I'll tell you. You're pretty intense."

You have no idea.

When he didn't begin right away, she raised her eyebrows.

"Keep in mind that this is a terrible idea, and I'm only telling you because you insisted. In no way am I suggesting that you should do it. You should not do it."

"Stop stalling and tell me." She leaned forward in anticipation.

Will set down his coffee, exhaling loudly. "Okay, so there's these, uh, young women—who may or may not be eighteen—who've started showing up when I go out in public. I don't know if it's a club, or if they know each other, but they have a similar look. They basically act like Liz did by the elevator, sometimes a lot worse." In response to the smile creeping across her face, he shook his head. "I'm not exaggerating."

As amusing as it was, she didn't like where this might be going. "I'm guessing here, but are you asking but not asking for my help dealing with your gang of fourteen-year-old stalkers?" She managed to ask the question without laughing.

For a few seconds he said nothing, and Jen was afraid her joke had gone too far.

"You could call them that, I guess. Anyway, some people say crazy fans are the price of success, but I don't accept that. And yes, I've tried telling them to leave me alone. Let's just say they don't listen too well—and if I react negatively, I'm the asshole making a scene. I don't want to walk around with security everywhere I go. I make it a point not to. What can I say? I'm too old for the bullshit, and I'm willing to try something else if it means they leave me alone."

Now she wished she hadn't teased him. "I'm sorry. That sounds terrible. And you're not old, by the way."

Will pretended to be annoyed with her, but there was a glimmer in his eyes. "You know who says that?" He paused just long enough for her to get curious. "Old people!"

"What did you call me?" She was losing the fight to keep a straight face as the laughter rose inside her. "You haven't even asked me the favor that's so morally questionable you're not allowed to mention it, and I'm already offended!"

Jen hunched over the table, laughing so hard her stomach hurt. When she sat up, slowly regaining control, he was laughing too.

"Thanks," she gasped. "I haven't laughed that hard in as long as I can remember." She tried to be serious. "But I have to say, I'm not sure you're taking the level of my superfandom seriously. I may have more in common with the fourteen-year-old stalkers than you think."

He shook his head. "No, those teenagers throw themselves at me because I'm on TV. You only did it by accident." Stopping so she could absorb his gentle ribbing, he smiled at her.

She cringed at the reminder of her clumsiness. "Maybe it's not only because you're on TV. Maybe they honestly like you. You're okay looking—even if you are old." Again, his mouth sat ajar in surprise. It was all she could do to keep from laughing all over again. "What? You called me old, and I'm younger than you."

"And you think you know how old I am?"

The question was a challenge if ever she'd heard one.

"Of course. Your age is public information, and I'd be a failure as a superfan if I didn't know that much. You're thirty-eight. Don't forget, I've done my research." Pretending to stop and think, she added, "Possibly enough that you should be concerned."

"Well, at least you're honest about it. But I'll tell you a secret. I've actually been dying to tell someone this. You're wrong."

"Wrong about what?" She frowned uneasily. "I get lots of things wrong. That's not a secret."

"My secret is that I'm not thirty-eight. I'm forty-one. It's a funny story."

She was glad to be sitting down then because her muscles went weak. Her reaction wasn't about having his age wrong. This was much bigger than that; this changed everything.

In three years of following him on social media and reading every article about him that she could get her hands on, she had never come across any discrepancy about his age. If she'd gotten something so basic about him wrong, she could be wrong about any of it. Maybe he had a dark secret after all. Maybe he had never been the honest guy he seemed to be. Maybe it was all an act. *Maybe this assignment was not a mistake.*

While the thought of him having a dark secret might make it a little easier on her conscience when it came to killing him, the idea was incredibly . . . disappointing.

First question: Why do you care so much? Second question: Does that mean you'll channel your ridiculous disappointment and do what you're here to do?

Willing herself not to show any outward reaction to Stephanie's words, she waited for him to explain.

"When I was twenty-one, I wanted a certain part in a movie. I wanted it badly. It was a high school drama, and they were only casting teenagers—with no exceptions." He paused, enjoying the memory. "Everything wasn't digital back then, and somehow I convinced my agent to fix all my paperwork. I became a few years younger, got that part, and it was my big break. After that, it was easier to let people continue to believe the information I'd already put out there. Also, I wanted to keep a good relationship with the people responsible for my success. Honestly, I'm not sure how it has slipped through the cracks this long. After all, that was twenty years ago."

So his age is a lie. If he lied about his age, what else did he lie about?

"That has to be the lamest deep-dark secret in Hollywood. You don't have anything better?"

"Nope. No juicy gossip here. I'm about as boring as they come."

"Alright, enough stalling. Tell me the rest already. The favor you told me not to say yes to. You're scared of your fourteen-year-old stalkers. So what?"

He glared at her, but there was laughter behind it, and he fought a smirk. Then, glancing away from her, his words came out faster than they had before, as if he wanted them out and over with.

"So, my sister suggested ever so helpfully that if I went out with someone and brought that someone along to these things, maybe the little groupies would relax. As if that hadn't occurred to me." After staring at the table, he finally peered up at her reluctantly.

"Why don't you? It's simple enough. Though from the sound of it, it may not work."

"But going out with someone I'm not interested in just to get the, uh . . . to get them off my case seems pretty low, though, doesn't it?" he asked. "I don't want to feed into the stereotype about actors."

Please tell me he's not this honest. "Oh, well, yeah. I hadn't thought of it that way." Jen still didn't like where this was headed. She needed to keep herself as low profile as possible, and if her guess was right, the favor he had in mind was very high profile—and she'd unknowingly begged him to ask her. She tried to preemptively steer the conversation away from her.

"So, you want me to find someone to pretend to be your date? Unfortunately, I have no contacts here in LA. I got in last night and I'm staying in a hotel so far, because that's how new I am. You are the only one I've talked to for more than two minutes since I arrived. Well, you and Curtis."

He smiled at her and shook his head. "No, Stephanie. The inappropriate favor that I'm definitely not asking of you was to pretend to be my date tonight when a big group of us goes out to dinner."

CHAPTER 10

JEN STARED BACK AT WILL across the small table, processing what he'd just said. "You want me to pretend to be your date?"

"I did say it was a terrible idea. I'm not actually asking you to do it. Just so we're clear."

Even though she'd seen it coming, when she tried to reply, all that came out was, "I . . ."

Sighing heavily, he turned serious. "I know it sounds ridiculous, but I have to do something. I've tried hiring a security detail, and I hate it. I'm just a guy, not a diplomat or a rock star. I've flat-out refused to let them assign me a detail on set. It's intrusive. I'm not going to have someone following me around, but I also don't want to be the jackass who has to yell at teenagers to leave me alone."

"Wow. Tell me how you really feel." She studied him and smiled, stalling. Obviously, sharing his extra-bright spotlight would be a bad idea. While she had no intention of saying yes, she didn't trust herself to open her mouth just yet, in case "yes" popped out on its own.

I do have to get to know him in order to do my job properly.

Being asked to be Will Bryant's date, real or not, would've been a dream come true last week. But last week was a lifetime ago now. In this week's reality, no matter how much she wanted to accept, it was out of the question. Even though he didn't expect her to say yes, she was determined to convince him that she had a better idea.

The words started flowing. "I see your point, but you don't need the paparazzi frenzy that I assume goes with bringing a date— pretend or otherwise. All you need is to create some uncertainty."

"You have something in mind?"

"Yeah. Similar, but not as complicated," she said. "Think about it. When people are scrutinizing you that carefully, you don't need someone with their hands all over you to make people talk. You show up with someone no one's ever seen before, and that starts rumors. Even without anything really happening. There's no need to make a big deal of it." She paused. "Unless you wanted an excuse for someone to have their hands all over you." Stifling a grin, she raised her eyebrows.

Will rolled his eyes but didn't acknowledge her teasing otherwise. He shook his head. "Didn't we just test that theory by the elevator? I hate to point this out, but you were standing right there when Liz walked up to me. She ignored you. They're at least as bold as she is."

"That's true. But she knew we'd just met, and we weren't out in public. If you show up at dinner with someone, you talk to each other as you walk in, that should be enough. It doesn't have to involve a performance."

"So, you're not against my appalling idea in theory? You just don't like the pretend date part?" His creased forehead suggested that he might be offended. "I'm not that bad of a date."

He probably doesn't get turned down too often.

She chose her words carefully. "The idea isn't as bad as you made it sound. I just don't think it's necessary to go that far. You can keep it simple."

"It's worth a shot. The 'someone' you were talking about was you, right?"

"I guess so."

He broke into a grin. "You'd do it?" Before she could answer, he kept talking. "No pressure. It's still probably a bad idea. Very bad. You know what? Never mind. Don't do it."

I should avoid the spotlight altogether. But then again, I can't learn more about him and find his weaknesses if I'm not with him. Her logic was flawed at best, but she didn't care.

"You're bad at selling this idea, you know that? But yeah. I'll do it." *For recon purposes only.*

Then there was the small matter of the "dinner with the group" part of the outing, which made her cringe inside. She didn't like groups, especially when she didn't know anyone. Things got out of control too fast with that many variables. In her experience, people were not worth the inevitable disappointment.

What did I just agree to?

"Oh, but one thing. I don't really . . . I'm not . . ." She stared into her coffee again, as if it held her confidence. "I'm not good with groups of, you know, people." Her face flushed at how ridiculous she sounded. "You'd probably be better off getting someone else to do it."

I'm Stephanie, not Jen. Stephanie's not the anti-social one. The lines were blurring badly.

"You're kidding, right?" His gaze became increasingly serious. "I may have just met you, but I don't believe that. Between you and Liz, I would pick you, no contest."

His compliment only made her chest ache. *If you only knew.* She released the air in her lungs deliberately, hoping he didn't get any sappier. He was either an even better actor than she'd thought, or he was a truly decent guy. It would be just her luck that the only decent guy she'd encountered in years was one she was assigned to kill.

"Liz was a little pushy," she conceded.

"That might be the understatement of the year."

She chuckled awkwardly.

As her awkwardness faded, she realized she had another problem. "So, what's the dress code tonight? Because most of my clothes are in boxes somewhere. I don't have much to wear."

"I can help you with that. I know exactly the right person for the job. Just give me a minute." He took out his phone and typed rapidly.

I can't believe I'm hanging out with Will Bryant.

Not hanging out with him. Surveilling him.

Finished texting, Will's head snapped back up. "Alright, I've got Erica, Rachel's assistant, on the case. Rachel is willing to donate Erica's time to the cause, so we have a plan."

"Time for what? What plan?"

"You and Erica are going shopping, and she'll help you find something to wear tonight."

Her uncertainty must have shown, because he added, "Don't worry. Erica's great. Rachel has no patience for the fake, LA type, so they interviewed about a hundred people for the job of her assistant last year. Maybe more. Apparently, applicants who are both competent and nice are hard to find in this town."

They veered back to more comfortable small talk, and Jen gradually relaxed. But now she had a new concern, and it wasn't anything to do with Stephanie, or even shopping with Erica. This was worse: in the space of an hour, she'd become aware of a strange new sensation.

That unfamiliar feeling is a connection with another human being. You'll need to get past it.

Five minutes later, a tall, well-dressed brunette in skinny jeans and a flowing purple top appeared in the kitchen, her wrists jingling with bracelets. She smiled brightly as she approached the table where Will and Jen were chatting. "Hey, Will."

"Hey, Erica. Thanks for helping out. This is Stephanie."

"Hi, nice to meet you." Erica extended her hand, which Jen shook with Stephanie's self-assurance. "I'm Erica Conway, Rachel's assistant."

"Nice to meet you, too," said Jen, studying her carefully.

Erica had a warm, friendly air about her, and she made wide gestures with her hands as she spoke, her enthusiasm bubbling over.

"This was not what I expected when I came in this morning. I'm so excited!" Turning to Jen, she added, "Is Will behaving himself today?"

Jen pretended to consider the question. "Well, it's been a rough first day so far."

"I'm sure." They both peered at Will, who stared from one to the other defensively, holding his hands in front of him.

"Hey! What'd I do now?"

"Good question, Will. What did you do?" Erica had a playful glint in her eyes. "You're always starting trouble."

"Erica, how was your hot date on Saturday?" Will shot her a retaliatory smirk, at which Erica rolled her eyes.

"Thank you for reminding me that I'm not going to talk about it."

"He's not coming out tonight so we can meet him? That's disappointing."

Erica shook her head emphatically. "Even if it had gone well, I'm not cruel enough to subject an outsider to this crowd. You just worry about your own dates."

Jen did her best not to laugh, glancing from Will to Erica and back. "Will, if you need a date, I'm sure Liz would go out with you." For Erica's benefit, she added, "She started today in Hair and Makeup. She was hoping to make out with him by the elevators, but Curtis had the nerve to talk to her. Then she tried to shoot lightning at me with her eyes because I got to walk down the hall with him and she didn't."

"Oh, poor Will and his adoring fans." Erica's voice was full of exaggerated sympathy. Will went to the sink to rinse his mug and crossed his arms with a pout. Jen watched, amused, as the other woman strolled over to Will and squeezed her right arm through the crook of his left amicably. His mock annoyance dissipated.

Erica's smile was bright as she bumped her shoulder against his. "Will knows how much I like him. It's just so much fun to tease him, I can't help myself."

Jen's chest ached as she watched the two friends. It had been years since she'd had anything like that. She had too much baggage to trust people, and her job didn't help.

Jen put her mug in the dishwasher and rested against the counter.

The other two were now teasing each other about something she'd missed.

"So, Stephanie, as you can see, he's really terrible." Erica grinned as Will pretended to scowl at her again. "Anyway, I'm ready to go if you are. I just have to grab my purse."

"Sure." Jen retrieved her things from the table and followed the other two into the hall and down to the elevator. Will pulled Erica to the side and spoke quietly with her just far enough away that Jen couldn't hear him. He slipped something into Erica's hand, looking especially pleased with himself, before the pair rejoined her, sharing one more conspiratorial glance.

"I've got you covered—don't worry," said Will.

Her forehead creased. "Meaning?"

"Erica will help you find what you need. It's on me."

"I'll be right back," said Erica.

Jen stared at Will in disbelief, not even noticing the other woman's departure. Though she started to protest, his words came out faster. "Steph, no arguments. It's the least I can do."

All she could do was shake her head. "But—"

"I'm not taking no for an answer."

I've known him for about an hour, and not only are we on a half-name basis, but he's buying me clothes.

"Well, thanks."

"I'd go shopping with you myself if I wasn't stuck here filming. I mean, I wouldn't be any help, but I'd offer my completely useless opinion."

"I'm useless myself when it comes to shopping." Jen imagined how much she would've enjoyed having Will go with them. Before she could stop herself, she added, "Maybe next time."

Excuse me?

She stood in front of the elevator, blushing just like she had when she'd bumped into him in almost the same spot earlier. It had been so easy to talk to him in the kitchen, but once again she'd lost the power to form intelligent sentences.

"You can still change your mind about tonight. If you want to. I mean, Erica's not wrong. I'm terrible."

"Shut up, she obviously adores you." Color flooded Jen's face. *I just told Will—my new boss—to shut up.*

He just shrugged, as if he had no idea what Erica thought of him. "Some actors give the rest of us a bad name, but I try not to be one of them. Sure, I've been called obnoxious. Hardheaded. Stubborn. Maybe I am, a little." He rolled his eyes. "I do have a bad temper sometimes. That I can admit."

A shadow crossed his face, but it disappeared just as quickly as it had come. "And I admit that I leave dirty clothes on the floor. I've been accused of eating the last Oreo, more than once, though I continue to maintain that I was framed . . ."

With every word out of his mouth, the reason she was standing here with him became more and more of a distant memory.

"Those sound like reasonable flaws, especially the last one. It's impossible to leave the last Oreo. That's common knowledge."

He shook his head. "I told you, I was framed."

"Either way, I don't mind helping you out. If walking into the restaurant with you is helpful, well, that's one of the easier favors I've ever done for someone."

"You sure you don't want to pretend to be my date? I'm not as bad as Erica makes me sound."

I want to say yes more than anything I've ever wanted in my life. The intensity of his smile threatened to undermine the entire operation, but she held firm, studying him carefully. "Why? Is it bothering you that I'm not throwing myself at you like everyone else?"

"I can see that you, Erica, and Rachel are going to get along great." His eyes narrowed, but the sparkle in them remained. She was both relieved and disappointed when he let the question about being his date go without protest.

Something occurred to her then. *If he doesn't have a dark secret, that means something serious is going on here and he's mixed up in it.*

If you believe he's the victim, you're an idiot.

"Dinner will be great. You'll get to meet tons of people. It's not a big deal, I swear. You being willing to help me, on the other hand, is a big deal—to me."

Something stirred in her chest, and she tensed. *These emotions are unacceptable. They only make things harder.*

But something isn't right here. I can't just ignore that. What if I find proof?

Fine. If you're so sure something sinister is going on, prove it. If you can't, you stop whining and kill him. Connection or no connection, you were hired to do a job. You're not risking your own life just because you have a crush on him. Remember, it's not just about you. Mom's life is on the line, too. Remember her?

Fine. She ignored the accusation about her feelings for Will. She definitely didn't have a crush on him.

"Ready?" Erica appeared between them out of nowhere with her keys jingling in her hand.

Startled, Jen looked up. "Oh, uh, yeah." She still wasn't sure about the shopping trip with someone she'd known for five minutes. As Erica hit the down button, Jen wondered if this was a mistake.

"Have fun," Will said. "I'll be lucky if I'm done by the time you get back."

All at once, Jen was conflicted. Spending the day with a stranger didn't sound nearly as interesting as watching Will filming. "I'm sorry to miss that."

Will shook his head. "Don't be. We have lots more to film this week."

Once inside the elevator, Jen and Erica turned and faced him as Jen pressed the button for the lobby.

"See you later." Will gave them a goofy wave. His eyes darted from one of them to the other, stopping on Jen and holding there until the doors closed and he disappeared from her view.

Focus. Stephanie's tone was sharp and unfriendly.

Between the nagging doubts about her not-so-distant future and constantly dealing with the two competing voices in her head, it was getting harder and harder to play the game, but she had no other choice.

Jen shifted to face Erica. "This is the craziest job I've ever had."

"It can be. But Will's one of the good ones. He's just a real person, you know? And he's hilarious. You guys seem to have hit it off."

Jen's mind rewound to the first few minutes after she'd bumped into him. As embarrassing as that was, she'd been more comfortable with him than anyone but her mom in as long as she could remember. "I think I'd known him for twenty minutes when he told me he had a crazy favor to ask, except that he wasn't going to ask me. He made the mistake of saying 'HR would never approve of it,' so then I had to drag it out of him."

"That sounds like Will," said Erica. "He loves to talk about his goofy ideas, and he has lots of them. But however outrageous he gets, he's as genuine as they come—which makes him the exception in this town. You'd be right if you were suspicious of him, with all the wild stuff you hear about actors. But that's not him."

Jen became increasingly uncomfortable talking about her target with someone who thought so highly of him, so she changed the subject. "So, are you going tonight? To dinner?"

"I'm going to try. I have a few things to do first. We'll see."

As they stepped out of the elevator into the lobby, Erica glanced back over her shoulder as if something had caught her attention. A strange glimmer of recognition flashed across her face, and then was gone just as quickly. Jen was immediately suspicious, and with good reason—being suspicious had kept her alive plenty of times on other jobs, and she had no idea what she was dealing with. While she was supposed to be the dangerous one in this situation, that didn't mean she couldn't be in danger as well.

Relax. You're not exactly helpless.

Something's off about Erica.

Maybe. Or you could be imagining it. You're a little paranoid right now.

Outside, she followed Erica to a silver sedan parked in front of the building. As she opened the passenger door, Jen squinted against the reflection of the morning sun on the shiny metal sign beside the building.

What have I gotten myself into?

Only time would tell.

CHAPTER 11

SIX HOURS LATER, ERICA PARKED her car back in front of building ten, and they climbed out into the sunshine. She was as lively as ever, whereas Jen had found the excursion draining.

"Here we are, home sweet home," said Erica. Even after their shopping marathon, her chattering hadn't slowed. "What did you think of your first day out and about in LA?"

"It really is as sunny as it looks on TV," Jen said, then blushed. That had seemed like a normal thing to say, but as soon as the words came out, she heard how corny they were.

But Erica just shook her head. "You're not the first person who's said that to me. But I'm glad we could live up to TV, at least for one day."

"Do you like working here?"

"Of all the shows I've worked on, this one is my favorite," said Erica. "What about you? Have you worked on any others?"

Jen proceeded with caution, keeping her voice light. "I'm sure you've never heard of it. It was called *Call You Tomorrow.*"

Having binge-watched the obscure show a few weeks before when she was stuck in bed with the flu, Jen's memory of it was fresh, making it the perfect addition to her cover.

"You're right. I don't know that one. I'll have to check it out."

After moving the shopping bags to her own trunk, Jen joined Erica on the sidewalk where she stood tilting her phone against the glare of the sun and scrolling through notifications.

"They may still be filming because I don't have anything from Rachel about being done. Do you have anything from Will?"

"I'm not sure. I don't even know if he has my number." Jen fished her burner phone out of her purse. Not expecting any messages, this was the first time she'd checked it all day. She had two, both from Will.

The first one was from only an hour or so after they'd left.

Hi Steph, it's Will. Curtis gave me your number. I hope you and Erica are having fun.

The second one was from a few hours later.

We are running late, as usual. If we're not done by the time you get back, Erica will show you where we are.

"Nothing that says he's finished, but I have one that says they're running late."

"They were filming together this afternoon, so most likely they're still at it. Let's head over to the set."

Jen's eyes lit up. "I know I'm a dork, but it's just so exciting," Jen said, unable to hide her excitement.

As they walked down the sidewalk and across the parking lot under a cloudless sky, Erica pointed ahead. "It's just on the other side of the warehouse."

They followed a cluster of extra-thick cables around the side of a large building that did indeed resemble a warehouse, and as they rounded the last corner, Jen's jaw dropped. Not more than thirty feet in front of them, the cables connected to several large power boxes. A collection of spotlights dangled from a wooden structure, high above the mess, and a smoky smell that she couldn't identify hung in the air. With so many things to concentrate on at once, her feet stopped moving.

Belatedly noticing that Jen had stopped, Erica backtracked to retrieve her. "This episode takes place in Afghanistan," she said in a low voice. "We can't go there to film, so . . ." They wove around several bulky pieces of equipment blocking their view, and Erica gestured dramatically at the chaos now in front of them: a vast, empty parking lot had been transformed into a desert. "Welcome to Afghanistan. They'll shoot the wider shots in an actual desert, of course, but . . ."

Jen missed the short explanation, already lost in what was happening in front of them. Giant cameras were set up not far ahead, and beyond them, the faux desert wasteland made her momentarily forget she was in more temperate Southern California. They stopped near a small group of crew members who stood watching the action.

Will and Rachel, along with at least ten men and women dressed in either black or camouflage combat gear and topped with bulletproof vests, were filming an intense firefight. They were all dripping with sweat and caked with sand, holding an assortment of weapons.

From behind a pair of armored SUVs, Matt, Mel, and the members of their team pointed their guns at a row of bullet hole–ridden cars that were half covered in sand, about twenty feet away. The opposition force poked their heads from behind the cars, taking aim at the team. As people from both sides were picked off one by one, Jen was conscious of nothing else around her.

Though she'd been transported into *Gemini Divided*, for a brief moment she was dragged backwards on her own timeline. She'd been lucky during her time in the Army. She saw a lot, but she'd never been stationed in Afghanistan, unlike others she knew. The ache in her heart reminded her that while the scene was fictional, it represented a reality that could have been hers if different choices had been made. For the sake of her current mission, she filed those thoughts away. This was not the time.

The last member of the opposition held a grenade above his head, and Jen held her breath. Without hesitation, Mel took aim and shot the man just above his vest, but not before the device had left his hand, sailing over the SUV that Matt and Mel were using for cover. The last thing Jen saw was the pair leaping to the side, Matt pushing Mel down into the sand before falling on top of her.

The booming explosion sent out a rush of air and spewed sand everywhere, obscuring everything from view. After that, silence. Jen fidgeted as she waited impatiently to find out what had happened.

She was annoyed to find Stephanie's voice in her ear again. *Will does as many of his own stunts as they let him. You need a filming schedule and a script; then all you have to do is rig the right set of explosives to be extra powerful. You have the basics, and whatever else you need to learn isn't hard to find. If they're not going to search your car, you can easily bring explosives on the set. The only trick is getting them in place.*

She stiffened, unnerved. *I can't think like that right now.*

Without warning, invisible hands wrapped roughly around her throat. *That's exactly why you're here! This isn't a vacation. The only thing you should be thinking about is where and how he'll be the most vulnerable!*

Bit by bit, Matt and Mel became visible through the smoke and sand, with the help of a few giant fans located off camera and pointed at the actors. Groaning, Matt pulled himself up to a sitting position, as Mel did the same. They leaned back against the tire of the SUV that had provided their cover, coming to rest with their shoulders touching. When they turned to look at each other, their surprise at the unexpected contact shone in their eyes, along with relief, confusion, and a sudden awkwardness. Jen held her breath. Despite the animosity between them, she'd been rooting for them to get back together since the second episode.

A few long seconds later the two characters broke eye contact without saying a word, scanning the immediate area as best they could with their limited visibility. They were either too tired to move apart or they'd wordlessly agreed not to. Around them, it was still deathly quiet. When they glanced at each other again, the awkwardness was gone, replaced by a familiar intensity.

"We need to clear the area." Mel's voice was raw and strained as she struggled to get to her feet.

Matt put a hand on her arm. "Mel, wait. Are you okay?"

"Yeah, I'm fine." She had trouble getting the words out, which made them less than convincing.

"That was a little too close." Matt's hand was still on her arm, and his voice was suddenly lower and more serious.

Neither of them broke eye contact as Mel spoke. "Why does it seem like it always is, with you?"

Jen's heart thudded in her chest. Mel could've been talking about their nearly having been killed for the thousandth time, or about the fact that their shoulders were touching and his hand was on her arm. That, of course, was the point. They didn't say anything else, simply continued to stare at each other.

"Cut!" a voice yelled from somewhere nearby, an abrupt reminder to Jen that once again, she'd been sucked in by the show. She blinked, only now fully taking in her surroundings.

The rest of the crew had moved to their next task, but she and Erica stood watching Will and Rachel have what appeared to be an uncommonly serious exchange. From everything Jen had read, this was out of character for them—both were infamous for goofing off on set. Something was wrong.

Will glared angrily into space, every muscle tense as Rachel tried to talk to him.

He did say he had a bad temper.

Rachel moved until she was sitting in front of him, her face full of concern. That was when he snapped, jerking away from her and jumping up, his hands clenched in fists at his sides.

The two assistants shrugged at each other and then looked back at Will and Rachel with the same confused expression. Erica's voice came out in a whisper. "I have no idea what that's about."

Will approached them, stomping on and ignoring numerous calls of concern from those around him. Only when he was already in front of the two assistants did it occur to Jen that she was blocking his way out of the makeshift set.

"Move, Stephanie." The angry man now growling at her was nothing like the good-natured one she'd stumbled into a few hours before, the one who'd bought her a dress and shoes like it was nothing.

She stood motionless, unable to command her muscles to move. Impatient, he grabbed her roughly by her shoulders and shoved her to one side, releasing her before she'd regained her balance and bumping his shoulder against hers as he passed. Luckily for Jen, Erica thought quickly and put out an arm to steady her.

By the time Jen's feet were firmly on the ground, Will had disappeared. He hadn't pushed her hard, and she wasn't hurt—not physically, anyway. Shocked and numb, her eyes were still fixed on the corner he'd just barreled around.

"Hey, you're Stephanie, right?"

Jen would know that voice anywhere, and all she could do was nod, still staring after Will.

"I'm Rachel Sudak."

Jen was too stunned to react to the fact that she was meeting yet another of her favorite celebrities. "What just happened?"

"I can't say, I'm sorry. It's not my story to tell. Just know it wasn't about you. It wasn't even about me."

Calm down. Of course it couldn't be about me. I haven't done anything to him—well, not yet, anyway. But the words didn't help.

Did he hurt your feelings? Well, I'll bet it would hurt his feelings to know you're here to kill him.

Rachel was still studying her with concern. "I know it's a lot to ask since we don't know each other, but trust me, okay?"

Jen's head bobbed obediently, though believing Rachel was easier said than done. She couldn't even understand why this was bothering her, and she certainly couldn't explain the emotions it stirred up.

"The director got what he needed, so we're done for today. I'm going to give Will a little while to cool down, and then I'll go talk to him." Then, recalling the shopping trip that Erica and Jen had been on most of the day, she asked, "Hey, did you two find something for Stephanie to wear tonight?"

"We did." Erica spoke for them, smiling at Jen. "She's going to be the best-dressed one there."

"Do you think Will is still going?" Jen forced the words out, hating that she cared. *It's my job to get to know him. I have to care if he goes or not.*

Rachel's face softened. "I'm honestly not sure. I've never seen him like this. Let's assume he is, and if he decides he's not up for it, you can ride with me. But go get ready, because either way, you have a ride. Between us, I'm more fun than he is, anyway. But he'd never admit it."

Jen appreciated the sincerity of Rachel's invitation, but she could no longer imagine getting dressed up. All she could picture was Will's anger.

Well, it's sure a lot easier to picture him as a guy with secrets now.

She tried to take it all in rationally. Will's outburst hadn't been serious enough that a similar outburst would make someone want to put a price on his head.

Not this time. But what else has his anger led him to do? He mentioned this morning that he has a bad temper. Maybe it's gotten him in trouble in the past.

"I need to get going soon. Stephanie, do you need anything?" Erica asked.

"No. Thank you for all your help today. It was an unusual first day for sure, but it was good, overall. I just need to get my footing. Figure things out." She chose her words carefully so she didn't have to lie; the others would assume she was referring to her job as Will's assistant, but she was thinking about the real job that had brought her to Los Angeles. "I'm a planner, so I don't like improvising."

"You sound like me my first week or so," said Erica. "You'll be fine. Don't doubt yourself. Take one thing at a time, don't be afraid to ask questions, and you'll get there."

"Thanks." Jen gave Erica the biggest smile she could manage.

Erica clicked her tongue at the vibrating phone in her hand and cursed under her breath. "I need to take this. Sorry. Hopefully I'll meet you at the restaurant."

"And I'm going to take a shower," Rachel said. "And then I'll talk to Will. I don't want you to worry about this, okay? I'm serious. This show is like a family. I've known Will for three years now, and he's like a brother to me. Actually, he treats me better than my brother does. Maybe today wasn't the best introduction to him, but I know him, and he's going to feel terrible about it."

Maybe he has everyone fooled, this woman most of all. Maybe she just thinks she knows him.

"It's fine." The words flew out of her mouth, even though it wasn't at all fine.

After spending years learning everything about him, it turns out I only know what he wanted the public to know, and that was apparently all lies. I can't even trust what he says to my face.

Not that his innocence matters in all this, but do you feel better about doing this job if he's not as innocent as you insisted he was? Either way, he's the target until you come up with proof of whatever conspiracy you think is at work. Which you won't.

Once she was alone, it occurred to Jen that she had no idea what time they were leaving or where they were meeting. She didn't want to text Will and she didn't have Rachel's number, so she figured she'd wait a little while. She was in the mood to be alone anyway. This whole mess had reminded her why she shied away from people in general. It never seemed to work out.

She trudged back to building ten. Most likely, either Rachel or Will would find her there or text her. Eventually.

Maybe I should call it a day.

No, you don't get to sulk. You're here to do a job. So get it done.

She did her best not to think. This was who she'd been for years, and yet not since her first job had she been conflicted about it.

Jen retrieved her shopping bags from her car and made her way inside. For that short time it took the elevator to reach the fifth floor, she didn't have to pretend to be anyone else, which was a relief.

One thing at a time. Go out tonight and gather intel. The next step is getting closer to him. If you find the right moment, great, but otherwise keep your eyes and ears open. Rigging explosives is an option, but you may find a better one.

Frustrated with her uncharacteristic weakness, Jen cleared her mind.

Back on the fifth floor, she ducked into the first bathroom she found with the idea of getting changed, but stopped in her tracks at the sight of herself in the mirror. Her heartbeat drowned out everything else as she stared at her reflection, which had taken her hostage without warning. *What the hell am I doing?*

Your damn job. She stepped away from the glass, suddenly disgusted with herself. Without another thought of changing her clothes, she stumbled through the door back into the hall.

Running wouldn't do any good, she knew, because she couldn't run from herself, but at that moment she couldn't bear to look herself in the eye.

CHAPTER 12

JEN WAS HEADED FOR THE kitchen on shaky feet when her phone buzzed with a text from Curtis: *Come down to my office and pick up your employee badge if you're still around. Otherwise just stop by tomorrow.*

Having that badge would allow her to drive onto the lot without having her car searched, so she composed herself and made her way to Curtis's office.

In the kitchen a few minutes later, she set her things on the floor by the far wall and busied herself making coffee. While it brewed, she leaned back against the counter and let her mind wander. Just that morning she'd sat at one of these tables with Will, laughing her head off. In his presence, it had been easy to forget why she was here—but he wasn't here now, and she could think of nothing but her assignment.

She took her coffee and sat at a table across the room. The liquid in her mug smelled like coffee, but it had no taste. *Have my senses gone haywire?*

The perfect blue of the sky was obscured by a layer of thin, wispy clouds. It wasn't quite late afternoon, but the light was already changing.

I can see almost the whole lot from here. How did I miss this view this morning? Oh right, I was distracted. By Will.

The thought of Will made Jen's stomach lurch. Her first response was to hope he was okay, which was ridiculous. *I am seriously messed up.* The problem was that no matter how she tried to convince herself otherwise, this assignment was different.

For the next forty-five minutes Jen sat at the white square table, drinking tasteless coffee, doing her best to keep her mind blank and toying with the idea of giving up on going to dinner—not that she particularly wanted to be at her hotel.

Don't be stupid. You're going to that damn dinner. You're the one who wanted to play Scooby Doo and solve the mystery.

What she'd learned about Will so far wasn't much—and now she didn't believe any of it anyway. Erica and Rachel were convinced they knew him well, but he could be lying to them too. *Does anyone really know anyone?*

Jen tapped her fingertips against the table in rapid succession. *This is why you do not connect with your target, dumbass.* Impatient, she checked her phone to confirm that she had no new texts or calls. Erica was busy, and texting Will was out of the question, so she scrolled through endless pages of internet nonsense, retaining none of it.

A noise made her head snap up, and even though the wait for him to show up had felt endless, seeing Will standing just inside the kitchen door now, she wasn't sure she was ready to face him. His eyes brimmed with sadness deeper than Jen had ever seen in another human being, and he approached her hesitantly, his expression silently begging her forgiveness. The fangirl within demanded that she at least smile to put him at ease, but her blank expression didn't waver. Stephanie gave her a standing ovation for not going gooey-eyed at the sight of him.

You're doing great, and you know I'm all for unemotional. But unless you're going to somehow kill him right now—and make it appear accidental—you have to at least pretend to forgive him and play nice until you figure out how and where you can do it.

I'm trying. She inhaled a shaky breath as she answered her own command.

Studying Will objectively, she tried to pretend he was a stranger. He was showered and clean, now wearing dark pants and a white button-down shirt with the sleeves rolled up to mid-forearm. He moved slowly in her direction, as if she might run if he got too close too fast. Finally standing in front of the table, he paused. She noted that even the scent of his cologne caused no reaction in her.

"May I join you?" His words were uncharacteristically meek. Unable to summon even one word, she bobbed her head slightly.

He pulled out the chair opposite her and folded himself into it, not speaking again right away. Genuine distress radiated from him, and a spark of concern ignited in her chest against her will.

You're worried. About your target. Really?

"I'm sorry for the way I acted, Steph," he said. "It was unprofessional of me. I was angry, but not with you. I promise."

Her hurt had turned to anger, though she wouldn't say so out loud. *Unprofessional? I think you mean to say that you were an asshole.*

Shhh. Focus.

She could only direct her blank stare at him. Inside, the numbness faded little by little.

You kill people for a living, and yet some sad guy is making you question whether you can do your goddamned job. You're pathetic.

He's not just some sad guy. Jen wasn't sure why she was defending him.

"It's okay." The words came out in a whisper, and her head shook quickly back and forth.

"No, it's not. What was going on in my head had nothing to do with you. But that doesn't excuse how I acted."

I bet this isn't even a sincere apology.

I believe him.

Of course you do. But so what if he's sorry? You're going to do your job. Despite her anger, her insides roiled at those words.

They sat in silence, Will's eyes bouncing between Jen and the table, while hers remained fixed on him. His features sagged, matching the way he slouched, worn down, in his chair. Meanwhile Jen sat perfectly straight, every muscle tense. She couldn't think of a thing to say; he obviously didn't want to talk about whatever was wrong, or he would've brought it up.

"I'm really sorry I pushed you. And I'm sorry if I scared you. I've been told that I come across as scary when I lose control like that. Sorry doesn't cover it, but I . . ." He paused, searching for the right words. "It's not a good impression for your first day. Or any other day, of course, but . . ." Giving up midsentence, he hung his head with a sigh.

"Let's forget about it, okay? It's fine. We're fine." The words fell out on their own. She always tried to minimize her feelings to avoid conflict, but this time it felt ridiculous. To her alarm, his apology had melted her anger and dislodged the stoniness inside her, and now she was conflicted all over again.

As if reading her mind, he skipped directly to the subject she'd been pondering for the past hour or so. "So, uh, if you want to change your mind about tonight, I understand."

"Oh, Rachel did tell me to get ready, but I wasn't sure. She volunteered to give me a ride if you weren't going." To her annoyance, none of her sentences were coming out right, and the growing ache in her chest was becoming concerningly common.

"I'm still going, if that's what you're worried about. But if you don't want to go, or if you want to ride with her, it's fine."

He hadn't told her the thing she most needed to know, so she had no choice but to be direct. "Do you still want me to go? With you? Because I—"

"Yes. Of course. Steph . . ." His voice caught on her name, and she peered up at him when he paused. "I'm sorry," he said again, this time in a voice ragged with emotion. "Really sorry."

A warm, pleasant sensation had barely formed in her chest when she was jolted by Stephanie's no-nonsense bark. *Get him out of your head. Imagine him dead on the floor. Because that's what he's going to be.*

Bile rose in Jen's throat, and the corners of her mouth twitched as she struggled not to flinch or to imagine him dead, on the floor or anywhere else. Exhaling deliberately, she forced the image away. "I know. So, it's time for me to go change." She said it mostly to stop him from saying anything else that would rupture her composure.

Shaking his head, Will's forehead creased. The turmoil in his eyes made her chest tighten. "I don't want you to think this is what it's going to be like to work with me. That guy this afternoon, that wasn't me. I know you have no reason to believe me, but—"

A tiny but sincere smile crossed Jen's face, and it took all her energy not to lay a comforting hand on his shoulder. "Would you believe me if I told you this is still nowhere near my worst first day of work?"

"Wow. I'd love to hear that story sometime—if you're not too traumatized by it." He sounded more like himself.

"Maybe one day." The knowledge that it would never happen was reassuring and yet also made her sad.

Enough.

"I'll be right back." She retrieved her bags and left the kitchen without allowing herself to turn around. The numbness inside her had abated, but that left the floodgates open for her emotions.

He should not be able to affect you this much.

Will's apology repeated in her head and warmth filled her chest, making her rational side even angrier. *Oh, you're relieved because he apologized. That's great! Now go get dressed up for dinner, so you can be Cinder-fucking-rella at the ball. Then you can kill him at midnight.*

Safely inside the bathroom stall, she took deep breaths and forced herself to change her clothes without thinking about anything else.

When she emerged to face herself in the mirror a few minutes later, now wearing the dress, she was already having second thoughts, which only intensified as she inspected the image before her.

The dress was shorter and tighter than anything she'd worn before, and it felt like it had shrunk since she tried it on that morning. The material was a shimmery black silk, with wide bands of fabric wrapped over each other randomly at all different angles. It was sleeveless with a scooped neckline, and the bottom hem was uncomfortably far above her knees. She tried not to imagine how high it would go when she sat down.

The shoes were also black, with tiny flecks of silver, and had three-inch heels. While she liked them, she would've liked them even more on someone else.

This isn't me. She frowned at her reflection.

Of course not. You're Stephanie, not Jen.

She tucked the clothes she'd worn to work that day in one of her shopping bags. Pulling the straps over her shoulder, she tugged the bathroom door open before she could reconsider.

"So? Let's see." Will pushed off the wall across the hall where he'd been leaning, hands in his pockets as he approached. His face was no longer burdened by sadness or guilt. Now his smile radiated sincerity. His eyes were locked on her, and he stopped within arm's length.

"May I hold the bags for you?"

His fingers had already landed against her bare shoulder by the time she realized she could have handed him the bags, and before she could give the order to her brain, his fingers had lifted the straps and moved away. An emotion that was either disappointment, relief, or a mixture of both pumped through her as he stepped back.

Don't get all soft just because he's grinning at you like an idiot. You're too smart for that. He's an actor, for God's sake!

In spite of her best efforts, the corners of Jen's lips rose as well. Her mouth had gone dry. This was a whole new level of self-conscious for her, and considering her awkwardness in middle and high school, that said a lot.

"I hope it's not inappropriate for me to tell you that you look . . ." He shook his head, apparently at a loss for words. "Wow."

His opinion is irrelevant. You are not here to impress him.

"So, it's okay?" She crossed her arms self-consciously.

"No, it isn't 'okay.' It's perfect for you." He paused, watching her, which only made her more insecure. "From the way you're fidgeting, I'm guessing you're uncomfortable though."

Glancing down at her traitorous crossed arms, Jen dropped them to her sides. Her cheeks flamed. She was terrible at accepting compliments, and he'd given her a big one—it was all she could do to stand still now.

When she managed to force her hands to be still at her sides, he nodded, adding, "Better." Desperately uncomfortable with the intensity in his eyes, she made a face at him, but he only stared harder. "Seriously, you look beautiful."

"Thank you." It came out in a whisper. "You clean up pretty well yourself."

The same wide smile she'd seen so many times on TV stared back at her. "Thanks. And now, one more thing. Come on."

"Where are we going?"

"It's a surprise." He tipped his head toward the elevator, indicating that she should follow him.

They rode down two floors, then wound their way through halls she didn't recognize, Will's "tour" never having made it past the kitchen.

At the end of the hall they came to a door labeled *Hair & Makeup*, and she stopped, her mouth forming an *O* shape. She'd barely had more done to her hair than letting someone trim the ends. As for makeup, she wore an absolute minimum. Anything more than the basics baffled her.

Will had arranged for Hailey, the head of the department, to do her hair and makeup for the evening. Thankfully, Liz was nowhere to be found.

A little more than thirty minutes later, the two reemerged. Jen was now significantly more glamorous; her hair had been arranged with the top pulled back into a series of complicated knots. The rest was down, and Hailey had made it fall perfectly in place. Her makeup was tasteful yet dramatic, accentuating her eyes without being over the top.

Back in the elevator, she beamed up at Will against her better judgment.

I think this may be the best and worst day of my life, all rolled up into one.

When he gazed back at her, she was sure of it.

CHAPTER 13

JEN WASN'T QUITE COMFORTABLE AS they settled into Will's blue sports car. Things were better between them, but the afternoon still cast a shadow she couldn't escape. Even so, at least now she could smile at him again. It was something.

She was okay until she reminded herself what she was there to do.

"All ready?" He buckled into the seat beside her and started the engine. The scent of his cologne was even stronger here, in the enclosed space. She did her best not to enjoy it, but it was a losing battle.

"Yes." She hoped her increasing anxiety wasn't obvious. Trying to figure out how to kill someone she didn't want to kill was bad enough, but on top of that, she was about to spend the evening in a dress too short for comfort with a group of complete strangers. It was all rapidly approaching too much.

She tugged at her hemline in vain, trying to be logical. *No big deal. We're getting dinner. Worst-case scenario, I glare at some teenagers. I try to get ideas about*—a shiver ran through her—*how I should do it.* She couldn't bear to think the words.

His voice brought her back to the present, and she looked up to find him studying her.

"You okay? You look like you're being led to your execution. Are you wishing you hadn't agreed to this?"

"Yeah. I mean, no. I mean, I'm fine." She scowled at her hemline once more before glancing up at him. His eyes sparkled with laughter, though only a hint showed on his face.

"It's not the dress's fault."

"I know." She sighed heavily and stared out the front window.

"You have nothing to worry about." Will's voice was soothing, even though he was wrong.

"Like I said before, I'm just not good with big groups of people. I'm better with a few people at a time. Or one-on-one." *Or none. I'm best with none.* "And I suddenly hate this dress—it's way too short. With my luck, it's a wardrobe malfunction waiting to happen. I don't want to back out. I just want to crawl into a hole."

They stopped at a traffic light just past the studio lot gate, and he peered at her so thoughtfully she worried he'd be able to see inside her head. But since he wasn't horrified, he obviously couldn't.

"So, you're a little stressed right now."

She scoffed at him. "That's an understatement."

"I get it." That was impossible, of course, but she didn't correct him. "You're out of your comfort zone. I would be anxious too, in your shoes. Especially the shoes you're wearing right now." With only a hint of a smirk, he went on seriously. "The thing is, I'm pretty sure you're going to surprise yourself. Whatever happens, I'm not going to let you crash and burn. I promise. Okay?" His eyes hadn't moved from hers, and she was now completely unnerved.

This has to be the longest traffic light in the world. It needs to hurry up and change so he'll have to concentrate on the road, not me.

Jen squirmed in her seat. "I wish it was that easy."

The traffic light was now green, so at least she could relax without the weight of extra scrutiny on her.

"Tell me the truth. Do you want me to turn around? You don't have to go. I'll even help you dig a hole if you want."

When she stared at him in confusion, he added, "To crawl into."

A genuine smile stretched across her face. *Dammit, Will, why are you so nice?*

"No, I'm not changing my mind."

"I admit it's not exactly a low-key dinner, so it may be baptism by fire, but you can always just ignore the other people and talk to me. Hell, you can ignore me if you want to."

"Ignore a restaurant full of people, huh? Right. As for ignoring you? I'm guessing that would drive you crazy after five minutes, max. You like attention too much."

He opened his mouth as if to argue with her but didn't.

"Ha! You know I'm right." They both laughed.

After that, they chatted about unimportant things: LA traffic, TV shows, movies, hobbies, and their families, among others. The comfortable banter that had flowed between them that morning resurfaced, and the time passed quickly. By the time they arrived at the restaurant, they'd been driving for an hour—and yet she wished they had farther to go.

Bright-green lights illuminated the sign on the building facade. The sidewalk overflowed with people, the crowd spilling into the road. Only when a police officer stopped the never-ending stream of pedestrians could he drive up to the valet station at the curb.

Jen took it all in, wide-eyed. "This is a lot of people for eight on a Monday night."

"Yeah, but luckily even when it's busy, they accommodate us—no matter how big our group is—because Rachel's favorite cousin owns the place."

The car stopped at the valet stand, and she was startled when her door was opened by a young man with a bright smile, wearing a black polo shirt emblazoned with the restaurant's logo.

"Good evening, miss."

She evaluated her options, fairly certain that to get out she would either have to take off her shoes or let go of the dress hem to pull herself up, which would make her dress ride up even farther. It was possible she'd have to do both.

"Miss?" The valet offered her a hand to help her up.

Jen wasn't even aware that Will had gotten out of the car, but all at once he was standing beside the valet, clapping him on the shoulder and greeting him by first name as if they were old friends. To her relief, the stranger withdrew his hand to greet Will.

She was still trying to figure out how to get out of the car without causing a wardrobe malfunction when she glanced up to find the valet gone, and Will now standing there alone. His right forearm rested against the upper edge of the open door, and he leaned down, trying not to grin.

"Obviously you're doing fine on your own, but would you like a hand?"

A deep sigh escaped her, and she was certain her cheeks were dark pink. "Yes, please."

His expression softened from teasing to sympathetic, and he held out his right hand. She held her dress down with her left hand, took his hand with her right, and allowed him to pull her to her feet. Rocking awkwardly on her three-inch heels, she muttered curses at both her dress and her shoes—and herself for picking them, for good measure.

She ignored the sound of his amusement, refusing to meet his eyes. As soon as she had her balance, their hands fell back to their sides.

"Thanks. I was kind of stuck there."

"Anytime." His voice came from closer than expected, and she looked up to find their faces only a few inches apart. His eyes sparkled with laughter, and her giddiness returned. She forced herself to turn and take in her surroundings, starting with the brightly lit building in front of her.

"Ready?"

"No. But let's do it anyway."

The wattage of his smile increased, and he moved closer to her as they squeezed onto the sidewalk, making their way toward the entrance. Her skin prickled, but she forced herself forwards. She'd always hated being the center of attention. She was also hyperaware that putting herself on display like this could jeopardize her anonymity in the long run. But even with every logical and emotional argument against what she was doing, she simply could not completely hate moving through the chaos with Will by her side.

Stupid.

Two giddy teenage girls called out to ask for Will's autograph, and he stopped to sign the pieces of paper they were holding, obliging each of them with a smile and a few words. Three more girls joined them, and the process repeated itself, ending with a group selfie before he left the teenagers bouncing happily on the sidewalk in his wake. The speed with which their fingers tapped on their phones and their delirious grins suggested that they were already posting those pictures to Instagram as he walked away.

Will and Jen continued along the sidewalk, and she tilted her head toward his so her words weren't drowned out. "Were those the fourteen-year-old stalkers? Because they weren't that scary."

"Trust me, you'll be able to tell which ones they are. And I'm sure they're here. That's the thing about being a regular. I'm not hard to stalk." His trademark charm never wavered as he spoke, which reminded her just how many eyes were on them.

Will straightened to take in the scene, then bent to speak into her ear again. "Over your left shoulder. Those three have been here before, and they're hard to miss, especially right now." He chuckled, adding, "They're definitely not happy with you."

The three girls stuck out from the crowd. Will was right; they were glaring daggers at her. They couldn't have been more than sixteen, and their minidresses left very little to the imagination. One of them held her phone in front of her, deliberately clicking the screen and mouthing, "Gotcha." Jen felt the malice in the otherwise innocent action, and she could only imagine what these three or anyone else would be posting online about her that night.

Jen gave them the same smirk she'd given Liz that morning, then turned around. "Wow, they're pretty intense."

He held the door open for her as she walked through in front of him. "Yes. And yet so far tonight, no one has needed to tell them even once to keep their distance. So I guess you're officially my good luck charm." He was obviously joking, but his light words were lead weights on her shoulders.

I am not a good luck charm. Nausea rose in her throat as they stepped through the front doors, her vision tunneling to a pinprick in front of her. Light-headed, she had no choice but to stop and grab the doorframe between the vestibule and the lobby to hold herself up.

Will's hand landed on her arm, the same way it had that morning after she'd backed into him. "Hey, Steph." His voice came from nearby yet also from far away, full of concern. "Are you okay?"

She didn't answer, so he swung around in front of her, his face full of worry.

"Sorry." She wasn't sure she was loud enough to hear over the din of the congested restaurant. Her vision returned to normal, and she let go of the doorframe, determined to keep moving. Unable to come up with a plausible reason for nearly falling over, she brushed it off. "I'm fine, I promise." She maintained eye contact with him in order to make her point, while he stared back as if trying to decide if he believed her.

He leaned down to speak in her ear, and she found his proximity didn't bother her as someone else's would have. "If you're sure," he said. Based on his skeptical expression, she doubted that he believed her, but he released her arm and turned to move forward again. The two women at the hostess stand greeted him and waved them past.

Back in the far corner on a raised platform, a large group of people sat at a long table. Jen assumed that was where they were heading. First, however, they had to make it through a particularly packed area by the bar. As she prepared to squeeze through the throng, Will, who'd been walking beside her, pressed his side against hers without warning.

She glanced at him to find him distracted by someone or something up ahead. The same darkness that had been in his eyes earlier, when he'd pushed her, was there again, except this time she read tension more than anger in his face. He seemed fixated on a Barbie doll–perfect woman moving toward them. Will had stopped to let her squeeze past them through the narrow space between groups. Though blonde like Jen and roughly the same age, the woman was infinitely more glamorous. She was tanned and toned, and wore a tight, low-cut red dress.

You're really outdoing yourself with the jealousy thing. They must have some kind of history. After all, don't all the beautiful people know each other?

The woman was only a few feet away now. The closer she got, the more hostility she trained on Will. Each glared hard at the other, both appearing determined not to be the one to look away. When the stranger had moved past them, Will restored the small space between himself and Jen.

"Sorry." He motioned for her to go ahead.

Before she'd gone five feet, she checked over her shoulder to find that he hadn't followed her. He was standing exactly where she'd left him, now facing the front entrance. With a sigh she retraced her steps, pausing behind him. Peering around his shoulder and craning her neck, she watched the woman disappear past the hostess stand and out of sight. Still, he didn't move.

"Will!" She tried to yell over the noise of the restaurant, but he didn't react. Twice more she tried, with no result.

Pushing aside her discomfort with the idea, she reached up and rested a hand on his left shoulder. The unexpected contact made him pivot faster than she'd expected, and her hand sprang back. Though he was now facing her, his mind was clearly still elsewhere.

"Will? Are you okay?" Perhaps it wasn't the wisest move after his earlier angry outburst, but she stood on her tiptoes, bringing herself almost to his eye level.

"What?"

"Are you okay?"

He focused on her for the first time since the other woman had appeared, and a grateful smile stretched across his face. "Yeah. Thanks."

She reminded herself not to enjoy his proximity, easing down off her toes and stepping back.

"Let's go." He gestured ahead. "I'll be behind you this time—I promise."

This time she didn't go far before checking behind her to make sure he was there. As if to reassure her of his presence, he laid a hand lightly on her bare shoulder. Far from making her flinch, sparks danced across her skin from his hand as she moved forward. As soon as they passed the congested bar area, the hand dropped and he was back at her side.

He bent his head to murmur, "Sorry about that whole thing. I'll explain later."

At last they made it to their group's table. Rachel was the first to spot them as they approached, and she waved them to the two empty chairs across from her at the center of the table. "Hey, look who finally made it. I saved you the best seats in the house!" They sat, and Rachel teased Will about being late, and he teased her right back about something Jen didn't catch.

At least twenty-five people were seated around the long table. Rachel turned and shouted, "Hey, everybody! This is Stephanie, Will's new assistant."

Far too many people for Jen's liking now studied her, and a chorus of greetings were shouted over each other. She located Erica among the unfamiliar faces, five or six seats to Rachel's left.

Will shifted until he was leaning near her ear. "Okay so far?"

Usually, every part of this experience would've made her uncomfortable: the noise, all the people, the attention, and most of all, having someone so far into her personal space. But for whatever reason, none of those things bothered her at that moment. She was afraid to admit that it had everything to do with him.

"Yeah, so far. Better when everyone's not staring at me, though."

"Don't worry; they were staring at me, not you." He winked at her, grinning. It wasn't true, of course, but she appreciated that he was trying to help her relax.

A waitress arrived, setting down glasses of water and asking for their drink orders. Without thinking, Jen said, "Could we please have a rum and coke, and a bourbon, neat?"

She flushed instantly. His favorite drink was one of only a few things that she'd learned about him while researching for this assignment, and she was mortified to have exposed her knowledge.

The waitress departed, and Jen rotated to face Rachel, watching the tiny candle in front of them and clenching her hands together on the table. She wished she could hide, well aware that Will was studying her with interest. He'd turned to face her, his right arm resting on the table and his left draped over the back of his chair. She pretended to ignore him, but he moved again into her personal space to speak over the increasingly loud music.

"Well, this time you were right. But is my favorite drink really common knowledge for superfans?" The words came out playfully. He was not upset.

Exhaling slowly, Jen narrowed her eyes at him. "Who said one of those drinks is for you? Maybe I wanted to order two for myself. The waitress just didn't wait to hear yours."

The delight on his face multiplied as he watched her. She, on the other hand, became increasingly uncomfortable, and at last she sighed in defeat, accepting that she was going to die of embarrassment. "Okay, fine. They're not both for me. But what part of 'I'm a creepy stalker-fan' is confusing?"

"You're not creepy."

"Let's just say, your favorite drink isn't on your IMDb bio, but it is online, and I found it." She began to calm down, studying him reluctantly as she sipped her water.

"As long as you're not planning to use any of the information you found to kill me in my sleep or anything like that, we're good."

The timing of her drink of water was unfortunate because it sprayed right back out, onto the table. Mortified all over again, she frantically patted down the area with her napkin as her eyes threatened to bulge out of her head. She forced herself to laugh, playing off her reaction as simple bad timing.

She jokingly pretended to consider the idea. "I wasn't planning on it." It was technically the truth. She had considered killing him in his sleep, but there were too many logistical issues. Plus, it was impossible to make it appear accidental if an autopsy came back that he'd been suffocated. Someone on his right called his name, and he turned toward them. The momentary distraction gave her a chance to compose herself. As she scanned the group for anyone she recognized, a loud, distinctive sound erupted from the far-right end of the table. She located the source of the sound—a man whose laughter itself was comical. He had to be in his forties, with dark hair and thick-framed, roundish glasses. Something must have been hilarious.

They ordered food, and Will drew her into conversation with the people around them. For whatever reason—alcohol or exhaustion or because she liked hanging out with him, or maybe a combination of those things—she began to relax and enjoy herself.

Leaning back in her chair, she sipped her refilled drink and inspected the group around her, just as she'd done at the airport. Her gaze barely settled on one person before moving to the next. This time it wasn't Adam Lewis, the aggressively charming man from the plane, staring at her but rather a balding man in his fifties at the end of the table, all the way to her left. His unwavering gaze jolted her back to high alert.

Jen grimaced back at him, rapidly becoming uncomfortable. The man did not blink, nor did he act embarrassed and look away as most people would.

Does he know something about me? Is he the one who hired me? The one who gave me the fake reference?

If he is, then all the more reason for you to pull yourself together.

Now rattled, Jen moved on, studying each person at the table in turn. She sensed the man still watching her, and it made her skin crawl. Taking another gulp of her drink, she unconsciously inched closer to Will.

CHAPTER 14

JEN WAS UNAWARE THAT SHE'D shifted into Will until his voice was in her ear. "Everything okay?"

Don't overreact. It's probably nothing.

"Yeah. Sorry." She tensed as she straightened, picking up her glass and fixing her gaze on the table as her stress level skyrocketed.

"I don't believe you."

This time she did not hesitate to twist toward him in her chair, her back squarely to the bald man. "Is that guy still staring at me? The bald guy, at the end of the table?"

Will moved his head to the side to glance behind her. "You mean Tom? He's talking to the guy next to him. Tom's one of the executive producers."

"He was staring at me, though. Even when I looked right at him, he didn't stop. He didn't even blink, which was really creepy." Her heart was still pounding. She had the urge to lean into him again but denied herself permission.

"I'm not sure what made him stare at you, but I'll bet he had no idea he was doing it. He's generally an awkward person." Will's lack of concern about Tom's staring was both comforting and maddening.

Maybe it's nothing. Or maybe he knows something.
Or maybe he knows everything.

Her lips were a tight line as she kept her eyes on Will, unsure she believed it was nothing but without proof either way. All she had was a bad feeling. Since she couldn't do anything about it, she let him change the subject.

In a move that she could only assume was meant to distract her, he asked the people around them to tell amusing old stories about him. Rachel was especially delighted to oblige. Little by little, Jen forgot to be stressed, laughing at Will's embarrassing antics. The evening wore on, and between the food and more drinks and stories, it became impossible to believe she'd been introduced to these people not even fourteen hours ago.

You have a job to do. Remember?

Dessert had been ordered but had not yet arrived, so the evening wasn't quite winding down yet. *Maybe if I can get him alone, I can at least learn something useful.* "Hey, do they have a back patio or something here? Anywhere I could get a little fresh air?"

"They do, but they also have a courtyard, which is even better. The fourteen-year-old stalkers don't have access to it." He grimaced. "Sound good?"

"Yeah." Once again he was making jokes at his own expense to put her at ease.

He raised his voice to be heard above the din. "Hey, Rach, we'll be back in a few minutes. Text me if dessert gets here before we get back?"

"I'll text you pictures of me eating your dessert." Rachel's grin was a mile wide as Will and Jen got to their feet.

They made their way through the bar area, which had grown even more densely packed. Like before, he insisted that Jen go in front of him, reaching over her shoulder to direct her to a door past the bar. He again rested a hand lightly on her shoulder as reassurance until they'd made it out the other side. She hoped he couldn't feel the shiver that ran through her when he did, or the fact that her heart rate increased.

They emerged from the air-conditioning into the warmth of the square courtyard, the sounds of the restaurant falling away as soon as the door latched behind them. The only sound out here came from a small bubbling fountain at the center, where the paths from each of the four sides met. Benches had been placed at regular intervals, spaced far enough apart to make private conversations possible if you kept your voice down. Only one other pair was out there, seated on a bench at the far end.

Will and Jen sat near the middle of the bright-green cushion on the nearest bench, their knees separated by less than a foot. She would never have guessed that this tiny oasis existed in the center of a loud, trendy restaurant.

"Better?" Facing her, he rested his arm on the back of the bench. As far as she could tell, he was equally at ease in the quiet as he had been amid the chaos.

"Much. Thank you. Sorry to drag you away from the action."

"No, it's been a long time since I was out here last, and I love it. I'm glad to have an excuse to take a break."

"It's been a strange day, but in a good way. And I can admit tonight has actually been sort of fun."

"See? I told you you're a people person."

"I'm not sure I'd go that far. But I'm still glad you talked me into this." As she spoke, however, she imagined the bio sheet with his picture on it that she'd received under a week ago, and the reality that came with it.

That's better. It's about time you got your head in the game.

"Oh, I promised to explain about the woman giving me the death glare earlier." His face became serious.

"It's fine. You don't have to."

"I want to. It's kind of a long story, though, just to prepare you."

"Okay. I'm ready." She turned and mirrored the way he was sitting, her arm draped beside her on the back of the bench.

His eyes darted around the courtyard, then back to her. "It's related to the incident this afternoon on set. I wanted to explain earlier. You deserved more than an apology. I just wasn't quite ready. That last part we filmed today touched a nerve. It's not something I talk about much. Or ever, I guess." He paused.

When he spoke next, it was in a slow, quiet voice. "Ten years ago, my friend Ryan, my best friend since I was a little kid, was killed in Afghanistan. Only one guy from his unit survived, and he . . . he described it really similarly to that scene. I used to have nightmares that were almost identical to what we filmed. When I read the script the first time, I threw it against a wall. Hard."

No wonder he snapped.

"I'm sorry." Jen's voice came out in a whisper.

"Thanks. These days, it's like it was all another lifetime, or something I dreamed that didn't actually happen. And it took a long time to get to the point where what happened to him wasn't in the front of my mind all the time."

He took a breath. "I know no one lives forever. I've lost all my grandparents, but it wasn't the same. It's not supposed to happen like that. So early. So suddenly. And no, I'm not the only person to lose someone that way, but when it happened to me, I felt like it. It didn't matter what anyone else said or did. People tried to help me. Nobody could get through."

She had the urge to comfort him but held herself back. *Don't even say it; I already know how ridiculous it is to want to help him.*

"The people around me at the time were great. I was lucky. I didn't feel lucky, though. I took a lot out on them before I got my head back on straight. Today brought it all back. It wasn't that I couldn't do it, because while I'm in character, I'm okay. Matt can take it. Me, on the other hand . . ." The sadness in his eyes when he finally raised them to meet hers was infinite.

"I didn't sleep all that well the past few nights. I had dreams of Ryan dying, and of me being there for real to see it. I'm generally a positive person, but I guess I've been trying to overcompensate, be extra cheerful. And poor you, you arrived right in the middle of that. Today probably gave you whiplash."

She wanted to protest, but he wasn't wrong.

He didn't give her time to reply. "I really thought I was okay with filming it. I thought I could compartmentalize it. Obviously, I was wrong."

"I'm sure no one would expect you to be totally okay with it. Even now. Did they know? The director? Any of them?"

"Only Rachel."

She nodded, at a loss for words. *That explains Rachel's reaction.*

"So anyway, that's why I was such an asshole this afternoon. I couldn't get out of there fast enough. Not that it's an excuse. I'm really sorry."

"Stop. We're good." As disproportionately hurt as she'd been, now her heart ached for him. Her expression dared him to contradict her, and he just nodded as peace settled on his face.

The sting of the earlier confrontation had faded, and his sharing such a personal story made her affection for him stronger. Which, of course, made everything more complicated.

"Okay. Good." But he was frowning again. "Anyway, that brings the story to the angry blonde."

"You don't have to explain."

"I might as well tell you the whole story. You've heard the worst part."

His openness only made her more aware of the depth and breadth of her deception, but it could not be helped.

"Her name is Skye, and we met at a party. We'd been going out seriously for a while when Ryan died. She couldn't understand what I was going through—or I was convinced that she couldn't. I recognize now that she wanted to help me, in her way. But she'd never been good with conflicts, and I was so angry. I wanted to fight so I'd have somewhere to channel my anger."

He paused, and she considered the idea. It made a lot of sense.

"Neither of us understood that was what I was doing. It got to a point where we couldn't talk to each other without fighting, so things fell apart. I almost never run into her, but I guess it figures that it would happen today."

Jen had had her share of heartbreak, disappointment, and betrayal, but she had no idea what to say to a story like Will's. No words were enough, so she said the only thing she could think of. "I'm really sorry."

Will peered into the distance, lost in thought. "I believe that some things aren't meant to work out. She and I were one of those things. It's obvious now. So that part, at least, is okay."

Something buzzed, and he pulled his phone out of his pocket, then laughed, shifting to sit shoulder to shoulder with Jen so he could show her the screen. It was a text from Rachel: she'd sent him a picture of her peering down at his dessert, spoon in hand.

"We'd better get in there." Jen shifted her eyes back up to him and noted that the distance between them was a fraction of what it had been. Her cheeks flushed once again. "I barely know her, but I think she's serious about eating it."

"She's doesn't play around when it comes to food, it's true."

When she moved as if to stand up, however, his hand landed on her shoulder again. She stiffened, glancing back at it, eyes wide, then into his face. A million things went through her mind as she willed herself not to overreact.

He quickly withdrew his hand. "Sorry, I didn't mean to startle you."

She was perched on the edge of the bench, her mouth twitching. The smile she wanted to give him wouldn't come. *Deep breaths.*

"What I was going to say was that I accidentally hijacked the moment. We didn't come out here to talk about me. Did you get enough of a break from the madness? Is everything okay?"

He told me an emotional story about his dead best friend, and then turned around and asked me if I was alright. Meanwhile, my primary reason for bringing him out here was to try to find out something that would help me kill him.

She raised her eyebrows at him. "Me? What about you? You've had a hell of a day."

He managed a slight smile. "Talking about that part of my life doesn't usually make me feel better. But this time it did. So, thanks."

She tried not to cringe at his gratitude. "I didn't do anything."

"Not true. You're a good listener. Not everyone is, especially around here. So now you answer the question. Are you okay?"

She smiled self-consciously, searching for the right words. They were both true and a lie all at once. "I admit that I was a little overwhelmed. I've spent a lot of time outside my comfort zone today. Sitting out here was a nice break. But I can hang out with the group a little longer. Especially if chocolate is involved."

"Well then, we should get back in there before Rachel eats her dessert, and mine. Maybe yours, too."

"That would be impressive." She made sure to stand before he had a chance to offer her a hand again.

CHAPTER 15

BACK INSIDE, RACHEL GRUDGINGLY SLID Will's plate back across the table as he and Jen reclaimed their seats. "Sal and Tom were looking for you."

"Thanks." He turned to Jen. "Tom was the one who was staring at you before. Sal is the producer. The big boss. He's standing with Tom over there."

Her earlier uneasiness about Tom came rushing back, and she recognized Sal as the man who'd been laughing so hard earlier. Both men were serious now.

"Sal, the guy with the glasses, comes to these dinners a lot. This is Tom's first one, I believe. I'm guessing they want to discuss this afternoon, so I'll go over and talk to them in a second. And you're coming with me."

"Why? Am I being punished?"

"Not punished. But you work for the show, and you haven't been introduced to them yet. And you're my good luck charm." His playful tone and that charming smile could not counteract her fear.

Curtis's words replayed in her head: *It looks like you come very highly recommended by one of the show's executives.* She'd been so distracted by Will that she forgot to worry about who had "recommended" her for this job. She didn't know how many executives the show had, but one of those two could be the one who hired her. *Are they here to keep track of me?*

Picking up her drink, which had been refilled again, she took a larger than average gulp. She no longer felt the sensation of butterflies—now it was more like bats beating their wings wildly against her insides.

When Jen didn't move, Will's face softened with encouragement. "They're not going to bite, I promise. Even Tom. Come on. I'll protect you."

He stood and raised his eyebrows expectantly. Since she couldn't get out of her current predicament, she finally rose as well.

The two men had been joined by two women, who were both even more glamorous up close than they'd been from across the room, perfectly made up and wearing very expensive suits. One had thick, chocolate-colored hair that fell in tight curls, while the other's black hair was as smooth as silk, flat, and bluntly cut at her shoulders. Jen smiled nervously as Will introduced her to all four of them. The two women were also executive producers, like Tom. Each of them shook her hand and welcomed her to *Gemini Divided*.

Sal didn't waste time, looking pointedly at Will. "After what happened this afternoon, we wanted to speak to you—privately."

For an instant, Jen was relieved, assuming she was about to be dismissed. But no such luck.

"We don't need to talk privately. Stephanie knows the story." He went on to tell them the same account he'd told her in the courtyard, minus the emotional details and the part about his ex. Afterwards, the executives mumbled their understanding and concern.

"We wanted to make sure you were okay," said Sal. "Both of you." Will apologized again for his behavior, and both he and Jen assured them they'd already talked about it, and everything was fine. As they started back toward the table, one of the women pulled Jen aside and pressed a business card into her hand, telling her that if she needed to speak to them privately, all she had to do was say so.

Jen smiled at Will as she rejoined him at their table. In answer to the question in his eyes, she rested her hand on his shoulder as she pulled out her chair, then forced herself to remove it as she sat beside him. They ate their dessert and talked while people rotated in and out of the seats around them. Around eleven o'clock, their group began to thin. A few people had already left, some were clustered together at various intervals along the length of the table, and some had retreated to other parts of the restaurant—a small table in the corner, the bar, the courtyard, or the outdoor patio.

As they had all evening, Jen and Will sat and talked like old friends, gradually closing the space between them without touching. Rachel was now at the other end of the table, talking to people Jen had never met, and Erica was around somewhere. The other people who'd been sitting near them had moved into one small group or another, but the two of them were perfectly content to stay put.

You've never had a weakness before, but this time you do, and it's obviously him. Which is another reason he needs to die. Soon.

Rachel flopped back down across from them, leaning forward with a grin. "Hey, you two! Stephanie, you're a trooper to put up with him this long on your first day. If I didn't know better, I'd say you were having a good time. Have you taken acting classes?"

Maybe the people who swore he was so genuine were right.

Jen laughed with Rachel before shifting her gaze to Will, who acted wounded.

In another life, the three of us could have been friends. If it wasn't all a lie.

"But I am having a good time. And he's not that bad."

"Not that bad?" Will pretended to be upset. "That's the best you can say about me?" Jen couldn't help but smirk at his reaction, and he winked at her.

"I see you've already brainwashed her, Bryant." Rachel shook her head at him.

"If I had brainwashed her, she'd say I was a lot better than 'not that bad.'"

Rachel ignored Will and spoke to Jen. "You survived your first day in the nuthouse. Congratulations."

Jen sighed dramatically. "Yeah, it was rough, I mean, look at me. Someone"—she paused, her eyes darting to Will's, then back to Rachel—"sent me out shopping with a guide to the city, bought me an expensive dress and new shoes and had someone else do my hair and makeup. It's like I'm Cinderella, but without the curfew or the forest animals. Yep, it was a rough day."

Rachel winced, her expression serious. "Please don't compare him to a prince, or we'll never hear the end of it."

Considering him thoughtfully, Jen said, "Actually, I think he's the fairy godmother in this equation." At that, the laughter began. Will slowly shook his head back and forth without a word.

Rachel pushed her chair back. "Alright, I'm calling it a night. I also had to put up with you all day, and I'm exhausted. Stephanie's new here, so she's too polite to say it."

Will grabbed a napkin, balled it up, and threw it at her, though it missed her by a mile. All three of them laughed this time.

Rachel was standing now. "See you both tomorrow."

"Bye, Rach," said Will.

Jen stifled a yawn. "Good night, Rachel." Waving over her shoulder, the actress disappeared into the crush of the bar area.

"I saw that yawn. You about ready to go?"

No, I don't want to go. But of course she couldn't say that. "Yeah." They both stood up and stretched. "Are all your days this exhausting?" she asked.

"Nope. Some more, some less. It evens out." After saying a quick good night to the people still at the table, they headed for the door.

She tried to stay awake on the drive back to the studio but quickly lost the battle, waking up, disoriented, as they pulled onto the lot.

The sleepy haze lifted, and there was Will beside her. She was not complaining.

Wipe that stupid smirk off your face. Stephanie's voice jolted her fully awake.

"Good morning." Far from being annoyed that she'd fallen asleep, he was grinning at her.

A quick check out the window told her that no, it wasn't morning, and she peered at him sheepishly as they approached building ten. She'd slept through the entire drive.

Her voice was raspy. "Sorry, I was afraid that would happen."

"No big deal. It's been a long day. You needed a nap."

Will parked beside her car. "Oh, I have something of yours in the trunk." He got out. She took off her shoes so she could get out without assistance, then joined him at the back of the car where he was leaning over to rearrange the contents of the trunk.

Right here. Quickly, while he's distracted. Catch him unaware, knock him out, and make it look like you've been mugged. Maybe he tried to be a hero and the assailant went too far.

Before she could process the thought, he turned and straightened with a smile. In his hand he held her two shopping bags.

"Wow, thanks. I'd forgotten about those." Jen pulled the long handles of the bags over her shoulder.

It wouldn't have worked anyway. First of all, this place probably has cameras everywhere. Second, I don't have a weapon of any kind. This is why plans should be made with more than five seconds of lead time.

Will shifted uneasily. "I'm sorry again about this afternoon."

"Don't be. Everything worked out."

You still don't have any evidence that he's a victim of anything, which means you're going to kill him, like you were hired to.

Chills ran through her.

While she stood trying to simultaneously process her assignment and Will's sincerity, he stepped forward and wrapped her in a hug, mumbling tiredly over her shoulder, "Thank you, Steph. You did great."

The hug was neither too tight nor tentative. She might have expected it to be awkward, but it wasn't that either. The conflict raging inside her fell silent as she hugged him back. Though she wanted to both thank him and apologize at the same time, she did neither. Too soon they were letting go and stepping back, smiling tiredly as they said good night.

Back at her hotel, she kicked off her high heels the moment she opened the door to her room. Peering down at her aching feet, she inhaled sharply. A small white envelope that must have been slid under her door filled her veins with ice. She dropped her bags, instantly on guard, and closed the door behind her. The envelope screamed for her attention, but she didn't go near it until after she'd cleared every inch of her room. Finally satisfied that only the envelope had entered her room uninvited, she returned to the entry to retrieve it.

Nothing was outwardly suspicious about it, and yet neon warning lights flashed in her head. Staring down at the stiff paper between her fingers, she walked to the middle of the room and perched on the edge of the bed.

On the front, her room number had been scrawled in thick black marker. From inside the envelope she pulled out a matching white card. She flipped it over, holding her breath. The two-word message on the other side, also written in black marker, tightened a vice-like grip around her throat.

Two Days

She had two days to kill him.

CHAPTER 16

THE BED WAS SOFT AND warm, but Jen was awake. Though dead tired after a night of tossing and turning, her body refused to stay asleep another minute. She couldn't explain the pleasant buzz in her head as she lay stuck in that place between sleep and consciousness, but it was far preferable to the dread that had weighed on her every waking moment lately. A voice whispered to her from the night before:

"I'm pretty sure you're going to surprise yourself. Whatever happens, I'm not going to let you crash and burn. I promise."

"It's obvious that you're doing fine on your own, but . . . would you like a hand?"

"You're my good luck charm."

As it had the night before, the last sentence hurled her headfirst into the brick wall of reality. Her mind had now rebooted, and she groaned, rolling onto her side and pulling a pillow over her head. Her feelings about him were complicated. What wasn't complicated was the fact that she didn't want him to die.

But I don't have any more of a choice than I did in the beginning.

The note that had been delivered to her hotel room was a reminder that she was in danger if she didn't complete her assignment. A tiny murmur in the back of her mind adamantly reminded her that she had several options, no matter what she told herself. The most obvious option was to kill Will, collect the money, and move on. It was what she'd done every other time, never looking back. The second option was to back out. It wasn't a great long-term plan, because they were both likely to end up dead by the end of the two days. Either way, he died. The only difference was whether she did too.

I refuse to accept that there's no other option, the small voice shouted from the back corner of her mind. *It's not right. Think harder.*

But no solution emerged. Instead, she saw her mother's face, as pale as the last time she'd visited her, just after the last chemo treatment. It was painful to see her so weak, so unlike the person she'd once been—full of life and activity.

Who are you going to save? Mom, or a stranger?

In a perfect world, she would save them both, but this was not a perfect world.

Her emotions flowed out of her like water down the drain. In an instant, she was numb again.

Now stop whining and do your damn job. For some reason, the fact that you love Will's show has rendered your brain unable to function correctly. You're a killer. So kill.

Too restless to lie still another moment, she opened her eyes to find that it was after 7 a.m. She got out of bed, impatient to get the whole thing over with. It was a relief not to be conflicted as she went through her morning routine. She felt more like herself than she had in days—even if she still felt a little nauseous.

When she checked her phone, she found a text from Will from the night before. *After such a late night, I don't expect to see you before 10:30 tomorrow.*

The extra ninety minutes gave her time to pack all her belongings and wipe down every surface in the room so she didn't leave traces behind. The note from the night before had rattled her. She couldn't stay here any longer; she'd find a new hotel that night.

Long before 10 a.m., ready to go and tired of sitting around, she gathered her things and left the hotel room. She picked up lukewarm coffee and a stale bagel from the free breakfast off the hotel lobby and stowed the duffle bag containing her go bag in her trunk. To compensate for being on the road far too early, she took another roundabout route toward the studio. Finding traffic to slow her down was easy.

I can do this. Everything will fall into place if I stay focused. I just can't act radically different from yesterday.

The tiny voice in her head that insisted there was another way resurfaced from wherever it had gone. *Is this really who you want to be?*

By the time Jen was riding the elevator of building ten at 10:29, she still wasn't sure how to stay in control of her thoughts and yet act like she had the day before. *Isn't that exactly what I've been trying to do from the beginning?* She'd failed at it so far. Being around Will made her forget everything else.

I have to stop letting him get into my head.

Her determination renewed, she emerged from the elevator, both relieved and disappointed when she saw no sign of him. Where was she supposed to meet him, anyway? She decided to get some coffee first, and the mystery solved itself.

"Good morning," Will said as soon as she entered the kitchen. He stood leaning against the counter beside the coffee machine, sipping from a mug.

"Good morning." She reminded herself not to let his smile affect her. "So, this is where you're hanging out."

"When in doubt, always look for the coffee."

She was already having trouble staying focused. This didn't bode well.

"That's the best way to find me, too." *I can do this, as long as I—*

"It must be, if you've got coffee on your key chain."

"What?" Her eyes darted down to find she was still holding her rental car keys, to which she had attached a key chain decorated with the artistic swirl of the coffee-cup logo for Jane's, her favorite café back home. It was the only thing from her real life she'd allowed herself to bring, and he'd just seen it.

Dammit!

"That one's nice, but it doesn't have enough caffeine." He put down his mug and poured coffee into a matching one on the counter. Her keys tucked away, she was impressed when he doctored it exactly the way she liked it.

He was paying attention yesterday.

"Here." He handed her the coffee as if it were the most normal thing in the world. "You look like you need this."

"Do I?" She raised her eyebrows.

Color rose in his cheeks. "That's not a criticism. I—"

"Thanks." She took the mug from him with a grin and took a sip.

Realizing she wasn't upset at his comment, Will studied her and chuckled. "I was trying to figure out what was different about you." Jen froze, afraid he could somehow read her mind. "Then it hit me. You were taller last night."

"Oh, yeah." She hoped her relief wasn't too obvious. An image from the night before rushed into her mind: the two of them standing only inches apart at approximately the same eye level after he'd helped her out of the car. She blushed, poking her fingernail into her palm to break the spell.

"Too bad those shoes don't go with my outfit today." She was grateful for the excuse to scrutinize her feet, even briefly, and therefore avoid his eyes.

"Too bad."

"Wait. I'm your assistant. Wasn't I supposed to make you coffee, not the other way around?" She gave him her most accusatory glare. "You're making it hard for me to do my job correctly."

"We can probably agree that yesterday proved I'm no good at having an assistant. Besides, I already have my coffee, and you needed some."

She shook her head, pretending to be distressed at his logic, as he continued.

"I guess I should've warned you. I've been told I'm impossible, and that I don't catch on quickly. I believe the exact words were 'so damn oblivious.'"

They ended up at the same table where they'd sat the morning before. For her own sanity, she tried not to peer at him for more than a few seconds at a time.

"Ouch." She gritted her teeth and winced.

His shrug was almost too small to notice. "And that's why she's an ex."

The urge to hug him flitted through her mind. It was gone in an instant, but the damage was done, and she was right back to square one. An awkward silence descended between them, stretching on until he cleared his throat.

"So, about last night."

"I don't think that's something you're supposed to hear on your second day of work." She kept her tone light, trying to dispel the tension that had come out of nowhere, and was rewarded with a tight smile from him.

"I replayed the day in my head. Sometimes I get these crazy ideas that are perfectly reasonable to me but in reality are pretty out there. It occurred to me last night that having some random guy you just met asking you to pretend to be his date in front of hundreds of people and everything that went with it . . . might have been too much."

"It turned out okay, though." She noted his relief at her casual reply. "And to be fair, you're not a random guy. And you did tell me that I absolutely should not agree to do it. I'm a big girl. I can say no to peer pressure."

It would've been fun. The thought formed before she could stop it, and she had to force the image of walking with his arm around her waist out of her head.

"Can we agree never to speak of that one again, starting now?"

Jen bit the side of her lip and tried not to laugh. His eyes pleaded with her, but he said nothing else.

"Isn't it the superfan—that's me, by the way—who's supposed to be the flustered and speechless one, not the celebrity?" She sat back in amusement to take in his reaction, picking up her mug in both hands and sipping slowly, savoring its warmth.

"Well, maybe, but in this case the actor is a complete dumbass, so this happens more than you might expect."

She raised her eyebrows at him and said nothing, a smirk on her face.

Will shook his head. "No, not asking random people to pretend to be my date. Me putting my foot in my mouth. I'm good at that, as you may have noticed."

You're letting him get inside your head, and it hasn't even been fifteen minutes. You're pathetic.

Jen held in a laugh. The seriousness disappeared then, and his face lit up. Glancing at the clock on the wall, he moved back from the table. "Anyway, I need to get going. We have to film a few scenes this morning, but after that we get the whole afternoon off."

"Oh yeah? How'd you get so lucky?"

"How did *we* get so lucky? Because that includes you. Well, our free afternoon is the good news. The bad news is we're filming tonight. Late."

"How late?"

"We're scheduled to start at ten, and it'll probably take at least a few hours." He grimaced. "I'm sorry, did they not give you the filming schedule?"

"No, Curtis said it was being revised but that he'd get me one. And the time is okay. I'm not busy. How often does that happen? Filming at night, I mean."

"It depends. If a script has a lot of night scenes, we film more at night. It doesn't happen all the time, but more than once in a while." He was standing now, so she did too. "Do you want to come along?

I still have nothing else for you to do. I keep forgetting to ask Rachel what an assistant is supposed to do around here."

"Wait. Did you just ask me—the self-professed superfan—if I'd like to tag along? While you're filming? I can't believe the answer's not obvious."

"So that's a yes?"

"Of course! For the record, just assume my answer is always yes."

"So, having an assistant is kind of like having a puppy? Following me everywhere?" Perhaps in anticipation of a playful slap, Will folded his arms across his chest and stepped back out of her reach, smiling mischievously.

Jen's mouth opened, but no words came out, and she narrowed her eyes at him. "I'm trying to decide if I'm offended or not."

"While you're pondering that, do you want more coffee? I definitely need more."

"Good idea." Before she could react, he'd picked up her mug and walked away with it. "Hey!"

"Yes?" He was already refilling her coffee when she got to the counter, and he added the extras before turning around to hand it to her, obviously pleased with himself.

"Thank you. But may I point out that once again, you made your assistant's coffee? And I'm pretty sure you did it on purpose—both times."

He poured his own coffee as well, only then raising his eyes to hers. "I'm terrible at this." This time he couldn't stifle a grin.

"Liar."

His smile drooped slightly. "Okay, fine. I wanted to be nice. I still feel bad about yesterday."

Dammit. He has guilt issues about hurting my feelings, and I have no emotional reaction to killing people.

"Anyway, ready to go?" he asked. "We can take these with us."

"Lead the way."

Jen had been determined to remain objective around him when

she walked in that morning, but so far, things were not going according to plan.

CHAPTER 17

HAILEY, THE SAME STYLIST WHO'D made Jen's hair and makeup so glamorous the night before, got right to work on Will. Jen stood off to the side, surveying the room.

"How was last night?" Hailey asked in her direction.

Jen tried hard not to contemplate just how much she'd enjoyed herself. "It was great. Thanks again for your help."

The stylist stood in front of Will, concentrating as she smoothed gel into his hair to achieve the slightly messy look of his character. Jen observed the process with interest, her concentration faltering when she caught him smiling faintly at her in the mirror. As the corners of her lips rose, she forced her attention back to Hailey.

"This group is a blast, aren't they?" said Hailey. "Well, most of them anyway." Peering down at the actor in front of her, she added, "That one who plays Agent Greene, though. He's a bit of a—"

"Hey!"

"Someone told me he's a nice guy," Jen said, adding, "When do I get to meet him?"

Will's mouth dropped open, and Hailey turned away from him to stifle her laughter. Others in the room were snickering too, and Jen held her breath, suddenly unsure if she'd gone too far. She was relieved when his face lit up with laughter, even as he pretended to be offended.

"Wow. So that's how it is."

Hailey resumed her work. "I like her." She picked up a makeup brush and pointed it at Jen. "She can hang out here anytime."

Jen blushed, evaluating the other people in the room in the mirror's reflection. Only one person hadn't appreciated her joke, nor had she gone back to work—Liz, the same petite redhead who'd been all over Will by the elevator. After glaring at Jen from across the room, she fixed her gaze on Will and began her approach. Jen was on high alert.

Relax. She's harmless.

Liz came to a stop beside Hailey, and Jen imagined having to jump across Will's lap to block her. It made her want to laugh, until she realized that would put her sprawled out across Will's lap. Her skin grew hot from the image, which she forced out of her head.

"May I do something to help?" Liz asked, smiling innocently.

Hailey moved a makeup brush rapidly over his face, replying without turning or slowing her work for a second. "Thank you for the offer, but Agent Greene is done. He's low maintenance. The actor who plays him, on the other hand . . ."

Will's mouth fell open again in mock indignation.

"What did I do to deserve this treatment?" The question wasn't directed to anyone in particular. The room buzzed with amusement, and Liz scowled at them all for laughing.

"But thanks for offering," Hailey added to the disappointed young woman. "I could definitely use your help with the next one."

Shortly thereafter, Jen and Will left the room. Neither of them spoke until they'd made it down the hall and around the corner, at which point they both burst out laughing.

"You don't have to give Liz the death stare on my account," said Will.

"I was giving her a look?"

He laughed even harder than before. "Oh yes, you were. She didn't catch it, but I did. I'm glad I wasn't the one it was directed at."

"Oh, uh, I didn't even . . ." She was thankful that he seemed to find the whole thing hilarious.

He flashed a grin at her but let the subject drop. "So, we're filming outside this morning. We can walk over, or we can drive. It's not far—maybe a ten-minute walk, max. Up to you."

They headed out of the building to find a cloudless day, the temperature hovering near seventy degrees. Jen turned toward the sun, letting the heat soak into her skin. "It's a beautiful day. Let's walk."

"You are definitely not from LA. I love it."

They hadn't gone far when she craned her neck to study him as they walked.

"What's up, Steph?"

"I'm trying to figure out what's different about you."

Will looked amused. "That depends who I'm supposed to be, right? Myself, or Matt?"

She smacked her palm against her forehead. "Oh my gosh! It's so obvious! You're a Matt/Will hybrid right now." Despite the strong resemblance, Will and his character had different hairstyles, mannerisms, and personalities. At that moment, his appearance was all Matt, but his behavior was Will.

"I won't ask which one you like better. Matt always wins that contest."

"You both have your moments." Scanning the large grassy field sloping slightly downward before them, her face creased in confusion—they had run out of sidewalk. "Where are we going, anyway?"

"Not much farther. See all the commotion at the edge of the trees over there? That's it." A group of people had indeed gathered along the tree line at the far edge of the field.

"Interesting. So the studio has its own forest?" *How did I not notice that before?*

"Sort of. It's not big enough to be a real forest, but I guess you could call it that. Basically, the studio spent a ton of money to cover up some undesirable land features by planting a lot of trees and the field in front of us, since they couldn't build there anyway. They spend a fortune on the irrigation system."

Almost as soon as they arrived at their destination, Will, Rachel, and a few guest stars tramped off into the trees with the director and a handful of the crew. Jen remained behind with everyone else. Their view of what was being filmed wasn't great, but she was excited to catch whatever glimpses she could.

Stop it. Deactivate fangirl mode and do your job.

She took a deep breath and emptied her mind of distractions. *Okay, possible hazards in the woods include snakes, spiders, and bugs. Slipping, sliding, or falling. Being poisoned by toxic plants. Infection from wounds. Dangerous animals like bears, bees, or other things that bite or sting. Forest fires.*

But none of them applied here, in daylight in a manmade "forest" on the studio lot surrounded by a TV crew. This assignment was proving harder than expected, logistically and otherwise.

In the meantime, she attempted to keep track of Will and Rachel as they darted between the trees as Matt and Mel. They were chasing an arms dealer and his associates who'd fled after the team had found their drop point.

Filming eventually moved deeper into the woods, and they were no longer visible from where she was waiting, so she sat in the shade with her back against a large tree. Though she tried to keep her mind on her job and off the previous night, it was almost impossible. Eventually, the actors and crew emerged back into the midday sunlight.

Maybe the cover of darkness in the woods would provide a better opportunity. It's the best option so far, anyway.

Erica stood nearby, having spent a large part of the last few hours on her phone, "taking care of things" for Rachel. Will and Rachel were heading their way as Jen rose and brushed herself off.

"Hey, ladies," Will said. "We are now free until 9:30 tonight, when the two of us are due in Hair and Makeup. Whatever shall we do with those eight hours? After I get a quick shower, of course."

Rachel was quick to speak up. "Lunch! I'm starving!"

"You read my mind, Sudak. Who's in?"

Erica shook her head. "I can't. I have a bunch of stuff to get done this afternoon." She checked her watch and her face tensed. "Speaking of which, I need to get going." She directed her next comment to Rachel. "I got through everything that needed to be done. You have copies of all the emails."

Will was poking Rachel in the side and trying to get a reaction. So far she'd ignored him.

"Thanks, Erica. See you later."

Rachel elbowed Will in the side after Erica left.

"Hey, what was that for?" he asked indignantly, as if he hadn't started it.

Rachel shook her head, then said to Jen, "Stephanie, you know how they say that in kindergarten that if a boy's mean to you, it means he likes you? Well, here is a boy who hasn't left kindergarten. And he's acting like he likes me—"

"What? Me? Like you? No way! You have cooties! And you started it."

Jen had a rare flashback to her much younger self. "You two remind me of my cousin and me when we were kids." Her stomach growled. At the rate these two were sparring, finding lunch might take a while if she didn't intervene. "Do I need to separate you two?"

Both of them froze, dropping their arms to their sides and feigning regret even while they bit back laughter.

"That might be a good idea." Rachel took an exaggerated step away from Will. "Otherwise we may not make it to lunch."

Will grinned sheepishly. "Sudak, you never answered my question earlier," he said as they headed back to building ten.

"No, you are not the handsomest man alive," she said without missing a beat. Jen burst out laughing.

Will stopped in his tracks, shaking his head with a solemn expression. "That was not my question. And you're officially uninvited from lunch—even if it was your idea." Both women's laughter echoed across the field. Once their laughter faded, he addressed Jen. "So, what about you, Steph? Want to go get lunch?"

Jen glanced at Rachel, who was still working hard not to laugh, then back at Will. "Sure. Hey, Rachel, you want to come to lunch with us?"

"I'd love to." The two women cackled at their own hilarity all over again.

"The things I put up with." He grumbled about them under his breath, but the glimmer in his eyes was unmistakable. Before they could respond, he added, "I'll race you back to ten—and I'm going to win!" Without another word, he took off running.

"Oh no you're not!" Rachel charged after him, and suddenly Jen was walking by herself, watching the other two growing smaller and smaller.

Being around Will and Rachel reminded her of something she hadn't had in a long time: connections. It was hard to keep up friendships when she had as big a secret as she did, after all. She'd almost never confided in people before she started at this job, and those few connections withered to nothing when her entire life became top secret.

Stop it. You have a job to do. It doesn't matter how much you like any of them. Even Will. Especially Will.

Not losing another second, she sprinted after the two actors as if her life depended on it.

CHAPTER 18

THEY WERE SHOWN TO A sunny corner booth at a diner near the studio. Rachel slid onto the bench on one side, and Will took the other, leaving Jen standing in front of them uncertainly. While her first instinct was to sit with Will, her better judgment warned her to do the opposite. It didn't occur to her until after she joined Rachel on her side of the booth that facing him wouldn't make things easier for her.

"Uh-oh." He glanced from one to the other. "Double trouble."

Rachel winked at him. "You'd better believe it."

Jen smirked, but she studied him objectively. He was solidly built but naïve, and she believed she could overpower him. While he definitely worked out and she couldn't deny he was probably strong, she had years of combat training on her side. If she timed things right, she'd have the element of surprise. That would be crucial. She just had to find the right time and place.

She peered up at him again, that deceptively calm mask frozen on her face to disguise her thoughts. Rachel's mile-a-minute play-by-play of something that had happened to her the night before briefly held Will's attention, but now he turned to Jen. It was hard to assess his weaknesses when he was gazing back at her.

He's not Will; he's the target. She conjured up the image of her mother's face in her mind, hoping for the same clarity she'd achieved in the early-morning hours. It worked, and just like that, for the first time when face-to-face, she didn't see Will but instead her mark.

The trick was to hold on to this feeling.

Jen smiled and laughed in all the right places as Will and Rachel joked and chatted, but inside she held firm—for approximately five minutes. The sincerity in Will's repeated glances caused her ironclad resolve to waver. Only a little, but still too much.

After lunch, the three of them wandered back outside, still discussing what to do for the afternoon. Jen's goal was the same wherever they ended up: to observe and wait for the right time. Either the opportunity would present itself, or she would have to create one.

"We could go to the beach club," Will said.

Drowning is an option. But not an easy one to pull off without a plan. An athletic guy like him can definitely swim, and no one has bathing suits with them. This idea probably isn't feasible, at least right now.

Rachel considered it briefly. "That kite festival is happening near there today, so it'll be crowded. Hmmm. It's a beautiful day for Disneyland, but we don't have enough time."

"We could start with our own favorite places."

At this suggestion, Rachel made a face at him. "Weren't you there with your nephew last weekend?"

"I never get sick of the Griffith Observatory."

She rolled her eyes and addressed Jen with a grin. "It's no secret that Will is a big kid. So let me clarify. He's a big dorky kid."

In response, he crossed his arms tightly and glared at her. "Space is cool."

Jen couldn't help but smile at their bickering. "I've always been interested in space. And I've read about the Griffith Observatory. It's on my list of places to visit here."

"Ha! See? The dorks are in the majority!" He smirked at Rachel.

"Wait, are you calling me a dork?" Jen demanded.

"It's a compliment, I swear."

Rachel let out a heavy sigh. "Alright, if we're going to make the drive to the observatory, then let's go, *dorks*." She sidestepped Will's playful punch.

Back at Rachel's car, Will nudged Jen toward the front. "My turn in the back."

"What? No, it's fine."

"Nope. Fair is fair." His expression said he wasn't backing down.

"Okay, if you insist," she said.

Stop smiling at him. Now. Unfortunately, she'd become addicted to the giddy sensation she got when she was around him.

Rachel and Will's teasing didn't stop as they drove. When Jen twisted in her seat, she was startled to find his face only inches from hers. He'd leaned forward into the space between them. Laughter filled his eyes as it so often did, and again she had to force herself to look away.

Around 4 p.m. they parked as close to the observatory as they were able. Will put on a baseball cap when they climbed out of the car. "Nice hat," said Jen. "Part of the plan to dodge the fourteen-year-old stalkers?"

He tensed. "Yeah, why? No good?"

"No, I like it."

Too much.

"Don't feed his ego, Stephanie." Rachel walked around the car toward them, grinning.

However pleasant it was, she needed to stop the buzzing sensation inside her head. It wasn't hard to figure out that it was because of him. Turning away, she halted at the sight of the structure at the top of the hill, which looked even more impressive than she'd expected.

"Wow."

Will stopped beside her on the sidewalk. "We're still a mile away.

Wait 'til we get up there." Peering from Jen to Rachel and back, he asked, "So, do we want to walk up or take the bus? It stops across the street."

"I vote we walk," Jen said, still staring up the hill.

Rachel agreed. "And you want to walk, don't you, Bryant?"

"Of course."

At the end of their climb, Jen slowed without warning. The massive white structure before them was striking, with tall, narrow windows lining the front, and domes protruding from the roof at both ends, as well as one in the center above the entrance. Over her shoulder, the view of the city below took her breath away. She spun around to face it, wishing she could take a picture. In her old life, she loved taking pictures.

Don't even go there. The last thing you need is unnecessary evidence that you were here. It's bad enough that you have a badge with your picture on it.

Inside, she sighed wistfully.

The other two had gotten a few steps ahead, and now Will walked back and stopped beside her. "It's beautiful, isn't it?"

"It's . . . incredible."

He is my target, not my friend.

But she could no longer numb herself to her feelings, even when she thought of her mother.

"Come on! It gets better." He bounced with excitement as he turned and continued onwards. Jen fell into step behind the other two. When she avoided eye contact with him, she could almost remind herself why she was there without making herself nauseous. Almost.

Will had been right: it was even more massive than it seemed from the bottom of the hill. Inside, she stared up at the ceiling, once again stopped in her tracks—this time by the beauty of a painting featuring the Greek gods. The trio wandered from one exhibit to another, with Will acting as their tour guide. Rachel examined it all with mild interest, but it obviously wasn't her thing. Since Jen was the more engaged of the two, he spent a lot of time pointing things out to her.

She alternated between inwardly chastising herself for her inability to complete her assignment and, to her dismay, grinning stupidly because, well, she couldn't seem to stop herself. They wandered through room after room, exploring the exhibits on four different levels. Jen could've sworn that barely any time had passed, and yet her watch said it had been more than an hour and a half since they'd entered the building.

"Hey, Will." She walked over to where he stood reading a panel on the wall. "Where's Rachel?"

"What?" He glanced around, but she was nowhere to be seen. "Oh. I'm not sure." After a few quick texts, he nodded at his phone. "She went outside to take a phone call. She said she'll catch up with us."

Jen stood with her back against the wall beside the panel he'd returned to reading, scanning the room out of habit. That was when she spotted them. Two young women whose form-fitting minidresses suggested that they weren't tourists or space enthusiasts. They lurked at the far end of the exhibit hall, staring at Will. Keeping them in sight, she took a small step forward so that she was almost next to him and stood on tiptoe, as close to his ear as she could get without her three-inch heels.

"Looks like you have two fourteen-year-old stalkers across the room." Standing so far inside his personal space and keeping her voice down gave an innocent situation an alarming amount of intimacy—or maybe it was her imagination. He shifted so he was in front of her, which only made it worse. The tiny space left between them was not nearly enough, and her pulse quickened.

"Where are they, exactly?"

With all his attention directed at her, she was glad to have an excuse to focus over his shoulder on the far end of the room. She told herself she wasn't enjoying his proximity. "They're by the far wall. They're not the same ones from the restaurant, but they must have studied at the same school of nasty glares and tight clothes."

Will laughed softly. "Thanks for keeping them away."

Jen waited, her eyes glued to the girls across the room as they whispered to each other. After directing their nastiest looks at her once more, they turned and walked up the stairs.

"The coast is clear. They went back upstairs. Do you think they're setting a trap?" She was mostly joking.

"I doubt it, but you never know." He stepped back from her. Now that they were gone, she had no excuse not to look at him. Leaning his shoulder against the wall beside them, he was still facing her, but not as directly. Even so, his gaze was even more powerful than a moment before. "That may be the most frustrating part of my job."

"Dealing with fans?" Jen pretended to misunderstand him, doing her best to counteract his intensity with a joke. "Because I can go . . ." She pretended to start walking away.

His hand landed loosely on her arm, tugging her back gently and then dropping back to his side. "No, you know that's not what I meant. And even if I did, it wouldn't include you."

Do not give him that ditzy, lovesick stare again.

She couldn't stop her lips from curling. *Traitors.*

"The worst part is dealing with people who have no concept of boundaries. Like I said, I don't want a security detail. But I'd also like to be able to go out in public." After a short pause he added, "You make a good security detail, without even trying."

"Me? Security? Right." She forced a laugh that she hoped passed for genuine, shaking her head as she surveyed the room out of both caution and discomfort. It was getting harder to maintain eye contact.

He straightened and turned to check the space himself. "Alright, I don't care if they haven't left yet. Your superpowers will keep them away. Come on, I saved the best part of this trip for last."

He strode across the room to the stairs, and she moved quickly to catch up with him. For those few seconds, Jen imagined being there with Will for fun, and not having to come up with the best way to kill him.

If only.

CHAPTER 19

"WE'RE IN LUCK," WILL SAID, squinting up at the board where times and descriptions for the various planetarium shows were listed. "The next show starts at 6:15, which is in twenty minutes. *Centered in the Universe.* Do you want to get tickets?" His excitement was contagious.

Absolutely not. Out of the question.

"We might as well, right? We're here."

"Exactly! Let me check with Rach and find out if she's coming back in." More tapping on the screen of his phone, and then a short wait. "She'll be in here in a few minutes. Let's stand in the ticket line."

A white-haired woman in front of them patted the small blonde girl beside her on the head. Jen guessed that the girl was about five years old, and probably the woman's granddaughter. The girl was spinning slowly in a circle, singing so softly that only a faint melody was audible above the noise of the tourists around them. All at once she came to a stop facing Will, and the greenest eyes Jen had ever seen locked onto him.

Will didn't notice, so Jen elbowed him gently, then tilted closer to him. "You have a new fan," she said under her breath. He caught sight of the girl, and a soft smile spread across his face.

When the grandmother turned to find the little girl staring at them, she laughed softly.

"Sorry," she murmured before tugging her granddaughter toward the ticket counter.

While her grandparents bought their tickets, the green-eyed girl gazed over her shoulder at Will. Another ticket agent called them to the counter, and with Will standing next to her but still distracted, Jen bought three tickets for *Centered in the Universe*. She'd already paid by the time she had his attention again.

"Wait, I didn't mean for you to buy the tickets."

Once they'd moved out of the way of the line, she peered up at him. "Do you have any idea how much you spent on the dress and shoes you bought me yesterday?"

"No, I forgot to look. Whatever it was, it was worth it."

She was momentarily speechless.

Dammit. Shut up, Will.

"I'm serious," he said.

Jen ignored his intensity as best she could. "Anyway, the maximum ticket price for these shows is seven dollars. I can handle that. You've spent way too much on me already."

She got the feeling he wanted to argue, but he must have understood that he wasn't going to win. "Well, thanks for getting the tickets."

"You're welcome."

"Hey, sorry." Rachel strode toward them. "Had to take a call. What's the movie?"

Will spoke up first. "*Centered in the Universe*. It addresses all the big questions: Who are we? Where do we come from? Why is the world the way it is? And all in one hour."

"Wow. That's impressive. How many times have you seen it?"

When he replied "Four," the two women shook their heads in disbelief, sharing a grin at his expense. "I like what I like," he said as Jen handed them each a ticket. Jen could certainly relate to that.

Soon they were inside the semi-darkened room with the domed ceiling. As the lights went down, they settled back in their tilted chairs. Jen hadn't been to a planetarium in many years, and she couldn't remember when she'd last been so excited for anything that wasn't *Gemini Divided*.

She swore no more than ten minutes had passed when the lights came back on and the room came to life. As the audience sat up and gathered their things, Rachel jumped to her feet, energized as usual. Will was the next one to stand, stretching. Jen managed to sit up but was staring straight ahead.

"Are you okay, Steph?" Despite the noise around her, she only began to blink at the sound of his voice.

"Yeah. That was . . ."

"It was good, right?" he finished for her. "I never get tired of that one."

"It was awesome." Rachel stretched her arms high in the air, squirming in place. "Ready to go?"

"Yes," said Jen, getting to her feet, and the three of them filed out of the planetarium.

It was now almost 7:30 p.m., and they walked through the front doors of the building to join a large group of people admiring the beginnings of the sunset over the city below.

"Wow." It was more a sigh than a word that escaped Jen. No words could properly describe the swirl of red, yellow, orange, and pink in the sky, and the three of them stood and admired it.

"We need to keep track of the time." Will tapped his watch. "It's about an hour to get back to the studio, though we should allow a little extra. And of course, we need to grab some dinner, too."

Jen was still mesmerized by the sunset when a female voice broke through her reverie, asking, "Hey, aren't you two on *Gemini Divided*?" Jen was suddenly alert, scrutinizing the pair of young women standing in front of them. One was blonde and fair skinned, the other her opposite with darker hair and a brown complexion. They were in their early twenties but resembled neither Barbie dolls nor spandex-clad stalkers. Jen breathed a sigh of relief to see that they looked like regular people. Still, she watched the interaction carefully.

"We are. I'm Rachel, and this is Will."

The two fans squealed, grinning in delight. "I told you!" one of them whispered.

"I can't believe this!" said her friend, whose attention bounced between the two stars, her eyes wide in anticipation. "Could we take a picture with you?"

"Of course." Will was as calm and friendly as ever. He was good at this.

In Jen's head, however, shrill alarm bells rang. In order to avoid being captured in one of their pictures, she sprang into action.

"Here, let me take it for you." She held out her hand for the other woman's phone.

"Oh, thank you so much! Could we turn this way, so the sunset is behind us?"

Jen took the device from her, and everyone shifted so the four were standing with their back to the sunset. She lined up the shot and clicked the button a few times.

They're so genuinely happy. It's surreal.

That's the normal way to be happy. They're not faking it, like you do.

She handed the phone back to its owner, who thanked her again. Backing away from the last bits of the giddy fangirls' chatter, she watched Will duck his head as if he were uncomfortable with being recognized. When he shot a shy smile at Jen, she shook her head at him in amusement.

The two strangers were walking away when Rachel elbowed her. "Don't let him fool you, Stephanie. He loves that stuff."

"Me?" Will pretended to be shocked at the accusation but beamed nonetheless. "I don't know what you're talking about. I didn't want to be rude to people with such good taste in TV shows."

Rachel narrowed her eyes at him, crossing her arms and speaking conspiratorially to Jen over her shoulder. "I don't know if you've noticed, but he has an ego the size of the moon."

Jen pretended to study him thoughtfully. "No, not the moon. Maybe just an asteroid."

Will sputtered with laughter. "That's how you defend me? Sheesh."

Rachel laughed long and loud, as usual. "Aw, you know we love you, Will. Right, Stephanie?"

Coming from Rachel, this spontaneous declaration of friendship was perfectly normal.

It would be awkward if I didn't agree.

"Of course."

Rachel now grabbed him in a violent hug that pinned his arms to his sides, squeezing him tightly.

"Okay, okay, enough love," Will said, shaking her off gently. She released him, satisfied.

Jen shook her head at them. "You two crack me up."

Rachel grinned and checked her watch. "Okay people, it's 7:45. I'm starving. Apparently a new burger place that's to die for opened thirteen minutes from here. Any takers?"

Will's stomach growled. "Sounds good to me. Steph?"

Jen went queasy at the words "to die for," but she swallowed her discomfort, her smile never faltering. "Perfect."

"Then let's go!" Rachel was never one to stay still for long.

After dinner they set off for the studio, arriving with coffee in hand since Will had warned Jen it would more than likely be at least 12:30 before they were done.

They paused on the sidewalk in front of building ten. "Rach and I need to go change. Our trailers are just behind the warehouse." He waved vaguely at the next building over. "So we'll see you in a little while."

"No problem. I'll go hang out with Hailey, since you'll end up there anyway. Unless you have something you want me to do in the meantime?"

"Nope." To Rachel, he said, "I keep forgetting to pick your brain about what Erica does all day. Because so far all Steph has had to do is hang out with me."

"Such a trooper." Rachel shook her head sympathetically at Jen before turning back to Will. "Whatever you need her to do. Maybe just hang out and be your friend, since you don't have any."

The two once again fell into their roles of playful siblings, Will's eyes going wide while Rachel ducked away from his good-humored swat.

"Can you believe her? Such nerve!" Will called to Jen as he turned to walk backwards away from her, grinning.

"I know! I'm much too smart to be your friend!"

Behind him, Rachel burst out laughing. Will narrowed his eyes at Jen. Pointing a finger at her and then waiting a beat, he shook his head. "Have you two been having strategy sessions or something? How to drive Will crazy in ten easy steps?"

"I don't actually think it takes ten steps," Jen mused. "Maybe four."

Before Will could respond, Rachel pulled him by the arm, adding, "Come on, time to get to work."

"See you soon, Steph." He beamed at her, and the bio sheet that had led her to this point flashed before her eyes. Somehow she managed to keep a smile on her face and breathe normally.

In the lobby of building ten, Jen fidgeted as she waited for the elevator. When her eyes locked onto one of the security cameras on the ceiling, her carefree afternoon left her mind. The camera was a reminder that she was under scrutiny, and that someone expected her to do her job. She had another twenty-four hours at best.

Icy calm descended over her as she crossed the threshold of the elevator. It was a rare moment when she didn't have to pretend to be Will's assistant.

That dopey, lovesick expression on your face all day wasn't always an act. It wasn't even mostly an act. You're not trying hard enough. It's almost like you want them to kill you. If you don't care about yourself, at least remember where that would leave Mom.

By the time she arrived at Hair and Makeup, she'd psyched herself up to withstand Will's charm again. She pushed open the door and greeted Hailey, smiling brightly, her mask once again in place.

CHAPTER 20

WHEN RACHEL AND WILL ARRIVED in Hair and Makeup, Jen and Hailey were sitting in the matching swivel chairs in the center of the room, laughing like old friends. Jen had finished recounting the events of the afternoon only moments before.

Liz stood by the far wall, straightening products on a counter and wearing her displeasure all over her face. Delighting in the fact that the sour-faced Barbie doll had to listen to her talk about her day with Will, Jen ignored her.

"It sounds like the three of you had a great time today," Hailey said as Will and Rachel sat in the chairs she and Jen had just vacated.

"We did." Will smiled at Jen.

Hailey chatted on as she set up her tools on a small table. "The Griffith Observatory is a nice introduction to LA. And not the obvious choice."

"Well, Will's a nerd, and it's his favorite place." Rachel's voice boomed across the room.

Will was not to be outdone. "Rachel's just jealous because I'm so much cooler than she is."

"They've been like this all day," Jen said to Hailey.

"I hate to break it to you, but they're like this every day." Hailey began the process of bringing Agent Greene to life while another woman arrived to transform Rachel into Agent Cleary.

Meanwhile, Jen scanned the long space and found Liz. Instead of looking away when Liz glared at her, this time Jen gave the other woman her best nasty smirk, then went back to ignoring her.

"Liz, why don't you help Jaz set up the table by Rachel?" Hailey called.

Liz gave her a tight smile. "Of course."

Jen's eyes met Will's in the mirror. He'd probably witnessed her exchange with Liz.

Oops. Oh well.

When they were done in Hair and Makeup, they made their way to the far side of the field, by the same opening in the tree line as earlier. Erica had beat them there. The area was now lit by a collection of floodlights where the crew and extras were gathered. "Will, we're ready for you now. Rachel, two minutes." The man who Jen assumed was the director walked away.

Will took one more sip of his coffee. "Hey, would you—" He stopped short and laughed because Jen was holding out a hand to take the cup from him. "Oh, thanks."

"Finally, something that justifies having an assistant."

His eyes sparkled with amusement, and he shook his head at her. "Catch you all later."

"What did you end up doing after lunch?" Erica asked as Will walked away. "Did I miss anything exciting?"

"Will's favorite place, then burgers, fries, and milkshakes," Rachel said.

"The Griffith Observatory, huh? His idea, I assume. Wasn't he just there?"

Rachel grinned at Jen. "See? It's common knowledge that he's a nerd." To Erica, she added, "The answer to both of your questions is yes."

"I had a lot of fun." Jen was suddenly defensive on Will's behalf, even though she knew the other women were joking.

Right, defend his honor as you're plotting how to kill him.

Erica laughed. "We're only kidding. I can't resist giving him a hard time."

"Even when he's not even here," Rachel added. A moment later, the director beckoned her over.

"How late do you think we'll be here tonight?" Jen asked Erica as Rachel headed toward the cluster of people at the entrance to the woods.

"At least 12:30. Maybe later. It always depends on what they're shooting, how many scenes, how long they are, whether they get the light and the angles they want, whether everyone gets things right, how picky the director is—all the usual factors. And no, we don't have a lot to do out here. Basically, we're here in case they need something last minute. Like glorified interns, I guess. But I'll take it."

"Yeah, I've had worse jobs."

Jen and Erica made small talk until Erica's phone rang again, at which point the brunette wandered off. Heading for the tree she'd sat under earlier, Jen was too far away to hear anything but distant strains of conversation from the crew who remained in the clearing. She caught glimpses of Will and Rachel dashing between the trees. Gradually the action moved farther into the dark and out of sight. When they'd disappeared from view completely, she gazed at the sky.

Hundreds of billions of stars are up there, and yet most of them are invisible to us. The planetarium show that afternoon had reminded her that there were far more stars in the galaxy than she could possibly see, especially from a well-lit metropolitan area. As focused as she was on everything in front of her, it was no wonder she'd lost sight of the bigger picture—both in the universe and her life.

A commotion at the tree line pulled her back to reality. She had no idea how much time had passed, but the crew had come back out of the woods. Rachel was talking to Erica, and a large group of people milled around. Jen got to her feet as a breeze kicked up and brought a chill to the air. She wandered into the crowd to find out what was happening, noting that Will wasn't among them.

Rachel saw her coming, and answered her question before she had a chance to ask. "We're taking a break. Will . . . needed a moment." When Jen regarded her curiously, she shrugged. "He didn't tell me anything this time. He plopped down at the edge of the ridge. They like to film out there because the drop is so dramatic and it isn't far from the path. They make us sign safety waivers to use it. I'm not sure what's going on with him. Could be more of the same as yesterday, I guess, though he wasn't mad this time."

"So, is filming done for the night?" Jen checked her watch to find it wasn't even midnight yet.

"I'm not sure. We weren't supposed to be done yet. It depends on Will."

The wheels in Jen's head were spinning.

"Oh, hey, Erica, we need to talk about . . ." Rachel's voice faded into the background as the other two walked away, talking about something Jen couldn't hear. Everyone around her was busy with something.

She walked as casually as possible, as if she were approaching the trees in search of something. At the tree line, slightly removed from the clearing that served as the main entrance and exit, she checked over her shoulder. No one was watching her, so she darted past the smaller trees on the perimeter toward the well-worn path. If anyone asked, she could always say she'd gone to make sure Will was okay. That was what she was doing—sort of.

Rachel said the ridge wasn't far from the path. I bet I can find him.

After confirming that no one was following her, she picked up her pace. She'd have to hurry.

Again she catalogued the hazards in the woods. *Things that fly, creep, or crawl—snakes, spiders, bugs, mosquitos. Slipping, sliding, or falling . . .*

He's sitting at the edge of a ridge.

A tingle ran through her. *This could be it.*

Jen strained to make out shapes in the darkness, which grew thicker the farther in she went. The outdoors wasn't exactly her comfort zone, and now she slowed, creeping along the path and trying without success to keep her footfalls from making noise. In the silence of the forest, the tiniest movement echoed in her ears like the trumpeting of an elephant.

She'd begun to worry that she'd gone too far when she spotted him, sitting in the only patch of moonlight filtering through the trees. It was so bright and framed him so perfectly that it could have been a spotlight.

Actors. She smiled before she could catch herself. Rachel had been right; Will was sitting on the edge of a ridge. His legs hung over the side, and his shoulders slumped forward.

This is your chance. No cameras and no witnesses.

Unable to determine how alert he was, Jen crept toward him, pausing after every step in an attempt not to announce her presence. She kept expecting him to turn around, but he didn't. Five feet away. Four. Three. Two. He still hadn't given any sign he knew she was there.

Peering past him into the darkness below, she catalogued the variables that would mean success or failure: how steep the fall was, how deep the trench went, what was at the bottom, or if the terrain along the sides provided anything to grab on to. Each of these affected whether he would survive the fall.

If she'd known about this earlier and inspected it in the daylight, she could've made an informed decision. But staring into darkness with no idea how far down it went? It would be foolish of her to make the decision now. She had no room for error, after all, because if he didn't die from the fall . . . Well, the range of nightmare scenarios was plentiful.

Do it, now. Before you lose your chance.

Jen concentrated hard on emptying her mind as the sounds of her surroundings seemed to amplify. Another step forward and she would be close enough. She was almost above him now, and the drop-off was sharp. All she had to do was take one more step, crouch down, and push forcefully, and over the edge he'd go. She imagined Will sliding down into the dark crevice, and the bottom fell out of her stomach.

I can't make this decision without knowing what's down there. Surely that was a good enough reason not to do it.

At that instant, his voice broke the silence of the woods. "Come and sit with me, Steph."

At first Jen was too stunned to respond, or even to move. When she finally found her voice, it was only to murmur, "Okay." She stepped out from behind him, on his left, and lowered herself to the ground, sitting with her legs dangling over the side of the ridge beside his.

"Fancy meeting you here." It was supposed to be a joke, but his voice was flat.

"Are you okay?"

You're pathetic.

He shook his head, his eyes on the darkness at their feet. The moonlight illuminated his face, where she read a tangled mix of emotions.

"Is it about . . " She couldn't bring herself to utter Ryan's name. ". . . the same thing as yesterday?" This time he didn't appear angry. The best word to describe his posture was defeated. His tone reminded her of his apology after his outburst.

"Sort of." He didn't elaborate.

"Do you want to talk about it?" She wasn't sure why she was suddenly channeling the concerned friend, a role she had no right to.

But I am concerned.

Shut up. Use this weakness of yours somehow. Just get him out of your head first.

Maybe I can get to the bottom of why someone wants him dead. If I can just ask the right questions—

Forget why. Why doesn't matter. You're here. You need to do it.

"Not now," he said.

She was relieved.

"Do you want me to go get Rachel? Or someone else? Because I can—"

He shook his head, his words coming out with surprising urgency. "No, I'm glad you're the one who's here, Steph. Would you sit with me for a few minutes? If you don't mind?"

"Of course." She couldn't force the words out any louder than a whisper.

Is this guy you have a crush on more important to you than your own mother? Because you have to choose, and so far you're choosing him.

She was grateful she didn't have to say anything as they sat listening to the sounds of the night. She wouldn't have been able to hold a conversation if he'd wanted to.

In the still and quiet, creatures who lived in those woods went about their nighttime business, rustling in the trees and on the ground. Her attention wandered to their legs dangling over the edge of the drop, where darkness wrapped around them, and then back to Will.

He'd acknowledged her before she'd decided whether or not to go through with it, but now she rationalized not pushing him. *Lots of witnesses could've placed me at the tree line, and they would've recognized that I wasn't with any of them when it happened. If he survived the fall and IDed me, I would go to jail, and that's not an acceptable risk.*

She took a deep breath, exhaling slowly. *I'll find a way to do it tomorrow.*

It had been at least five minutes since either of them uttered a word. When she hazarded a peek at him, this time she found his gaze fixed on her. He smiled sadly, saying nothing. Without meaning for them to, her lips turned slightly upward as well.

Not long thereafter, footsteps approached from behind them, and Jen peered over her shoulder. A flashlight beam bounced in the darkness, and Rachel took shape behind it.

"Hey." Jen kept her voice low. Rachel's eyes darted to Will, then back to Jen, who nodded. *Yes, he's okay.*

"Hey, Will." Rachel stopped behind him on his right. He regarded her over his shoulder but did not reply. "Should we call it a night, or are you okay to finish up? I don't want to rush you, but everyone's waiting."

He paused before responding. "Sorry. Let's finish up. By the time you bring them all back here, I'll be ready."

"You sure?"

"Yeah. Thanks, Rach."

Jen envied these two their close friendship.

After Rachel disappeared down the path into the dark, Jen turned to Will. "Are you sure you're okay?"

"Yeah." He already sounded more like himself. "Or I will be. Thanks for sitting with me."

She cringed, pummeled by her conscience. "I didn't do anything."

"I told you last night, you're a good listener."

"But you didn't even say anything for me to listen to."

He stared at her with an intensity that made her insides quiver. "I felt better just having you here. Sometimes that's all it takes. The right person at the right time."

CHAPTER 21

WILL'S KIND WORDS STUNG, AND she worked hard not to wince
as they taunted her, echoing in the silence. Jen's attention shifted
back to the darkness at her feet.

*I'm not the right person to help him, and I'm not the right person
for this job, either. That's why I couldn't do it. I shouldn't be here.*

This was not the time to wallow in self-pity.

*No, I'm the perfect person for this job. I'm a genuine fan of the
show, not a weird stalker fan. That's why he trusts me. I don't like it,
but I have to do it.*

A chuckle broke the silence, and her head snapped up at the
sound. Beside her, Will stood and brushed himself off, his expression
free of whatever had been tormenting him. "I guess 'lost in thought'
was contagious tonight. Are you okay?"

By the time she'd managed to send the signal to her muscles to
stand, he was offering her a hand. Jen studied it momentarily before
letting him pull her up. Once again she stared into his eyes, just as
she had when he'd helped her out of his car the night before, albeit
from several inches lower in her more sensible shoes.

"Thanks," she said.

"Thank you."

The ensuing silence crackling with electricity. She was so distracted she didn't immediately recognize that she hadn't let go of his hand. Blushing furiously when she did, she was thankful for the darkness of the woods as she turned toward the path to hide her face.

"I'll get out of everyone's way here." She darted away from him as she spoke. "I'll meet you out there whenever you're done."

"Sounds good." His words followed her as her feet hit the trail. *Dammit.*

She'd jogged halfway to the clearing when she passed Rachel and the crew on their way back to Will.

"Is he okay?"

"He seems to be. Or doing better, anyway. He didn't tell me anything. All I did was sit there." She needed to get away before Rachel read the truth in her face.

"Thanks for looking out for him. You two make a good team."

"Uh, thanks. I'll see you later." Jen hurried on, eager to get away from what had nearly happened.

Emerging from the trees, she spotted Erica halfway to the parking lot, still with her phone to her ear, and sighed in relief. At least she didn't have to make small talk for the time being. But her relief didn't last long because at that moment, Rachel's mild-mannered assistant caught sight of her and scowled as she spoke into her phone. Her stare reminded Jen of the unsettling way Tom had gaped at her the previous night at dinner. *What's going on?*

She glanced around to be sure Erica's glare wasn't directed at someone or something else nearby. But no one else was anywhere around or behind her. The other woman ended her call with an abrupt hand gesture and directed her displeasure at her phone as she paced back and forth, typing angrily.

What was that about?

With nothing to do but wait for filming to finish, Jen returned to her spot at the base of the tree. Pulling her knees up in front of her, she attempted to calm her racing heartbeat. Everything was going haywire. Time dragged on, and while Erica didn't do anything else that was remotely strange, Jen couldn't relax.

Familiar voices reached her, including one voice in particular. *I must have fallen asleep.* She lifted her head off her knees, getting to her feet wearily and making her way over to where Will, Rachel, and Erica stood talking.

"Hey, there you are." Will's expression said he was tired but genuinely glad she was there. "I was about to come and wake you up. We're done."

"Sorry for falling asleep on the job."

He shrugged it off. "With these hours and not much to do, it's understandable."

"So, guess what we're filming tomorrow?" Rachel asked Will in her most innocent voice. The smirk she gave him made it obvious that this was not the first time they'd discussed this.

"You don't have to remind me." He pretended to be annoyed. "You love it when I get shot."

Jen's eyes widened in surprise.

This is perfect! If you replace their blanks with live rounds, you could get this over with. Maybe it wouldn't be convincingly accidental, but it would get the job done. You had dismissed that option as too obvious, but at this point, you have to admit that the perfect scenario may not exist within your short window of time.

She would do a little digging tonight. The potential solution shot a surge of adrenaline through her, and she was awake and alert.

Mistaking her surprise for alarm, Rachel was quick to reassure her. "Oh, Stephanie, sweetie, don't worry. He'll be perfectly safe."

Jen nodded.

This is a really bad idea. They have safeguards that stop those things from happening by accident, and the investigation would be massive. Still, he'd be dead. That's the most important thing. And you'd be long gone.

She hesitated, uncertain, as she wrapped her mind around the idea. *As much as I don't like it, this might be the best plan. But I've never had to pull off anything like this before. I don't know if I can.*

Will was talking to her now. "Steph, you have nothing to worry about. They've shot me many times before, and I'm still here. You'll get used to it."

"Give it a few days. By the end of the week, you'll want to shoot him yourself, like the rest of us." Rachel smirked first at Jen, then at Will, who puffed up with indignation.

"She will not! She's on my side." Turning to Jen, he directed all his charm at her. "You're on my side, aren't you?"

Jen gave them both her best diplomatic smile and ignored the question. "Are you filming out here tomorrow, too?"

Will shook his head. "Nope, tomorrow we're in the warehouse. It's just past building ten. And best of all, it won't be in the middle of the night."

"Speaking of which, are we leaving this place before morning, or what?" Rachel was bouncing impatiently, as usual.

"Yep, let's go," he said.

"Hey, if anybody wants a ride back to ten, I'm parked right over there." Erica pointed to the nearby parking lot. It wasn't a long walk back, but given the hour, they took her up on the ride. When they piled into the compact car, Rachel ended up in the front passenger seat, Will and Jen in the back.

Erica's car was smaller than Rachel's, and with four adults, it was crowded. Only a small space remained between the pair in the back seat. They happened to glance at each other at the same moment, and a smile reflected from one to the other.

Stop it.

Within two minutes they arrived in the parking lot, and the three passengers extracted themselves from the car as Erica rolled down the window. "Hey, anybody want to go get a drink or something? It's still early."

Rachel spoke up first. "Sure. Sounds good."

Will nodded in agreement. "I can do one drink. Steph?"

"I can't keep up with you guys. I need to sleep—I think I'm still a little jet-lagged." She stood rummaging through her purse, pretending not to find the keys that lay at her fingertips. "I guess I left my keys upstairs. Will the system let me in the building to get them at this hour?"

Will nodded. "Yep. Lucky us, they let us come to work in the middle of the night. Do you want me to come up with you?"

It was crucial that he left. She shook her head. "No, no, I'm fine. You go. I'll run up and get my keys, then go back to my hotel. I'll see you in the morning."

Will's expression was conflicted. "Well, okay, if you're sure. But call if you can't find them, or if you have any trouble."

"I will, thanks."

"And tomorrow—10:30, like today. Okay?"

"You're the boss. Good night."

Rachel waved over her shoulder as she walked to her car. "Good night, Stephanie." Erica waved from her car without looking up, still staring at her phone as she waited for the others.

Will hadn't moved yet, and Jen's muscles were locked in a total system failure. He took a step closer to her. "Night." His voice was soft, and again they stood facing each other longer than necessary. With anyone else, she would already have looked away.

Move. You're planning how to kill him, for God's sake.

Jen suppressed a shudder, keeping her face neutral as she turned away, and Will headed to his car. She took three steps toward the door before she stopped to rummage through her purse again, grabbing her phone. She tapped her finger on the screen, then held the device to her ear, pretending to talk.

Rotating toward the cars, which were now backing out of their parking spaces, she waved, giving a theatrically dramatic shake of her head to suggest that it was a call she'd rather not take. One by one, the cars drove away. She paced on the sidewalk, pretending to be on the phone until the last of the three cars—Will's—was no longer visible from where she stood.

Her plan was last minute, though still more carefully thought out than simply "Push him off the ridge." She didn't like improvising, but time was short, and she had to make the most of the opportunities she had, no matter how flawed. This might be her best chance.

Putting her phone away, she walked back to her car. She had a busy few hours ahead of her.

CHAPTER 22

JEN CLIMBED INTO THE DRIVER'S seat of her car as if everything were normal. Instead of backing out of her parking space, however, she opened the welcome packet Curtis had given her the morning before. While her expectations were low, maybe she could find something useful in it.

The folder contained several maps, the first of which included the whole studio lot. *If I'd looked at this map yesterday and checked out the ridge in advance, tonight might have been a success. Oh well, can't do anything about that now.*

Behind the first map was another, more useful one. It detailed the three buildings used by *Gemini Divided*: building ten, building six, which was across the street, and the one called "the warehouse" nearby. Ten was mainly offices, and six had a lot of the storage on the upper floors, but she couldn't be sure about the warehouse. Will had said they'd be filming there, but it was also listed as storage.

This map also wasn't as detailed as she would've liked, but it was better than nothing. She hoped to find props, so storage was her best bet. Now with a general idea of her plan, her next task was to move her car. It was too conspicuous here by itself.

The squealing of brakes made her jump, and her head whipped around in search of the sound, freezing as a tractor trailer slowed at the stop sign a block down the road. She studied the vehicle, not daring to move a muscle.

She had no idea whether it was normal for a large truck to be arriving on the lot at all hours of the night, but it struck her as strange. The truck rumbled along, going straight through the intersection and continuing up the main road that led further onto the lot. Not even a minute later, the same screech of brakes was audible again. The truck hadn't gone far.

As her momentary panic eased, she consulted the map once more. She was relieved to find a parking lot for studio vehicles near the intersection the truck had passed through. Her car would be less obvious among other cars than it would sitting here by itself. Wasting no more time, she started the car and inched toward the intersection.

Not including the gate attendant at the main entrance a half mile or so to her left, who was probably either watching TV or on his phone, there was not a soul in sight. There was also no sign of the truck. She turned right at the stop sign, and made a left at the next driveway, where a sign read *Official Use Only*. As the map had indicated, it was a small parking lot full of studio-owned vehicles. But there was a setback—the lot had a fence around it, a camera pointing at the gate, and a padlock securing it.

So Jen did the next best thing, parking in front of the fence and crossing her fingers that the spot was outside the camera's range. It wasn't ideal, but it was better than her car sitting alone by building ten, announcing her presence. She backed into the space so the front of her car faced the road, in case a speedy getaway was necessary. Next, she took every last scrap of everything from the front seat and placed it all in the trunk so a peek inside the car wouldn't point back to her.

Jen opened the trunk and set down her purse, then unzipped a lightweight black backpack she'd removed from her larger duffle bag—her go bag. She withdrew the jammer that had been left for her at the hotel. Turning the device on, she stuck it in her left pocket with the prongs poking out. If it worked correctly, she would now be invisible to the security cameras.

Next, she reached into the bag for her gun. After tucking it into her waistband, she took out two extra clips and slid them into her right pocket. She pulled two latex gloves from a small box and stuffed them into her back pocket with her cell phone. The last item she needed was a lightweight gray sweatshirt, which she put on and zipped halfway up the front, concealing the contents of her pockets as well as the gun. She then locked the car and slid her phone and key fob in her pockets so she had her hands free.

After checking again for any signs of life around her, she ducked across the street and back toward building ten, staying in the shadows as much as possible. She would cut back along the side of building ten to the front, then across the street to building six.

But a light shone from between the buildings, somewhere past building ten, and a low rumble of activity came from there as well. Her better judgment advised her to avoid whatever the commotion was, but she was desperate to figure out why she'd been hired to kill Will. Maybe this was somehow related.

When "the warehouse" came into view, she understood why it had the name it had. Though it may have been built as a soundstage, it resembled an old warehouse. The lights and faint commotion came from around back, so she began her investigation at the front, which was dark and quiet.

As she approached the door, she thanked herself for having the foresight to hack into the security system and recode her badge to give her system administrator–level clearance under the name of a random employee. Used in conjunction with the jammer in her pocket, she had complete anonymity. If it worked, anyway.

Standing in front of the door, Jen pulled the gloves out of her back pocket and put them on, then held the badge up to the black square beside the door and sucked in her breath. A second later the door sensor let out the same chirp as always, and she pulled the door open. *As much as I love a challenge, that was so much easier than having to disassemble the sensor pad.*

Stepping inside, she was hyperaware of the cameras. Despite the jammer she was carrying, it was hard to trust that they couldn't detect her. She squinted as her eyes adjusted to the fluorescent lighting inside. The immense open area was filled with rows upon rows of large wooden crates. As far as she could tell, all of them were stamped *Gemini Divided,* followed by the letters *DUB.* She was inclined to doubt that this was normal. She'd witnessed criminal activity plenty of times in her line of work, and this felt suspicious.

Will said they're filming here tomorrow. They wouldn't have crates in here for that—or would they? As long as I'm here, I might as well find out what's in them.

Muted noises came from the back of the building. Whatever was happening out there was getting louder. Her eyes darted around the space and landed on a stairwell door and an elevator on the far wall, where the ceiling was lower. Something told her to make a break for the stairwell, and her feet were moving before she had time to wonder if it was the right thing to do.

If she was discovered, it would be hard to find a plausible explanation for walking around in a building where she didn't belong in the middle of the night, with an ID card that opened doors it shouldn't, and with tools that would incriminate her. There wasn't a good way to get out of that situation, so she'd just have to avoid being caught in the first place. Not her ideal plan, but really, nothing about this job was even good, never mind ideal.

Jen dashed across the large space, closing the stairwell door behind her seconds later without a sound. Multiple voices echoed on the other side of it, but she dared not peek through the small glass window. Now she had only one way to go, up the stairs, so she tiptoed to the second floor as swiftly as she could. The stillness on that floor was disconcerting, and the tiny squeak of her sneakers against the floor of the long, empty hallway made her anxious.

Pull yourself together.

The walls were lined with eight evenly spaced steel doors on each side. Moving quickly, she jiggled the knob on the first door to the right of the elevator. Locked. She tried the doors one by one, growing more and more frantic. *What if someone finds me up here?* Without meaning to, she'd backed herself into a corner.

As she approached the last two doors, the sounds of voices downstairs increased. She was desperate. So when the penultimate doorknob turned in her hand, she gasped in relief and almost fell through it, ready to fling herself inside.

She stopped short in the doorway. Whatever she'd expected, it wasn't a closet full of wooden crates identical to the ones downstairs, stacked neatly against the walls. Like the others, they were stamped with *Gemini Divided* and the same three-letter sequence.

DUB. It's an airport code. Dublin. We're going there next week.

Maybe the crates are being shipped out in advance. The props for the shoot could be packed in crates.

Maybe. But something wasn't sitting right with her.

In light of her discovery, Jen had almost forgotten that she was in a desperate hurry to hide. A muffled voice from nearby reminded her, and she jumped through the doorway. When the light switch on the wall made a clicking sound but failed to produce light, she sighed in exasperation and pulled her phone out of her back pocket. The tiny light the device produced didn't help much, but it was better than nothing. Before closing the door, she twisted the knob from the inside to be sure she wasn't going to be locked in—not that she had another option at that moment. The knob turned in her hand, which was the only thing that had gone right so far that evening.

The closet was pitch black except for the thin beam of light from her phone, which she shined on the crates. They were stacked to her eye level along both walls. *What's packed inside them?*

The *ding* of the elevator carried from down the hall. Suddenly frantic, she spun around, tripping over her feet. The sound of groaning metal and at least two muffled male voices came closer. Jen darted past the crates and was relieved that she had just enough room to crouch behind the pile on the left, her back flat against the wall. Now hidden, she swiped at her screen in desperation, extinguishing her only light as the sound of the approaching strangers grew louder.

She tried to catch what they were saying, but her heart was hammering too loudly, and she couldn't summon Stephanie's calm.

Panicking is not going to help. Now pull yourself together. It's not as though you've never been in danger before.

Before she had time for another thought, the door swung open.

Her eyes had adjusted to the darkness, and she squinted against the light, pushing herself lower to the ground. When her knees hit the crate in front of her, she clenched her teeth to avoid yelping in pain.

"Where's the flashlight? How am I supposed to change the light bulb in the middle of the night without a damn flashlight?"

In a defensive voice, another man answered, "Would it be easier if it was daytime? It'd still be dark up here."

"Do you have the flashlight or not? I need to get this done. The boss wants everyone out back in five."

Something clicked, and dim light filled the closet. After the sounds of creaking metal came whispered cursing, and then grunting, more creaking of metal, and even more cursing. From the sound of things, one of the men was now on a ladder.

Please don't let him be high enough to spot me over the crates.

The first man barked at his partner to hold the ladder still but also for him to move the flashlight to one side or another. The grumbling finally stopped, and the man released a stream of mumbled obscenities. The dead light bulb must have proven harder to remove than he'd anticipated.

After a long string of creative cursing, the man on the ladder spoke again. "Take this one."

"Boss, my hands are full," the other man protested.

"Just take it," snapped the man on the ladder. The man on the ground must have managed to do as instructed because the yelling stopped. "You got the spare?" Much cursing and creaking later, the closet was flooded with light. After a click of the flashlight switching off, the creaks of the ladder resumed, as did the grumbling as the first man climbed back down.

"There. Now they'll be able to get the crates out of here. Everything in these first two closets is going out in tomorrow's load, so they'll be coming to move it downstairs anytime now."

"They're not expecting us to move it, are they?"

"Don't you ever listen? Our exact instructions were 'Don't touch the crates unless you want to end up in one.'" The first man was losing his temper.

"Oh, right, they did say that."

The door creaked open, and she was plunged back into darkness when the light was switched off. After the bright lights, this darkness was even blacker than before. Now back in the hall, the men's voices were muffled as the door shut behind them.

She'd only just sighed with relief when a *click* signaled that the lock had been engaged from the outside. The men's footsteps grew faint as they lumbered away, the elevator dinged, and their voices faded. And then silence.

Did they just lock me in here? Jen's pulse pounded so hard it made her light-headed. Her breathing grew ragged as she flicked frantically at her phone to turn the light back on. She had only one thought. *I have to get out.*

CHAPTER 23

JEN SCRAMBLED FROM HER HIDING spot, wincing as she scratched her arm on the corner of a crate. Once the overhead light was back on, she slowly turned the doorknob without pulling, reassured when the lock disengaged. It was strange that they didn't have more secure bolts on the doors. Of course, if they had better security, she would've been trapped, so she silently thanked them for their lack of preparedness.

Breathing easier now, curiosity stopped her from pulling the door open. Yes, she needed to leave, but not before she found out what was in the crates. Wasting no time, she got in position and jammed the heel of her hand up against the board sticking over the corner of the top crate. Pain shot up her arm to her shoulder, and she gritted her teeth to hold back expletives, but nothing moved. The second time, she felt the corner board loosen, and finally it moved enough for her to pry it up and expose the contents. She ignored the pain radiating up her arm and peered inside.

The crate was filled with armor-piercing live rounds.

But they wouldn't need real bullets on a TV show, and certainly not armor-piercing ones. There's no reason they'd be sending these bullets to Dublin for the show. They can't be props. But if they're not props . . .

She took several pictures on her phone, then replaced the board as best she could. Unable to resist, she gritted her teeth against the pain she knew was coming and dislodged the corner board on the top crate of the other stack the same way. This crate held the guns the bullets belonged in, and she took pictures of those as well.

When she'd snuck into the building, her vague plan had been to find the prop gun they were going to use to shoot Will tomorrow and switch real bullets into it. If she hadn't been desperate, she never would've considered it. They would inevitably have safety protocols, after all. It was a stupid plan, and she barely believed she'd have actually gone through with it anyway.

All that was irrelevant now—because this changed everything.

Will's mixed up in this somehow, I'm sure of it, and I refuse to believe he could be the one responsible for whatever this is.

She made a concerted effort to ignore the voice nagging at her. *He's an actor, so he could easily be lying. Just like you are. He'd be a lot better at it.*

But she had more pressing dilemmas, like getting out of here before someone caught her.

Jen replaced the loose board on the second crate, her mind racing. Listening for noise from outside, she crept to the door and stood against the front wall. Her phone back in her pocket, she put one hand on the doorknob and switched the light off with the other.

Standing in complete darkness, she turned the knob in slow motion. There was no telling the consequences of being found in this closet, but it wouldn't be any better if she rushed out into a hall that wasn't empty. She pulled the door inward a fraction of an inch at a time, until she was no longer blinded by the hallway light.

Once her eyes adjusted, she pulled the door the rest of the way open and confirmed that she was alone. Closing the door, she sprinted to the stairwell. She was far from safe yet, but if everyone was still out behind the building, she should be able to slip out the way she'd come in. It was a big "if."

She scanned the warehouse from the small window in the door at the bottom of the stairwell. The loading dock doors at the far end were open, and about half the crates were gone, but as far as she could tell, no one was inside the building. From her angle she noted two different doors besides the loading dock and made her exit plan.

Closing the stairwell door behind her without a sound, Jen took off running for the exit that opened to the front of the building. She skidded to a halt when she reached it, then peered out into the shadowy parking lot as a black sedan crept by. She jumped back, away from the glass, flattening herself against the wall.

So many things didn't make sense: the black car, the commotion behind the building, whether it had something to do with the crates, what Will had to do with any of this, and why she'd been hired, among others.

Maybe I can get a peek at whatever's going on in the back.

Logically, she knew it was an unnecessary risk.

But what if this explains it all? I just need a peek.

The car was gone, so she inched the door open and slipped out. The sounds of a crowd reached her, as well as the rumbling idle of a large vehicle. She approached the first corner of the building, peering around it. Floodlights spilled out from the back parking lot, but whatever was happening was still not visible. She'd have to go closer.

Right, because what could possibly go wrong?

She was already halfway along the side of the building, pulled like a moth to a flame. Arriving at the next corner, her eyes widened at what she saw with her quick glance: it was a far bigger operation than she'd expected. The same lights that had been set up for filming now illuminated the parking lot and the tractor trailer that had rumbled through earlier, which was backed up to the loading dock.

Large men carried the wooden crates marked for Ireland onto the truck. They weren't the men who worked on the crew during the day—they looked, spoke, and moved differently. Rougher. A group of twenty-some people had been clustered in front of a dark-haired man, whose face was obscured from her angle. They cheered as if he'd just finished speaking, and most of them were headed back inside.

If I'd been in there much longer, I would've been stuck.

As she watched the men loading the crates onto the truck, her mind worked at the puzzle.

So they're shipping this stuff to Ireland. But—

Shouts interrupted her thoughts, and it occurred to her that she was pushing her luck more and more the longer she stayed there. She'd worked for criminals before, and she was smart enough to recognize when she was in over her head. This was one of those times. Slinking back along the side of the building, she hoped she could get away without being spotted.

She did not.

There was nowhere to hide and wait them out, so she made a break for it. As she dashed across the courtyard between buildings, two angry male voices rang out behind her.

"Hey!"

So much for a clean getaway.

The shouts did not die away. On the contrary, they multiplied. They were following her. Pushing her muscles to run faster, she began to feel sick. *I never wanted any of this.*

And yet, here you are. Her conscience had chosen a hell of a time to reappear. *Breaking and entering, planning to kill a certain celebrity you allegedly respected. No one forced you to do those things.*

The black car rematerialized, and she dodged behind the red brick building on the corner by the stop sign. Now directly across the street from where she'd left her car, she kept running.

I can do it. Just a little farther.

Behind her, more shouts. Just before she rounded the far side of the brick building, a bullet whizzed by and narrowly missed her. She did the only thing she could do—she kept running, pulling her car key out of her pocket.

One last open stretch remained, from the end of the brick building and across the street to the parking lot, and she had to make it without cover. Halfway across the street she clicked the key fob frantically to unlock the car, arriving seconds later. She threw herself into the driver's seat, wincing as she bumped hard against her sore right arm, and turned the key in the ignition, thanking her earlier self for backing into the parking spot.

Taking a left up the main road, she pulled on her seatbelt, driving like nothing was wrong because she was not yet out of sight of the guard at the main gate. She wondered if they'd heard the shot. Once she reached the next corner, she could floor it to the back exit. If things went her way, the jammer would scramble the surveillance video, and if she was really lucky, she wouldn't encounter a security patrol. However, at the moment it was more important to lose whoever was chasing her. She needed to get off the lot and disappear.

Before she'd gotten as far as the side street, both the black car and the two men on foot were behind her. The men ran hard, advancing at an alarming rate. The black car was steadily gaining on her as well. Her pulse accelerated in kind.

At last she made another left, off the main road and onto the side street. The moment the buildings blocked her view of the main entrance, she slammed hard on the accelerator, dramatically widening the gap between the vehicles. It also helped Jen that at that moment, the black car stopped to allow the two men on foot to jump into the back seat. She tore around the next corner as fast as she dared, putting as much distance between them as she could. Two more turns, plus a mile or so of road that wound behind the woods, and she'd be at the back exit of the lot.

She took the next corner faster than she should have and for a moment was certain the car was going to flip. All four wheels gripped the road none too soon. The black car had not yet reappeared behind her, but it wouldn't be long. Her next turn was only two blocks away, but she slammed her foot on the accelerator, then again just as hard on the brakes before pulling the car around the next sharp corner.

As she struggled to keep control in the turn, the black car screeched onto the road she was leaving.

She reminded herself to breathe.

Again testing the acceleration capabilities of her rental car, she reached highway speeds as she hugged the curves on the road along the back of the lot, the trees zooming past her on both sides. Thankfully the back exit was unstaffed, simply a high fence with an electronic sensor, topped with barbed wire and monitored by security cameras. The trick would be to get herself through while stopping the black car from getting out.

The final corner would be the hardest one. From this winding road that roughly paralleled the edge of the lot, she had to make a sharp right at the narrow exit, marked by a small sign. The pull-off to the exit was a few car lengths long at most and just one car wide, leaving little time for braking or space for correcting a too-fast turn. They didn't expect anyone to round the corner at forty-plus miles an hour, but she was about to try.

Jen could only trust that the thick wrought iron bars would open in time, because the black car would be back in her rearview mirror momentarily. A metal box stood on a pole beside the exit with a button and a speaker, but as soon as her tires squealed around the corner at the exit, the wrought iron bars slid open.

She launched the car forward the instant the opening was wide enough, thanking her lucky stars for the sensors that automatically swung it back to the latch once she was on the other side. The black car careened into view as the gate was secured. She had to act fast.

Window down and gun drawn, she twisted in her seat and aimed out the window. With one shot, she disabled the back exit's control box along the curb, sending up a shower of sparks as the black car made it around the last, sharp corner. The men in the car screamed obscenities and took aim at her.

Her mission accomplished, she jammed her foot hard on the accelerator again. Gunshots rang out around her, one bullet reverberating off the metal somewhere on her car and another shattering the driver's side mirror—much too close for comfort. The important thing was that they could not follow her.

As she squealed her tires around the corner at a traffic light a few minutes later, she recalled the previous night, when she'd sat at the endless red light with Will, wishing he'd stop staring at her. Her heart lurched at the memory.

I may be a terrible person, but I can do the right thing for once.

The part of her brain that took over when she was on a job—any job but this one—raged at her. *What the hell has happened to you? You've never let your emotions run rampant like this. It's like you're not even the same person anymore.*

Maybe I'm not.

Checking her rearview mirror constantly, she wove through the streets, her pulse pounding. She was compromised, and she needed to ditch this car as soon as possible—it was likely they'd be able to identify it. As for identifying her, blonde women weren't exactly rare in California, so her hair color alone didn't necessarily give her away. At least, that's what she told herself.

Up ahead, a neon sign for the same rental car company from which she'd rented her car at the airport blinked at her. Pulling into the parking lot behind the building, she got out and opened the trunk. After removing all traces of herself from the car, she condensed her belongings into her duffle bag, lifted the bag onto her shoulder, and clicked the key fob to engage the locks. The resulting chirp made her wince.

Wiping the keys clean of fingerprints and depositing them in the return slot, she shoved the latex gloves back in her pocket as she jogged around the building. Now out of sight of the road, she used her phone to search hotels in the area, settling on one about ten miles away. That way, even if they managed find the car, she wouldn't be nearby. First thing in the morning, she'd pick up a different rental car.

Now with a destination and a rough plan of action, she turned off her phone as she strode across the parking lot toward the run-down bar next door. It was all too easy for her location to be tracked through her phone, and she vowed to use it as little as possible going forward. She scrutinized every black car around her as she waited for the screen to go black, then shoved the device in her pocket.

The paint was peeling on the walls of the building, and a blinking neon sign announced its less than original name: *Margaritaville.*

These days it seemed that everyone used a phone app to summon a ride, so she wasn't sure of her chances of finding a plain old cab. She was in luck, however, because a decrepit taxi was parked by the door of the bar. Its driver stood against the cab and smoked, ogling her as she approached.

"Need a ride, baby?"

"Yes, actually." Controlling her disgust at being called "baby," Jen climbed into the back seat without reservation. She could subdue the man if necessary, so his sleaze factor didn't intimidate her. After rattling off the name and address of the hotel she'd chosen, she slumped in her seat as the car pulled onto the road. Now that she'd almost made it to safety, the adrenaline began to leave her system, and the pain in her arm and shoulder returned.

A jumble of questions swirled in her head. Among them was the most important one: *What do I do now?*

CHAPTER 24

A LITTLE AFTER 2 A.M., Jen paid the cab driver, squinting at the lights around the front entrance of the hotel. She hadn't taken her eyes off the road behind them for a second the whole way there, and she was as sure as she could be that no one had found her.

After checking every inch of the room on the fourth floor just as thoroughly as always, she lay in bed, staring at the ceiling and worrying. She worried about Will's involvement in whatever was happening at the studio. She worried about whether he was safe, even for the next few hours. She worried that someone had followed her. She worried about whether they'd located her rental car, or if she'd left a clue that would lead someone back to her. She worried about having to kill Will, and she worried about what would happen if she didn't. She worried about her mother—not only her health, but also what she would think if she knew the terrible things Jen had done.

Only after the clock had ticked past 3:30 a.m. did her brain stop spinning, and she dropped off to sleep.

The next thing she knew, Jen was rubbing her eyes, trying to figure out why her surroundings were strange yet recognizable. The details quickly filled themselves in one by one, as if she were inside a time-lapse video of a pencil drawing that went from a few lines to an intricate, full-colored design before her eyes. She was seated at a table with a white linen tablecloth, and Rachel took shape across from her, laughing and chatting excitedly. To the right and left, her surroundings appeared—this was the long table at which she'd sat for dinner on Monday night. The people who'd sat there, whose names she did not remember, were there too.

That was more than twenty-four hours ago. This must be a dream.

If this is Monday night, then Will is sitting to my immediate right. Her heartbeat accelerated.

A hand wrapped around the bare skin of her left shoulder, flooding her veins with warmth. She twisted to face Will, who gazed down at her with surprising intensity, triggering a rush of emotion. Her confusion must have amused him, because the corners of his eyes crinkled even more.

To her surprise, he tipped his face toward her until his stubble brushed her cheek, giving her chills. "You look beautiful," he said in her ear.

Instead of replying, Jen blushed and brushed her cheek against his, overwhelmed. For once he didn't tease her, simply chuckled as he nuzzled close to her ear. "Steph? You with me?"

She moved back just enough to study him. "Yeah. And . . . thanks."

As if in slow motion, he bent lower until his forehead pressed against hers. The next second, their noses made contact as well. This made them both grin harder.

The next second, Will was gone, along with the restaurant, and she was lying in an unfamiliar bed, alone in a silent room. The memory of her dream was already gone. She squinted into the darkness as she dove to the right to retrieve the gun she'd tucked under her mattress. Breathing hard and holding the weapon out in front of her, she pieced the previous day back together, recalling that she had changed hotels, and why. Her breathing slowed back to normal, and she set the gun on the nightstand.

The day ahead felt like a prison sentence. What was going on at the studio and what to do about it weighed heavily on her mind, and the biggest mystery of all was how Will was involved.

A chillingly emotionless voice filled her head. *Today, you're going to do what you need to do. No hesitation, no excuses. You don't want to end up dead, so you're going to do your damn job, and that's all there is to it. It's your last chance.*

But Jen was no longer certain. *Unless I can prove he doesn't deserve to die. Because something's going on—*

Shut up; of course he does. You're not paid to play detective.

Jen ran through her morning routine on autopilot, her insides swirling with equal parts impatience and dread over talking to Will. She was ready much faster than usual, but it wasn't fast enough for her. When she was done, she packed all her belongings again—the essentials and incriminating items such as her gun and jammer in her go bag, which was tucked with everything else inside her duffle bag. Like the day before, she wiped the room clean of all traces of her.

Just before 7 a.m. she walked out the front door of the hotel. The cab driver from the night before had offered her a card, and she called him from her burner phone before switching it back off. He took her to a nearby rental car agency that opened early.

Will had instructed her not to come in before 10:30 a.m., but no way could she stall that long. It'd been all she could do to stop herself from calling him in the middle of the night about what she'd witnessed. By 7:45 a.m., unable to deal with finding a detour to slow down her arrival, she pulled through the studio lot main gate, surveying the property warily. To her relief, there was no sign of the men, the black car, or the tractor trailer. Still, she was on edge.

When the elevator doors opened onto the main hallway, she braced herself—not that anyone was around at that hour. Her stomach was in knots as she approached the kitchen, which she was both relieved and disappointed to find empty. She melted into a chair at the table closest to the window, facing the door. It was best that no one sneak up behind her in her current state.

Staring out the window to her left, she paid no attention to the overcast sky. With a heavy sigh, she dropped her head into her hands, doing her best to will herself somewhere else. Her body was sluggish from lack of sleep, but even un-caffeinated she was jittery and couldn't sit still for long. Abandoning her seat, she stood and paced back and forth in front of the window until exhaustion won out over her nerves. She slowed to a stop and leaned her right shoulder against the wall beside the window, resting her forehead on the cool glass and closing her eyes.

One second, a hand was on her shoulder, and the next Jen was peering down at Will lying on his back on the floor in front of her. Her reaction to an unexpected touch had been to spin around, put him in a tight hold, and flip him on his back before either of them knew what was happening.

Her hands flew to her face in dismay. "Oh my God, I'm sorry," she said through her shaking fingers. She sank to her knees beside him, horrified. "Are you okay?" She could barely force herself to look at him.

"Well, good morning." His voice was weak, and he appeared genuinely shocked. "I guess you didn't hear me come in."

She shook her head, forcing herself to speak. "I'm so sorry." She kept repeating it in a whisper. "I didn't even— You were there and I—" The words were jumping out of her mouth, and she ordered them to stop, but it wasn't working. "I'm a little on edge today. It was an involuntary reaction, I swear."

He smiled at her but didn't attempt to move. "Where'd you learn to do that, anyway?" It was surreal to be holding a conversation with him like this, as if it were perfectly normal that he was lying on his back on the floor.

What could she say? The truth was off limits. Though she wanted to rest her hands on him as reassurance—his arm, maybe?—she no longer trusted herself to be gentle. Instead, she gripped her own knees hard enough to leave marks.

I threw Will on the ground. He should at least be annoyed with me. So why isn't he?

"Steph? You with me?"

Those words triggered something in her brain, and all at once the dream she hadn't remembered replayed in her mind on fast forward, the details so vivid that it could've been real. If she had to guess based on how her cheeks burned, she'd say her face was now purple.

"Hey, are you okay?" His voice sounded far away as he lifted his head to gaze at her, wincing as he tilted it to one side.

"What? Oh, yeah. My arm sort of hurts because I—" Realizing that Will was asking about her distraction, she stopped abruptly, since she did not have a lie prepared for why her arm would be hurting. She forced Dream Will out of her mind, then faced the real one sheepishly. "Maybe we should start today over? I promise not to throw you on the floor again."

"Good idea." He moved slowly, pushing himself up. "And that's the last time I sneak up on you. Not that I was sneaking up on you, of course."

She winced in embarrassment.

Already on her feet when he sat up, she offered him her hand. It was the least she could do.

"Thanks." He held on tightly as he pulled himself up, and though her shoulder protested having to lift his weight, her skin tingled from the contact. He gripped her hand for a half second longer than necessary before letting go.

No. You're imagining things.

"Okay, starting over. Hey, Steph. Good morning."

"Good morning." Now that her intense humiliation had begun to fade, she recalled why she'd been distraught that morning.

He was studying her, a curious expression on his face. "Don't take this the wrong way, but did you get any sleep? And why are you here three hours early?"

"No, you're right, I didn't sleep much. And maybe I shouldn't point this out, but you're here early, too." She tried to smile as if nothing were wrong, but it didn't work.

Will ignored her observation. "Do you want some coffee? We can pretend you made it."

She closed her eyes and took a slow breath, wanting to cry over the overwhelming unfairness of the entire situation. "No, thanks."

"So, you didn't get any sleep, but you don't want coffee? Steph, talk to me. I don't know you that well, but that goes against what I do know about you. What's wrong?"

She didn't deserve his concern. Pushing aside a rush of affection for him and avoiding his gaze, Jen was torn. She wanted to figure out his involvement in this mess before she decided what to do or how much to tell him. Did she talk about this here, in a relatively public place, or somewhere they wouldn't be overheard? Of course, if he was involved and she confronted him, it could be dangerous to go with him somewhere more private. It came down to whether or not she trusted him.

Trust was not her thing—it always seemed to backfire. She bit her lip, glancing around nervously even though no one else was there, and studied him for a few more heartbeats.

Please let me be right about you.

She went with her gut instinct. "What do you know about props being shipped ahead of time to the international shooting locations? Do they do that?"

Will stared at her, processing the question. "I've never given it any thought. If they need to send something, I assume they pack it and send it a little ahead of time. Then again, maybe it's easier to buy things wherever we shoot. I don't know. What does that have to do with anything?"

She studied him as he spoke, trying to read his mind.

He's an actor; he could easily be lying.

"But you don't suppose they'd take, for example, a whole tractor trailer of crates full of props?"

He was regarding her strangely now. Of course he was. She sounded like she'd lost it.

"I'm not sure what the usual amount is," he said. "But one time I did get a peek at some crates. Maybe they were props."

"You did?"

"Yeah, why? What's wrong?" His voice dropped as low as hers.

This was a red flag to her. *If he'd watched the crew packing crates on a regular basis, it would mean nothing. But only once, that could've been an accident. If he was behind it, he'd want it to seem like no big deal. He wouldn't be asking more questions.*

Or am I seeing what I want to see? Because I'll bet he can fake sincerity really well. It's part of his job.

When she didn't answer him, he took half a step forward, into her personal space, his face tense. His right hand moved as if he intended to use it to comfort her, but her head snapped toward the movement, and after an awkward second, he dropped it to his side. Considering that she'd flung him to the ground, she couldn't blame him for being afraid of her.

He should be afraid of me. The thought made her nauseous. *But I trust him.*

Her eyes darted around the room as if she expected someone to appear out of midair. "We shouldn't talk about it here."

She expected him to tell her she was being paranoid, but he softly said, "Okay, can we talk in my trailer?"

"Yeah." Her feet, however, had other ideas.

When she didn't follow him toward the door, he started back and stopped in front of her, lifting his right hand as if in surrender before inching it forward. "I'd appreciate not ending up on the ground again, if that's possible."

She winced at the mention of the incident, nodding slightly, and stared as he closed the distance between them. His hand landed on her shoulder, and instead of a violent reaction, she found herself leaning into it.

"Come on." Will's gentle voice steadied her as much as the hand that now slid to the middle of her back. "Let's go."

All her energy went into putting one foot in front of the other as they walked down the hall to the elevator. He kept his hand resting lightly on her back, the momentum urging her forward. Once in the elevator beside him, she gave in to the weight of her eyelids and concentrated on remaining upright, resisting the urge to rest her head on his shoulder.

Let's be realistic. Just because he doesn't deserve to die doesn't mean the two of us get a happy ending. The best I can realistically expect is to keep both of us alive. He goes on with his life, and I go back to whatever's left of mine. This isn't a fairy tale.

They walked out through the lobby and across the parking lot, following almost the same path she'd taken the night before. A breeze blew strands of her hair wildly in front of her, but her arms were crossed against her chest, and she made no attempt to tame it.

"Alright, here we are." They'd arrived at his trailer, and he pulled the door open for her. "Go on up; I'm right behind you."

She climbed the first step, then glanced over her shoulder to the empty parking lot behind Will, searching for immediate threats. But not a soul besides the two of them was there, so she turned and climbed the last few stairs, dread expanding to fill every inch of her.

Her feet stopped moving only a few steps inside the doorway, even when he moved past her. "Steph, come sit." He beckoned her to the couch a few feet away. Steeling herself, she sank down on the edge of a cushion, trying to find the words to say what needed to be said. He sat facing her, a small space left between them, while she stared blankly at the opposite wall. She sensed him watching her as she hunched forward, letting her hair fall around her face like a curtain.

You can't fall apart now. Still, no words would come.

Hey! Snap out of it! It's time to explain what's going on. You owe him at least that much.

Only when Jen managed to get out of her own head did his words reach her. She suddenly became conscious of how close he was to her, and of his hand moving tentatively back and forth across her back. Her insides flipped between serenity and alarm.

"Tell me what's wrong."

She was distressed at the worry on his face. It was the last thing she deserved.

"It's going to sound insane." She shook her head as she looked away from his unwavering gaze.

"Try me."

She sat up straight and regarded him again. "Can I ask you something? I know how random it sounds, but I swear it'll make sense."

"Of course. Anything."

Stop being so nice, Will. Please.

She exhaled and forced the words out. "Would you tell me about the crates? Where were they? And when?"

He raised his eyebrows at the change of topic but answered thoughtfully. "I was on the second floor of the warehouse last week. I forget what I was up there for. And yes, we have people who'll go get stuff for us, but I can easily do it myself."

It was such a Will thing to say, and Jen wanted to smile at him, but she couldn't. "Do you remember anything else about that day?"

"Well, the second floor is a long hall lined with storage closets. I'd just come out of one of them when some guy came out of the door across from it. He didn't look happy to see me there, that's for sure. He wasn't a tall guy, so I could see over his shoulder into the closet behind him. There were two stacks of wooden crates, maybe two feet wide and like five feet long."

Just like the ones I saw.

"And it was weird, because I'd assume crates are more for shipping than storage; but since we film internationally, I figured they had stuff packed to send ahead for our next shoot, like you said."

"What did the guy coming out of the other door look like? Did you recognize him?"

He paused, his forehead creased in thought. "No, he wasn't a regular on the crew, which was also a little weird. It's usually the same people around here. He grunted at me, and I said something like, 'Oh, hey man,' as he shut the door. He didn't say anything, just stomped back to the elevator." Will's shoulders rose and then fell. "That's all I know."

It made sense. Even though he had no idea what was in the crates, someone knew he'd seen them. In the mind of whoever was in charge, what little he knew was too much, and they wanted him out of the way.

That's why I was hired. He doesn't have a secret. He has really bad timing.

"Can you describe the guy?"

"Uh, heavyset white guy, short dark hair. We're all casual here, but this guy looked like he hadn't showered recently. Oh, and he had some kind of huge skull tattoo on his right arm, halfway between his shoulder and his elbow. It was hard to miss."

"You have a good memory."

"Well, it was a weird moment. It stuck with me."

His hand had stopped between her shoulder blades, his thumb still moving back and forth and reminding her of her dream. The corners of her mouth tilted upward the tiniest bit at the thought, but she pushed it away. It would only make things harder.

"Okay, your turn. What's going on?"

She sighed under the weight of so many secrets. But she'd promised to explain, and she owed him what little information she could give. This was the point of no return.

CHAPTER 25

"FROM WHAT I'VE PIECED TOGETHER, it's something dangerous."
Jen's eyes darted around the room and back to him.

His hand on her back tensed, as if he'd only just realized it was
there. "I'm sorry if I'm making you uncomfortable. Sheesh, I'm like
HR's worst nightmare." When he lifted his hand and scooted away
from her, a sinking feeling pulled at the inside of her chest. Her head
moved quickly back and forth.

"No, you weren't." She studied her knees. Just in case she hadn't
been clear, she added, "You weren't making me uncomfortable."

He stopped moving, and she knew he was watching her. "Was it
helping?"

She gave a quick and almost imperceptible nod. After a slight
hesitation, the couch creaked as he moved back to where he'd been,
closer to her. She would regret encouraging this, but her future was
already a disaster, so consequences be damned.

Staring down at her hands fidgeting in her lap, she didn't see
him reach out his free hand until it landed on hers. Inhaling deeply,
she allowed herself to enjoy the nervous energy zinging through her,
counting to five before she met his eyes. Again she worried that he

could read her thoughts.

"Tell me." That sincere look in his eyes stabbed at her conscience, but there was nothing she could do about the lies she had to tell him. Nothing, that is, except tell him as much of the truth as possible.

She inhaled the scent of his cologne, gathering her courage. Even though they were alone, her voice dropped to a whisper. "Last night, after I found my keys, I came back outside. A bright light and faint rumbling noise were coming from this way. I couldn't imagine what was going on so late at night, so I came over to find out." She stopped talking, momentarily mesmerized by his hand on hers, and had to remind herself to keep going.

"The sounds were coming from near the warehouse loading dock. And I'm stupid, and nosy, and I wanted to find out what it was, so I went around the front and slipped in through a door that was propped open. The floor was covered in long rows of crates that were all stamped *Gemini Divided*. They had an airport code on them, too. 'DUB.' Dublin."

"We're supposed to film in Dublin next week."

Jen glanced up at him again. "Yeah. In theory, it could have been props." Her tone suggested that she didn't believe it. "I'm not sure how many crates of props are a normal amount. Or would they buy things on-site, like you suggested? I don't know. Anyway, that space was full of them. It was impossible to me that they would need that many. I should have left, but for some reason I ran across the room to the stairwell."

Hazarding another peek at him, she tried to force herself to smile but ended up just making her lips twitch awkwardly. Her attention returned to her lap as she continued.

"The second floor was . . . creepy. The noise from downstairs was getting louder and I was afraid of being found up there. I had to find somewhere to hide."

His hand squeezed hers a little tighter.

Enjoy this while you can.

After a quick account of ending up in the closet, and what had come next, Jen shook her head at the shock on Will's face. "I know what you're going to say. And yes, it was stupid of me."

"Not stupid. Reckless, yes, but not stupid. What was inside the crates?"

"Ammunition. Not blanks, and not regular bullets, either. Armor-piercing bullets. Those would never be props. Oh, wait, I took a picture." She was reluctant to loosen her right hand from under his, but she did, then pulled out her phone.

He shifted for a better view of the screen. No longer facing her, his shoulder came to rest beside hers, and his hands shifted back to his lap. She told herself she wasn't disappointed.

In front of them was a dim, grainy picture of what she'd discovered. "I opened one other crate before I left."

He turned to gape at her in disbelief. "Steph, you shouldn't have been spending time taking pictures. You should've gotten yourself out of there immediately."

"This is the other one." She scooted closer so he could get a better view, and so she wouldn't have to look at the reproach in his face.

"Guns."

"Yeah."

He paused, taking it all in, but rebounded quickly. "So, whatever else is in the crates, it's not props."

She was amazed that Will didn't question anything she was saying. She had proof, but it was still unbelievable, and surely he didn't know enough about guns to know from the pictures that those things were what she said they were. She didn't deserve it, but she had his trust.

"I don't see how they could be."

"No wonder you've been freaking out." Quiet stretched between them. "How did you open them, anyway? Aren't they nailed shut?"

"Like this." She pantomimed the motion, wincing when pain shot up her arm even without hitting anything. "It hurt," she said, sheepish.

He looked at her hand, now back on her knee, and for a second she thought he was going to cover it with his again. Instead, his eyes found hers. "But you're okay."

"I wish that was the end of the story."

"It's not?"

Her eyes closed and she sighed. "No. Upstairs, one of the guys had mentioned something about the boss wanting everyone out back in five minutes. I figured that was my chance to slip out without being caught." She detailed what had happened truthfully, but ended with the black car's departure and slipping out of the building.

"Please tell me that's when you left?"

"I should have."

He shook his head at her. "Steph," he said in a frustrated grumble.

"I guess you're not the only one who's impossible." She grimaced when the spark of recognition lit his eyes. "I told you, I'm nosy. I need answers. So I snuck around the side of the building to find out what was going on."

"Seriously?"

Recounting what she'd seen behind the warehouse, she left out the part about the car chase and everything after that.

Will shook his head at her. "I'm glad you're okay, but what you did was incredibly dangerous. Anything could have happened to you."

She'd forgotten what it was like to have someone besides her mother worry about her. Though it was both undeserved and temporary, she craved the bittersweet feeling.

Whoever's in charge of this operation is the one who wants him dead. She managed to hold that part in.

"Why didn't you call the police? Or security? Someone?"

A normal person would have reported this, so she had to have a good reason why she hadn't. "I didn't want to get in trouble." That was true, just not in the way he would assume. "It was only my second day here, and I wasn't supposed to be there in the first place."

"I can't believe— This is crazy. Are you sure?"

"About which part?" She tried to laugh, but it came out as more of a choked sob.

She wanted to tell him about the threat to his life, but she had no proof except the fact that she'd been hired to kill him. He'd stumbled across some crates, which she'd later found as well, along with some others that had been loaded into a truck; there wasn't enough evidence to suggest repercussions were coming.

For a minute they were both quiet. Again Jen studied him, still anxious about his reaction.

"Steph, you put yourself in a lot of danger. What if they'd caught you? You should've been more careful."

"I'm fine."

"Can you describe the guys upstairs? Or any of them?"

"No. I kept out of sight, so I never saw them. But I'll never forget the two voices I heard in that closet." She shuddered as they echoed in her head.

Her long-held rule against admissions of weakness made her hesitate to share her next thought, but her desperation to tell him something that wasn't a lie won out. Focused on her lap, she said, "I'm not scared of much, but I don't think I've ever been as scared as I was last night." She bitterly realized that this confession also supported her assistant guise better than acting as if she were fine.

When she peered up at him, he was frowning at her. "Okay, I get why you didn't call security. But why didn't you call me?" He sounded hurt.

Her chest constricted. She needed him to stop being so nice. "It was the middle of the night. And I was fine. What could you have done?"

"You were fine?" he repeated, incredulous. "You just told me you'd never been so scared. And how did you sleep last night, after everything that happened?" Will was making a point because she'd already admitted to barely sleeping.

She sighed, saying nothing.

"Exactly. You weren't fine. As far as what I could've done? I don't know. I could've talked to you. I may have still been at the bar, which wasn't that far away from here. Even if I was at home, I wish you'd called me. We're friends, okay? You can call me in the middle of the night if you need me."

"Are you sure about that?" She'd never had that kind of friend before.

"It's obviously not an offer I make to most people. But I'm telling you that if you need me, you call me. No matter what. Okay? Promise me."

For a second Jen was speechless. Uncomfortable with his seriousness, she grimaced, her tone as light as she could make it. "Well, I was hoping that would be my first and last time in that situation, so . . ." When his expression remained serious, she sighed. Meeting his eyes again, she nodded solemnly. "Okay fine, I promise." Only then did he smile back at her.

I won't be around long enough for a "next time," but I'm going to do the right thing this time.

The problem was that she had no idea what the right thing to do in this situation was. "Wait and see what happens" was not an option. And yet, the alternative was to take control of a situation composed entirely of unknown variables. She wanted to scream in frustration, but that wouldn't help. In order to figure out her next move, she needed to think clearly.

Tuning out the noise, she went back to a familiar question: *What do I know?* Only one thing was certain. *I'm going to save him, or die trying. I owe him that much.*

CHAPTER 26

JEN FINALLY GAVE WILL A weak smile. "What time do you start this morning?"

"I have to go up to Hair and Makeup at 8:30." According to the clock on the wall, it was almost 8:15. "We need coffee." He went to the kitchenette. "And it's not a question this time."

She didn't have the energy to make another joke about him making her coffee—her brain was too busy spinning in circles. When he sat beside her again, he placed a mug and a paper towel–wrapped Pop-Tart on the coffee table in front of them. "The menu's a little simpler out here than in the kitchen. Sorry."

"Thanks. It's okay. I'm not hungry."

"Humor me, please."

She took a bite of the Pop-Tart and a sip of her coffee. Both were tasteless, which should've concerned her, but she had too many other things on her mind. A tense silence descended.

"Are you worried about the scene we're filming today, or about the crates?"

For a guy who called himself oblivious, he's amazingly astute.

"Yes," she said, aware that it wasn't a yes-or-no question.

He made a valiant attempt not to laugh, fixing a sympathetic smile on her. "Well, nothing bad is going to happen to Matt until after lunch. And I swear, you have nothing to worry about with that. It's like Rachel said last night, they've shot me many times before and I'm still here."

Since she couldn't tell him what really had her so upset, she had to let him believe she was being a little ridiculous. "I still don't like it." It wasn't a lie; it just wasn't the whole truth.

Will shook his head at her, and for a few minutes they sat in silence again, eating and drinking. He was the one to speak first. "Ready to go?"

"Yeah." She drained the last of her coffee and stood. "Oh, and it's probably best not to tell anyone else about the crates for now."

"Agreed."

Preceding him through the trailer door, Jen searched the empty parking lot for signs of danger, continuing to survey the area as they walked. She didn't let her guard down until they were safely inside the building ten elevator, where she released a long-overdue sigh of relief.

Will gave her a curious look, and she found her voice. "I can't stop thinking about last night at the warehouse."

"But no one got a good look at you, right? So you're as safe today as you were yesterday."

That's what I'm afraid of.

The elevator doors opened, and the tension returned. Her constant scanning of their surroundings resumed as they walked down the silent hall. He kept glancing back at her but said nothing. Finally, as they neared the door to Hair and Makeup, he spoke up.

"What's really bothering you, Steph?"

"I just have a bad feeling."

"Well, all I know is that I pity anyone who sneaks up on you." Before she had a chance to feel bad about having thrown him to the ground, he opened the door, and Jen was forced to put on her best "everything is totally normal" face.

She was grateful they didn't need to be there long; pretending everything was fine was exhausting. Of course, leaving the relative safety of Hailey's domain and walking back outside was worse. She was accustomed to exploiting vulnerabilities, not protecting people. Instead of choosing the best of multiple options for eliminating a target, she had to somehow foresee and defend him against a million potential threats.

There was not a single crate to be seen in the warehouse—instead, cameras and filming equipment cluttered the floor. Making sure she wasn't overheard, she leaned into him and lowered her voice. "I'm not crazy. I swear, this whole place was full of rows of crates last night."

"I believe you, Steph," he said softly. "They wouldn't have left anything for people to find."

As they moved farther into the room, Jen peered up at the rafters for the first time. One metal stairway on each wall led up to a thick grid of beams that crisscrossed high above their heads, like a ceiling loosely woven of metal. It stretched from one end of the room to the other, with lights and other equipment secured in the gaps.

She went cold with the realization that she was looking at a perfect hiding place for a sniper.

After studying the rafters as best she could from her position and finding no sign of anyone, she concentrated on the ground. Will was nearby, talking to the man she recognized as the director, while a few others stood and listened. She scrutinized each of the people around him, all potential suspects.

It's going to be a long day.

For the next few hours, her eyes only left him when they were sweeping the area and the rafters above. He'd caught her watching him in between takes more than once, his eyes always offering the same reassurance. *He probably thinks I'm being paranoid.*

The morning was painfully long. When the director finally sent them on lunch break and Will made his way toward her, the weight in Jen's chest eased a little. Ever vigilant, she scanned every inch of the floor and ceiling again before peering up at him.

"Hey," he said, now standing in front of her. "Everything okay?"

"So far."

"You hungry? Lunch is set up in the courtyard."

"No." She'd already started another sweep of the room.

He glanced around to be sure no one was nearby, moving a little closer before he said, "I guess I shouldn't have phrased that as a question. You need to eat. What if you have to do more ninja moves? You need to keep your strength up."

She smiled despite how stressed she was. "Fine."

"Let's get some lunch. I have an hour."

Jen gritted her teeth and tried to be rational, not wanting to think about what came after lunch.

How ironic that last night I had convinced myself I wanted him to be shot, and now I'm trying to stop it.

The food for the actors and the crew was set up in the courtyard beside the warehouse. While most people sat at folding tables set up nearby, Jen and Will sat on the ground with their plates, leaning against a low stone wall that shielded the backs of their heads—Jen's suggestion. That way, she didn't have to constantly check over her shoulders. Even so, she inspected the 180 degrees in front of the wall over and over.

They ate slowly, not talking much. Like her coffee that morning, the food had no taste to her, and she ate very little. He cracked a few jokes but couldn't convince her to relax.

If I concentrate hard enough, I'll figure out how to fix this.

They'd gone ten minutes without speaking when the loud *beep* of his watch made her jump, her heart leaping into her throat. He grinned at her, shaking his head.

"Jumpy? Me? Not at all," she said quietly, adding, "I guess it's time to get back in there?"

"Yep." He sat and watched her without moving. His next words came out in an unusually serious tone. "Steph, I know you're worried, but it's going to be fine. Unless you know something you're not telling me?"

Anguish twisted her insides. *I wish I could tell you.* The longer she stared into his eyes, the more the pain in her chest intensified.

"No, you're right. It's going to be fine." Standing deliberately, she rested a hand on his shoulder to keep him sitting while she examined all 360 degrees around them. Finding nothing, she moved away reluctantly so he could get up.

At the door of the warehouse, he stopped. "You're really not going to tell me what's wrong?"

"I hate feeling helpless. About the crates. I wish I could do something about it. Someone has to do something." She paused as she considered how much truth there was to what she was about to say. "And I admit it, the thought of you getting shot makes me nervous. Yes, I'm a bit of a control freak."

Will buzzed the door open with his ID and pulled it open a crack, but no farther. He turned to face her, his expression serious. "Does it help if I tell you that you're the least helpless person I've ever met? I'm not kidding." Her cheeks flushed as she remembered that she'd thrown him to the ground.

Dammit, Will. Stop being so nice. All she could manage aloud was "Wow. Thanks."

Once inside, they stopped not far from where the director was standing as Jen scanned the space again. Panic bubbled inside her, and she took a half step closer to his side as if her proximity could protect him. This was her last opportunity to talk to him before whatever was going to happen actually happened. But what could she say? The director beckoned him over, and she spit out the only words she could come up with.

"Be careful, please." She had to rely on the urgency in her voice and in her eyes to convey what her words could not.

"Come on." His words were joking and serious at the same time, and brimming with affection. "Who in their right mind would mess with me when I have you on my side? I have nothing to worry about."

She had never hated herself more than she did at that moment.

"Wow. No pressure, right?"

"It's going to be fine," he murmured, and she fought a sinking feeling.

Her stomach tightened as he approached the director. All she could do now was keep watch, so that's what she did. Standing with her arms crossed tightly over her chest, she scoured the area for anything out of place as Will and Rachel's characters snuck into the building they were raiding.

Movement in the rafters caught her eye. The reflection lasted a fraction of a second, but it was enough. Staring hard between the beams, she spotted a shadow where none had been before.

Someone's up there.

Her blood curdled at the realization that she'd been right. Someone was going to kill Will unless she could stop them.

Jen craned her neck to find Will, but he was somewhere in the labyrinth of false walls that had been constructed for filming. Not wasting time, she moved swiftly—but refrained from running, for fear of attracting attention. Up the metal stairway she climbed, taking care to keep her footsteps light while still moving quickly. Miraculously, no one seemed to notice her.

Not only did she have to get all the way to the top without arousing suspicion from below her, but she had to avoid being detected by the sniper and disarm him or her without anyone getting hurt, all before they took a shot at Will.

Get to the top. Get to the top.

With cat-like grace, she stepped onto the landing in slow motion. The distance between where she stood and the sniper's rifle pointed at Will was vast. Déjà vu surrounded her. She was used to being the one peering through the scope at a target.

Instead of rushing forward and tackling the man, as she wanted to, she slunk toward him without a sound. If she drew his attention, it was over. Holding a metal pipe someone had discarded by the wall, she advanced as quickly as she dared.

For once, something went right for her—almost. She was in range of the sniper, bringing the metal bar back to swing at his head, when he went absolutely still; he was about to fire.

No! I can't be too late.

Adrenaline surged through her, and she swung harder. The *crack* of the bullet leaving the rifle came half a second after the *thump* of the metal pipe making contact with his head. The force of Jen's swing rolled him over, and his weapon lodged where two pieces of the woven ceiling overlapped below them, preventing it from falling to the floor.

She could only hope she'd altered the bullet's trajectory.

The man lay still, stunned by the blow, and she couldn't tell if he was unconscious. Her question was answered quickly when, in the space of a few heartbeats, he was back on his feet with an angry fire in his eyes the likes of which she'd never seen. She backed away carefully, buying time to prepare herself for a fight. Blood leaked from a gash across the side of his head where the pipe had made contact.

Holding the pipe firmly in front of her, she stood her ground. Now that he was upright and closing in, the man towered over her— she hadn't expected him to be so much bigger. He swung his arm as if to pick her up, but she was lighter and quicker and sprang out of his way. With all her strength, she smacked his arm with the metal rod again. Now even more furious, he unleashed a tirade of muttered curses as he drew a pistol from the back waistband of his jeans.

Time slowed when he took aim at her. She gripped the pipe midway along its length in both hands, swinging one end and then the other in a fluid motion. Though she hadn't used the move in years, her body remembered what to do. She knocked the gun out of his hands, and it clattered away, disappearing from sight. This left them more evenly matched, or so Jen hoped.

She needed to disable the man and vanish before security swarmed the rafters. It wouldn't be long.

Angrier than ever, he charged at her. Her plan was to wait until he got close enough, then use his size against him. Unfortunately, his size proved to be more of an advantage than she'd taken into account, and when her foot slipped, he grabbed her before she could right herself. His fingers dug into her sides as she was lifted into the air and slammed into the metal surface. Her head vibrated loudly, and her whole body stung from the impact.

The sound of shouts and the pounding of shoes on the ladders reached her ears. They weren't at the top yet, but they were closing in.

Struggling to stop seeing double, Jen got to her feet. The shooter had already fled, and she had a horrible thought—*If they find me here alone, they're going to assume I was the one who shot at Will.* She squared her shoulders. *No. I don't have time to get caught. I have to save him.*

The entrance to an internal stairwell that didn't lead to the open warehouse floor was nearby. Security could just as easily be swarming this one as the others, but she had to risk it. She grabbed her trusty pipe from the floor nearby, wiped it off with her shirt, and set it back on the ground. Wrapping the bottom edge of her shirt around the door handle, she opened it. It wouldn't do to leave fingerprints behind on either surface.

She flew down the stairs back to the ground floor faster than advisable after how hard she'd hit her head, tripping twice and barely saving herself from careening headfirst into the cement of the wall or the floor. Blending into the throng of people below, she rushed back to the last place she'd spotted Will. The police had not yet arrived to take control of the chaos, and Will was nowhere to be seen. Her head swam.

The shooter got away. Will's missing. I failed. I'm too late.

She did not immediately register that someone was talking to her. It was Erica, who stood wide-eyed beside her. "What happened?"

Jen could only shake her head helplessly, still unable to catch her breath or form words. The brunette propelled them through the crowd to the front, where a large man dressed in a gray uniform blocked the way. From there they watched a woman in pink medical scrubs with a first aid kit kneeling beside Will. He lay on his back, talking to the nurse, who pressed a cloth against his shoulder.

He was alive. Jen's knees went weak with relief, and she put a hand on Erica's shoulder to keep from losing her balance.

"Sorry, ladies, everyone has to clear this area. Let's go." The security guard eyed them, stone-faced.

"Can you at least tell us what happened?" Erica sounded desperate.

Jen's thoughts momentarily drowned out the world around her. *They hired someone else to do my job, which makes me expendable. They'll come after both of us sooner than later. We have to get out of here!*

Erica had walked them back around the corner without Jen realizing it. "Stephanie?"

"What?"

"Are you okay?"

She ignored Erica's question. "Did someone call an ambulance?" She was already powering on her phone.

"I doubt it. We have an infirmary across the street, with at least one doctor on set or on call at all times. You saw the nurse with him. They won't send him to the hospital unless it's necessary." Erica looked at her strangely. "What happened to your cheek?"

Jen's hand went to her face, and the heat radiating from her skin reminded her she'd been body-slammed. Adrenaline from the fight was draining from her body, and even her own soft touch made her wince.

"What? Oh, it's nothing. I wasn't paying attention, and I ran into the metal pole over there." She waved her hand vaguely across the room. "Maybe I hit it harder than I thought. No big deal."

"Are you sure it doesn't hurt? Because it looks like it does."

Jen worked very hard not to squirm under Erica's scrutiny. "It stings a little, but I'm fine. Enough about me! I want to see Will."

"He was talking to the nurse, so I'm assuming he's okay. You're really pale. Come and sit over here. I'll go try and find out more. Do you want anything?" Erica sat her in the chair labeled *Will Bryant*, promising to be back with an update, some water, and an ice pack in a few minutes. Before Jen had a chance to protest, the other woman had jogged toward the main door.

She was thankful for the silence that fell when Erica left. Right now she desperately needed to concentrate. *He almost died, and he's still in danger. I can't protect him if I can't get near him.*

Focus. Okay, what do I know? For one thing, someone here is in on this. They have to be. The director, or someone on the crew maybe? It has to be someone here right now. Whoever it is, they wouldn't have wanted to miss that.

For a split second she flashed back to Erica checking over her shoulder with a strange expression as they made their way out of building ten before their Monday-morning shopping trip.

Something in her hand vibrated—her phone, which she'd forgotten she'd taken out of her pocket. A text from Will had just arrived: *What are the odds that my getting shot is related to whatever is going on with the crates? I'm thinking it could be.*

A quick burst of laughter erupted from her as relieved tears sprang out of nowhere. Too many emotions overtook her at once, and she covered her mouth with her free hand to hold them in. He was all right enough to text her, and with his usual sense of humor. Another text bubble popped up.

They're taking me to the infirmary. It's on the second floor of Building 6. Across the street from 10.

And then a third one.

I know you were worried before. Please tell me you're not freaking out. I'm okay, I swear.

Jen exhaled slowly to steady herself. Whatever this was, it wasn't anywhere near over, but at least he was alive. She could still save him.

She kept her response short, already on her way to the exit.

I'll see you there.

Moving quickly, she passed a confused Erica in the doorway. Jen was running across the parking lot as the other woman's shouts faded behind her.

CHAPTER 27

DISREGARDING ANY DANGER TO HERSELF, Jen sprinted across the street to building six. She took the stairs two at a time, her heart hammering in her chest, then ran down a hall and came to a stop in front of an ordinary door with a sign that read *Infirmary.* Even though Will had texted that he was okay, her hand paused above the doorknob, trembling.

The room was much smaller than any doctor's office, and the same young blonde in pink scrubs from the warehouse smiled up at her from a miniature reception desk. "Hi, you must be Stephanie."

"Oh, uh, yes. I am. Is Will here? Will Bryant? I'm his assistant."

"Yes, he's here. He told me to expect you. You sure got here fast!" Jen struggled to hold back her emotions, which must have shown on her face. "Don't worry; he's alright. Dr. Shaw should be finished with him soon. You can have a seat right over there." The young woman pointed to a few upholstered chairs in the corner of the tiny waiting area. With no other option, Jen perched on the edge of one, tapping her foot impatiently.

Each minute lasted an hour. *Whoever wants Will dead is nearby, and it's only a matter of time before they make another attempt on his life. If we're safe now, we won't be for long—especially here.*

After what might as well have been an eternity, a door opened further back in the suite, and two voices floated out to meet her. "And don't get shot again," a woman said good-naturedly.

"I'll do my best, but no promises." That voice belonged to Will.

Jen rolled her eyes. She had simultaneous impulses to hug him and strangle him. The sound of his voice wasn't enough, though. She needed to see him for herself, and she moved so close to the edge of her chair in anticipation that she nearly fell forward.

"Sounds like they're done. Let me check with the doctor." The nurse stood and disappeared around a corner. A few agonizing seconds later, Jen followed her to a door with a large 3 on it. "Here we are." She knocked softly, then opened the door a crack. "Go on in."

"Thanks," Jen muttered over her shoulder as she pushed on the door. Even more nervous than she'd been at the entrance of the suite, she forced her feet to move forward into the room, unable to look up as she shuffled in and the nurse closed the door behind her.

"Hey, Steph."

She stared at the floor, but the smile in his voice came through loud and clear. Those two words alone were almost enough to undo her composure, and she looked up at him.

He sat propped up against several pillows. The hospital-style bed took up most of the tiny room; three steps' worth of floor remained between them, which was both far too much and not nearly enough.

This is all my fault.

In the past, being Stephanie at work had allowed her to flip the switch on her emotions, but that didn't seem to work anymore.

I'm not going to cry. I don't cry. I shoot people from rooftops, for God's sake. What's wrong with me?

Though Will was fine, Jen couldn't stop her bottom lip from quivering. Even her insides were shaking.

"What happened to your cheek?"

She'd already forgotten the welt on her cheek.

"What? Oh, nothing. I bumped into a pole. In the warehouse." It was almost true. Her gaze wandered, inspecting every visible inch of him to determine where he'd been shot.

He must have understood what she was looking for. "The bullet hit my arm, near my shoulder." Careful not to move too fast, his right hand crossed his chest to tug the sleeve of his hospital gown off his left shoulder, revealing the bandage.

She nodded, her eyes glued to the white material wrapped around his shoulder. *He's okay.* Even though she could see him for herself, she could not force the bile in her throat to go back down.

"So, crazy day, huh? Steph?"

Her face fell, her head moving back and forth. She had the urge to back away, but she managed to keep her feet firmly planted. "I'm sorry, I—"

"Sorry? For what?"

Jen forced the words out, telling him how her bad feeling had led her to discover a sniper in the rafters. She simplified the description of the fight she'd had with him.

"So, by 'I bumped into a pole,' you meant a sniper slammed your face into a metal beam because you took it upon yourself to stop him from shooting me?" Will shook his head at her, his eyes and mouth both wide in confusion. "Why would you—"

She ignored his question and went on. "When I got up, he was gone. I lost him. I'm sorry."

"You're sorry? You saved my life."

She winced. "You wouldn't have been shot at all if I'd been faster."

"Stop it. You saved me. I'm sure he wasn't aiming for my shoulder."

"You were wearing a vest, though, when you were filming. Wouldn't that have stopped the bullet?"

Will shook his head. "Our vests aren't real. The real ones are a lot more expensive."

The full weight of it all settled on her shoulders. Even though his face was filled with gratitude, the words repeated in her head like a chorus: *I did this.*

"Hey. It's okay." His voice was quiet, and his compassion was more than she could stand. When she glanced at the floor, her shuttered eyelids released several tears she hadn't been conscious of holding back. Many more threatened to fall.

"Look at me," Will said, but she couldn't. If she looked at him, she would crumble.

"Steph." When Jen didn't respond, he tried to reach for her arm. "Would you come closer, please? Unless you want me to fall on the floor, trying to reach you. I think getting shot is bad enough for one day, don't you?"

The noise that escaped her was decidedly miserable sounding. She took the last three steps forward. Now that she was within arm's reach of him, his good arm slid around her back and pulled her into a careful but tight hug, pressing her into his uninjured right shoulder.

Despite knowing she shouldn't, she found herself hugging him back. The turmoil in her chest pressed outward with equal force until she feared she would burst.

I need to move away from him. I need to keep my feelings out of this.

My feelings have been in this from day one. That's the whole problem.

"Don't cry. Please?" He pressed his cheek against her hair. "You are not the bad guy here. I'm very lucky you were looking out for me."

It was time to give herself a Stephanie-style pep talk. *The only way to save both of us is to look at the situation rationally. Whatever I do, it's going to end in heartache, but better heartache than death. Since I already know it's going to end that way, at least I can make it mean something.*

He tried again to cheer her up. "How is it that I'm the one who got shot, and I'm consoling you? It's like with the coffee! I'm hopeless. I can't get it right."

That one earned him a real chuckle from her, and her resolve to stand up finally won out. "I should, uh . . ." She leaned back until he released her. It had to be her imagination, but she swore she saw disappointment in his face. Taking one more step back so she was out of his reach, she swiped at stray tears with her fingertips.

The distance between them left her both relieved and empty at the same time. "I'm going to talk to the doctor. We really need to get out of here."

"You're not just running away and leaving me to fend for myself, right?" His expression suggested that he was joking, but when she didn't laugh and deny it right away, his face grew serious.

I could walk away right now. I could disappear. The thought lasted only a second. *No, I couldn't live with myself if I did that to him.*

"No." Inside she cursed herself when her voice almost broke. "I just need to figure out how to explain to the doctor that we need to hide from whoever wants us dead without sounding like I've lost my mind."

"Okay. Good luck." His eyes revealed his complete trust in her, and she was assaulted by shame.

The only way to save him is to get moving, stupid. Jarred by Stephanie's sudden reappearance, she pulled the door closed and started toward the front desk.

The silence was unnerving, and she could tell before she reached the entry that something was wrong. It wasn't the quiet of an infirmary with only one patient, but of an infirmary that had been deserted.

The stillness reminded her both of the second floor of the warehouse and of that empty rooftop the night she'd shot Fish Lips. A quick peek around the suite confirmed that both the doctor and nurse were gone.

Oh God, did I put him in danger by leaving him alone?

Her pulse pounded in her ears as she made her way back to Will.

We have to get out of here. Now.

CHAPTER 28

BACK IN WILL'S ROOM, JEN closed the door without a sound and strode to his side. Gone were the hesitation and the tears. Her face was blank, as it would've been on any normal job.

She could tell he was confused by the abrupt change in her demeanor, but she had no time to explain—not that she could have. A silent finger went to her lips.

"What's wrong?" he mouthed.

"They're gone," she said breathlessly. "The doctor, the nurse. Wherever they are, they're not out there. I checked the whole suite."

Will's eyebrows shot up.

Her blank expression did not change. "We need to get out of here. Get dressed."

"Okay." He lifted himself off the bed, every move deliberate. "I could have used a nap, but never mind. Later." Though he was making jokes, his expression said he understood the danger. Moving slowly, he retrieved his clothes from the small cabinet in the corner.

She didn't expect him to be in peak condition after being shot and more than likely given pain medication, but she was concerned by his sluggish motions. Staying ahead of whoever was after them wasn't going to be easy.

Under normal circumstances she would've left him alone to get dressed, but she wasn't about to set foot outside without him, so she walked across the room and stood facing the door, her foot tapping impatiently. After several minutes and much rustling of fabric came an exasperated sigh.

"Hey, Steph, since we're in a hurry here, could you help me out?"

He was now wearing jeans, socks, and untied shoes, but the hospital gown still hung off his left arm. His shirt sat on the bed beside him. The sling had stopped him from sliding the gown off. "My range of motion sucks right now."

Despite Stephanie's steely reserve, it did not escape Jen's attention that he was shirtless. Evidence of many hours spent in the gym stared her in the face. Though his looks were not the only reason she found him attractive, under normal circumstances, she would've been bombarded by a tangle of emotions. Instead, she evaluated the situation objectively.

"Here, I've got it," she said as matter-of-factly as if he'd asked her for a pen. She tied his shoelaces first, then unclasped the sling and slid it off his arm with care. He winced with the effort of supporting his left arm. She freed him of the hospital gown, then picked up the black T-shirt.

She tried to be gentle, but there was no time to move slowly. Lining up the arm hole of the shirt with his left hand, she threaded it through. Using both hands to stretch the neck hole as wide as she could over his head was a challenge, and she stepped forward, now only inches from him, to maximize her reach. Still she had little reaction to their proximity.

I should feel something. Especially right now. Something's wrong with me.

Will had been silent since asking for help. He watched her, even when she couldn't reciprocate. Now as she teetered in front of him to hold his shirt over his head, his good hand landed lightly on her waist, helping her keep her balance.

With anyone else, she would've recoiled from the contact. With Will, in any other situation, she would've been bright red and stuttering awkwardly. But now her steady gaze met his curious one. A spark of something stirred inside her, but it was too weak to identify. As much as she didn't like being embarrassed and tongue-tied, she liked this robotic sensation far less.

As soon as his head was inside the shirt, she took half a step back, his hand falling from her side. Her face remained blank.

She helped him work his right arm into the hole, then tugged the shirt down for him. After retrieving the sling from the bed, she had it back in place around his arm and clasped over his shoulder with ease. When she checked again, he was still studying her.

He's better off disappointed than dead. Keep moving.

"Let's go."

He said nothing, just got to his feet slowly.

Jen moved in front of him, putting her arm out to keep him back. She pulled the door open gradually, peeking into the hall to find it as eerily still as before. Tilting her head toward the lobby to indicate that they should continue, she pulled the door open and slipped out silently. When she glanced back to make sure Will was behind her, he rested a hand lightly on her shoulder, as he had to keep from losing her in the crowd at the restaurant—a thousand years ago, and yet not quite forty-eight hours before. Her heart caught in her throat as she tiptoed forward.

The waiting room was in perfect order, with no sign of a struggle. The chair at the front desk had been pushed in and the computer powered off, as if the nurse had gone to lunch.

Which might have been believable if it wasn't 3:30 in the afternoon.

Her heartbeat boomed. *I can do this.*

Jen pressed her ear against the main door but heard nothing. Her fingers were curled around the door handle, ready to make a break for it, when the *ding* of the elevator made her jump back. She grabbed Will's hand on his good side and hauled him away from the entrance, only realizing after she heard him inhale sharply that she'd pulled too hard. They skidded around the reception desk and into the first available door.

Before she secured it behind them, she noted that they were in a supply closet. The sole source of light was the bright strip between the door and the floor. Their eyes hadn't yet adjusted to the dark, but they had no time to waste. Moving to her left, Jen's hand found Will in the blackness and she turned to stand in front of him, resting her palms on his chest.

"Okay, back up a little, against the wall. Good." She couldn't stop to worry whether her urgent whisper scared him. Her left hand moved quickly over his right arm to the wall behind him, using touch to ensure that he was clear of the door. "Stay right here so you'll be behind the door if they open it."

Before she could step away, his right hand flew up to cover her left.

"I'm sorry, I didn't mean to yank you so hard," she added. "Are you okay?"

"I'm okay. What are you going to do?" Will voice trembled, and strangely enough that made her smile in the darkness. The numbness was fading, her feelings bleeding back in, and the first to arrive was that ache in her chest again.

He cares about me. It was such a nice thought—until it occurred to her that he would very soon learn exactly what kind of a monster she was.

The main door creaked open.

"Don't worry about me. I can handle myself." She was thankful the darkness kept her from having to avoid his eyes. He squeezed her hand gently before letting go.

After that, things moved quickly. She forced herself to break contact with him, moving to the other side of the door. With her back flat against the wall, she was tense and ready to strike.

"Steph—"

"Shhh. It'll be fine." Hoping to reassure him—and maybe herself, too—she reached into the darkness one more time, found his arm, and rested her fingertips on it long enough to take a deep breath, then broke contact again. Whoever was after them, they were close now, and Jen and Will fell silent.

An angry male voice yelled from the far end of the suite. "What do you mean they're gone? How the hell can they be gone?"

"I have no idea. But they're not here."

"Well, the boss said they were here a minute ago. Now go find them, you moron!"

"Okay, I'm going." The second man sounded annoyed.

Heavy footsteps stomped through the small medical suite, moving closer. Jen stood still, ready to pounce on whoever opened the door.

Their boss knew I was here? How?

But that question would have to wait.

An instant later, the door swung open and light flooded the closet. Jen sprang into action, swinging a sharp left elbow to the stomach of the unsuspecting man before turning to face him. He doubled over, the wind knocked out of him, and before he could stand to his full height, she kicked him in the midsection. The force of the blow threw him backward, his back colliding hard with the wall, after which he hit the ground with a thud.

Will peered around the door in shock. Jen stepped out of the closet, and as the man regained his balance, she twisted her foot around his ankle and yanked it back, hard. The man landed with another thud on his back. Before he could recover, she wrestled his gun away from him and, with no second thoughts, fired two bullets into his chest. Though the silencer on the gun took the edge off the sound, the shots thundered louder in her ears than any gunshot had before. Everything was different this time.

Without turning all the way around, she spoke over her shoulder.

"Stay put. I need to take care of the other one." She was thankful not to have to look at him, knowing that she would now not only see fear in his eyes but disgust as well.

The dead man's partner rounded the corner without delay, and Jen was ready, gun raised. He stopped short and went for his own gun, but she was faster. Still, he managed to get a shot off before her bullet hit him in the chest, and for a moment she feared she'd end up on the floor along with the two thugs.

When a shelf of medical supplies exploded in the closet behind her as the man dropped to the ground, she jumped. The bullet had narrowly missed her, sending bandages cascading to the floor. The moment the second man was down, she lunged for his gun, then checked both men for a pulse, just to be safe. Neither had one.

Whoever sent them will send others.

She stuck both guns in the waistband of her jeans and patted each man down, but found no other weapons. Pausing to catch her breath, she stared at the ground as she walked back to the closet. She peered back over her shoulder to avoid Will's eyes, checking for more would-be assailants as she spoke.

"Are you okay?" He didn't reply, and she still couldn't bring herself to look at him. "We need to move."

Still he said nothing, but she heard his soft footfalls behind her as she moved away. For the moment, that would have to be enough.

Two red puddles had now joined to form one large and growing pool of blood, and they took care not to step in it.

"There will be more of them coming." She turned her head in his direction, but not enough to face him. "Whoever is doing this, they want you dead badly. Me too, by now. This won't deter them."

Will hadn't made a sound, simply followed her as they ventured into the hall and onward to the stairwell. They crept down the flight of stairs to the ground floor, then bypassed the lobby through a narrow passage to a secondary exit which opened straight into the parking lot behind the building. From there they walked along the rows of cars as normally as it was possible to walk when running for their lives with no idea of who wanted them dead.

Back across the street in front of building ten, they climbed into Jen's car without a word. Driving twenty miles per hour, the speed limit on the lot, she finally worked up the courage to make eye contact.

Fear was in his face, but that was an appropriate reaction. She couldn't tell whether he was afraid of what was happening or of her. Both seemed reasonable. What she did not find were the rest of the emotions she'd expected from him—disgust, anger, and betrayal.

Not yet.

"I have a few questions," he said. "But this might not be the best time."

Now he was the one making understatements. "Yeah."

They stopped at the security gate on their way off the lot, where the guard on duty nodded sternly at them. "You folks need to wait until the lockdown is over. The police told me no one in or out until I get the go-ahead."

Jen had not anticipated this wrinkle in her plan. "They just cleared us," she said without a hint of hesitation.

The shrill ring of the phone in the guardhouse interrupted whatever the man was about to say, and he held up one finger for them to wait as he answered.

"Hang on," Jen mumbled through gritted teeth, barely giving Will time to grab the door handle before hitting the accelerator hard. The bar blocking the entrance didn't break on impact, but the force of the car was enough to bend it. Jen veered sharply to the right, onto the curb and around the arm, getting away with only a deep scratch along the doors on the driver's side.

Tires squealing, Jen made several turns in quick succession, knowing it wouldn't be long before someone went looking for them— whether it was the police or the people who wanted them dead.

"We need to find somewhere safe. The question is where?" She was more talking to herself than to him, and she cursed the desperation in her voice. Allowing herself a glance at Will, she found him staring at her, wide eyed.

"Steph, I—"

Before he could say more, she was startled by her phone buzzing in her pocket.

CHAPTER 29

JEN FISHED HER PHONE OUT of her pocket and peered at the number on the screen. "Would you mind holding this for me and putting it on speaker? I recognize the number, but I'm not sure why." With some difficulty, Will turned far enough to reach for it with his right hand and did as she asked.

"Hello?"

"Hey, Stephanie? It's Adam Lewis."

Adam Lewis? Why does that name sound familiar?

When she didn't reply, he added, "We sat together on the plane on the way to LA on Sunday."

She already regretted having answered. She didn't have time for him just then. "Yes, right. Hi, Adam. How's everything?"

"Not bad, not bad." Adam's voice was as smooth as it'd been in person, and she caught Will rolling his eyes. "I wanted to call and find out how things were going, and make sure you'd connected with your friend. If you need a tour guide, I'm still available."

"That's sweet of you, but we're okay." A check of the rearview mirror revealed nothing out of the ordinary. Not yet, anyway. "Although since you're on the line, I do have a question for you."

Will was studying her. *Is he making that face because of something specific, or about Adam in general?*

"Shoot," Adam said.

She tried not to wince at that particular word.

"We're trying to find somewhere low key to hang out this evening. Something out of the way that only locals know about. Do you have any suggestions?"

"As a matter of fact, I do. It's unlisted, but let me find the address for you. I'll call you back in two minutes."

The call ended, and she glanced at Will holding her phone in his lap. For some reason that made her smile.

"So, Adam Lewis from the plane, huh?"

Jen rolled her eyes. "Don't start. He's nobody. I'd forgotten about him. I sat next to him on both legs of the flight to LA, even though we changed planes. He was irritating, so I pretended to sleep. But he was a nice enough guy, I guess."

"He sat next to you on both legs of the trip?"

"Yeah. It was weird."

Will frowned. "So, you told him you were meeting a friend out here?"

"Yeah. Talking to a random stranger on a plane, I figured it was better not to admit I was moving to a new city without knowing anyone."

"You weren't planning to hang out with him?"

She swore he sounded slightly hopeful.

"No. I told you, I don't like people." He regarded her skeptically. "Alright, I like a few people. He's not one of them." She did her best to ignore a sinking sensation, aware she was playing with fire.

"Do you trust him?"

It was a fair question. She'd just admitted he was almost a complete stranger.

He claimed he was a personal trainer, but then later he said something about his job not wanting him to be out of touch for even a few hours.

"He was a guy on a plane. He seemed nice enough—a little weird, but then I'm not one to talk."

"You're not weird." He sounded offended on her behalf. When her eyes darted to him, he looked as surprised at his response as she was. "Well, okay. You're a little weird. But it's the good kind of weird."

She smirked. "Are there good and bad kinds?"

"Of course. And you are definitely the good kind of weird."

"Um, thanks, I guess." Jen blushed as she wove through traffic, glad for the excuse not to look at him.

Her phone buzzed again, and they both stared at it. "Ready?" he asked.

"Ready." She attempted to give an encouraging smile.

He connected the call and put it on speaker.

"Hi, Adam."

"Alright, I got it," said the voice on the phone.

Something flashed across Will's face that hadn't been there before. *He's probably nervous about trusting a complete stranger.* She was now a little hesitant about that, too.

"It's down in Long Beach, if you don't mind the drive. You ready for the address?"

"The drive is no problem. Let me open the GPS." Of course, Will had her phone, and before he could open the app, her phone needed to be unlocked. Attention still on the road, she held up her thumb and aimed blindly for the phone, hoping they could manage this maneuver without talking. Will moved the phone to her hand, pressing his thumb over hers against the button and holding it there while the phone identified her. All at once her heart was beating frantically, both from the stress of being pursued and from the giddiness of this unexpected contact. She wouldn't have been shocked if it was audible to Will.

When the phone unlocked, he removed his thumb.

"Okay, Adam, go ahead." As Adam read the address, Will typed it into the search box, setting the phone down on his leg and giving Jen a thumbs-up when he finished.

"Got it," Jen said. "So, what kind of place is it, anyway?"

"A little hole-in-the-wall. Doesn't even come up on GPS maps by name, and they like it that way. Called the Surf Café. It's more popular with runners than surfers, though." Adam chuckled, and Will scoffed so quietly she wondered if she'd imagined it. When she turned her head, his face gave away nothing.

"The GPS says it should take us about forty-five minutes to get there." Jen was more and more hesitant about this plan but couldn't think of a reason not to go through with it other than uneasiness. They didn't exactly have a better option.

"If I get off early, maybe I'll stop by. I'm not too far away now."

"Great." She gritted her teeth. Adam showing up was one of the last things she wanted, but she would deal with him if it became necessary. "Thanks, Adam."

"My pleasure. I'll talk to you later." His smooth voice grated on her more and more.

The call disconnected, and at first they were both silent. The GPS advised them to continue straight for five miles.

"So, you do know one person in LA after all."

She shook her head. "He doesn't count. I told you, he's a random guy I sat next to on an airplane. I wouldn't even call him an acquaintance."

"Okay, but he's a guy who called you after you spent six hours together. So maybe he wants to get to know you better."

Jen sat straight up. A particular memory flashed through her mind. It'd been late Sunday evening at LAX when she and Adam had been saying goodbye. He'd given her a plain white card with only his name and phone number on it. What now occurred to her was a small but important detail.

Inhaling sharply, she signaled and pulled into the breakdown lane, which was barely large enough to accommodate her small rental car.

"Steph, what's wrong?"

"We can't go there." She put the car in park and turned to him, her eyes begging for help. "I'm not sure how I missed it before. I'm trying to come up with a logical explanation, but I can't. I never gave him my phone number."

Will's expression went from relief to worry. "But how would he have gotten it?"

"I— I have no idea," Jen said, becoming increasingly agitated. "I guess if someone . . . Or, no, they couldn't, but . . . I don't know!"

Maybe they've been watching you from the beginning, maybe they haven't, but this is not the time to worry about what already happened. The men with guns are not going to stop coming after you.

"What do I do?" Her voice was small, reminding her of a long-ago version of herself.

Will gave her a tense smile. "Steph, we don't have to go to that place. I do know LA, too, you know."

"I know. I'm sorry. It's not that I wanted Adam's help and not yours. I trust you, of course. I just thought it would be safer to go somewhere that couldn't be traced back to you—"

"My point was not for you to be sorry. My point was that you don't have to figure it out all by yourself. I'd like to help, too, if I can. I'm nowhere near the badass you are, but I'll pretend it's because I got shot."

"Okay." Jen managed a shaky smile at his joke—and the fact that he'd called her a badass. "But we need to move. They could be following us."

"Agreed." He picked up her phone and erased the destination address from the GPS.

"Please turn that off."

Will obliged, setting it in the console between them. "We won't need it anyway. I know where we're going. Just start driving, and I'll tell you where to go."

"As long as it's not your house. That'd be way too obvious." She eased back onto the road.

"No, this is a different kind of out-of-the-way place, in Santa Monica. It's not a hole-in-the-wall, but it is hard to find. It's supposed to be more exclusive that way. And if anything should happen to it—if it gets filled with bullet holes, or blows up or something—that's okay. It's my ex's favorite place in the world."

Her jaw dropped, and she shook her head. "That's not very nice."

"Who said I was nice?"

She paused before replying. "I say you're nice. And I don't like people. So you must be."

Regarding her fondly, Will didn't acknowledge her comment out loud. "It's the next exit."

As he directed her toward Santa Monica, Jen's stress level escalated again. She needed to get out of her own head but couldn't quite break the loop. There was too much at stake.

Will cleared his throat. "Now it's my turn to ask a very strange question. Or more of a request, I guess. Anyway, I indulged you about the crates, so would do the same for me and please give me your hand?"

He'd rotated to face her as much as he could. His injured left shoulder bumped the seat, and he winced as he straightened. While the position must have been excruciating for him, he extended his right hand to her, palm facing up.

"Why?"

Sighing, he shook his head at her, his mouth tilting up tiredly as if to show he wasn't offended. "It's okay, never mind." His hand fell back to his lap, and he faced forward again.

Though he'd let her off the hook, she considered his strange request. She didn't understand it, but she trusted him, so she kept her eyes on the road and slowly reached out her right hand. For whatever reason, it was easier to comply if she didn't make eye contact, but still she held her breath. This was the most vulnerable she'd allowed herself to be in a very long time.

Will pivoted in his seat again, caught her hand in his, and held it. Four fingers sat loosely under hers, and his thumb skimmed across her palm. Goose bumps broke out up and down her arms, and butterflies suddenly filled her stomach.

He's trying to distract me so I stop freaking out. After all, he needs me to help him stay alive. That's all. For a few minutes they drove this way in silence. He entertained himself with tracing lines on her hand, and she wasn't complaining.

"Any better?"

Actually, yes. Her cheeks heated as she nodded. "Yeah. You must be some kind of magician."

"Nah, just a lucky guess."

His thumb came to rest across the center of her palm, pressing gently, and without thinking, her fingers curled inward around it.

He was about to say something when Jen's eyes flicked to the rearview mirror, growing wide as she gasped. "Will, that car—"

A car was gaining on them with alarming speed. He checked over his shoulder, then squeezed her hand before letting go. She clamped both hands on the steering wheel, her knuckles turning white as she considered her limited options.

She couldn't make the car in front of her go any faster, and to her right there was only a narrow shoulder. The gap in the lane to her left would close any second as a car approached her blind spot.

"Hold on." Tires screeched as her car skidded to the left. The driver she'd cut off cursed at her angrily in her rearview mirror, but she'd made it. The car that had been approaching from behind veered off onto an exit ramp and vanished.

She exhaled loudly. "Maybe that was just an aggressive driver who was in a big hurry to exit."

"Maybe." Will studied the other cars on the road with increased suspicion. "But if they were looking for us, they could come back on at the next entrance ramp. Or there could be more than one of them. We have to stay alert."

Jen raised her eyebrows. "Hey, I thought you were the calm, optimistic one."

"I'm trying to balance calm and optimistic with cautious and realistic." He still had his back to the passenger window, staring past her at the other cars on the road and scanning behind them and to the side. "It's not that I'm not scared. I got shot, remember? I know the stakes here. But good decisions are easier when you're not stressed, so trying to keep our stress levels down is my way of contributing. After all, you obviously don't need saving. So I trust you to keep us safe, and I want to help you in whatever small way I can."

Caught off guard by his description of her not only as someone who didn't need saving but as someone he trusted, all she could say was, "Wow."

Too bad he can't save me from myself. Not that I deserve saving. Guilt stabbed at her insides. *I shot two men right in front of him, and yet he can still somehow find good in me. Or maybe he's afraid of me. Maybe he thinks I'll hurt him, and this is how he keeps himself safe.*

His voice brought her back to reality, its smoothness a sharp contrast to the scheming Will she'd conjured in her mind. "I'm an actor, remember? I don't have to feel calm to act like it."

Right. She gripped the steering wheel harder than ever, summoning all her concentration to stop from reacting to his words and crumbling then and there. *Of course it isn't real—any of it. I've known that all along. My lie is a thousand times bigger, so I can't begrudge him his own.*

Her thoughts were not taking her to a good place.

Neither of them said much after that, both sitting stiffly and focusing on getting to their destination alive. He stared past her, keeping a lookout, but kept glancing back at her. The only sound was when he occasionally told her which way to turn. They drove like this, quiet and tense, the rest of the way to Santa Monica.

CHAPTER 30

THEY'D BEEN ON A WINDING back road for miles when Will announced that their turn was coming up. Jen was confused until she spotted a wooden building nestled in a grove of trees. It was far grander than anything she'd pictured.

They pulled into a small, half-full parking lot, and parked on the far side of a large SUV where her car would be obscured from the view of those driving in.

Made of a reddish wood with a natural glow enhanced by floodlights on the ground, the large two-story structure resembled a glass-fronted house.

"Wow," she whispered, gazing in awe as she got out of the car.

"Yep, it's pretty stunning." He smiled back at her as she moved toward the trunk, where she grabbed the go bag from inside her duffle bag. Stuffing her purse in her go bag, she closed it and pulled the straps over her shoulders. Will watched her but did not ask questions.

A curving wooden walkway began at the edge of a steep hill that slanted down, out of sight. The building itself was built on stilts along the edge of the hill, and like a bridge, the wooden path climbed over open air and slanted gently upward to the front door.

Inside, a dark-haired young woman stood behind the counter. Her nametag read *Nora*, and judging by her face, she recognized Will. Jen could spot a fangirl anywhere. Her eyes swept the interior and studied every face in the room as Will turned on the charm.

"Hi, Nora. Is Michelle here?"

Nora nodded without a word, then disappeared into a back room, emerging a moment later behind a fifty-something blonde whose wavy hair fell to the middle of her back. The woman wore a pale-yellow sundress, and her overly tanned skin said she'd spent lots of time on the beach.

"Will!" Michelle rounded the counter, putting one hand on his back and giving him a kiss on the cheek. "How are you, sweetheart? It's been forever." She regarded Jen behind him with disinterest, and then, noting the sling on his left arm, she clamped on to Will's good arm. "You've hurt yourself, you poor thing. Come back into my office so you can tell me what you've been up to!"

In her "office," a large room that stretched across the entire back of the building, Michelle closed the door behind them.

"Michelle, this is my friend Stephanie."

Michelle's eyes flicked in her direction, but she again showed no interest in the younger woman. She seated herself on a short couch and motioned for him to sit beside her.

"And this was just the product of a little filming mishap," he added, pointing to his left arm as he lowered himself carefully, a little further away than she'd indicated.

Their hostess sat angled toward Will, while Jen sat off to the left side on a matching overstuffed chair. She wasn't sure how this arrangement was going to work out; it would be hard to plan out their next move with Michelle spewing inane banter and flirting with him.

That sounds a lot like jealousy, you know.

Jen sat in silence, her anxiety and frustration increasing by the moment. This wasn't what she'd had in mind. Will glanced at her and smiled. *I'm working on it,* his expression promised. *Bear with me.* Then he returned his attention to their hostess.

He laid things out carefully, telling Michelle why they were there without lying more than necessary and while being his usual magnetic self.

I'm willing to bet that charm never fails him. This certainty only added to her discomfort. *It's not just me. He's like this with everyone.*

"You were the first one I thought of, because this is the perfect place to get away from everything and everyone," Will was saying.

Michelle put a hand to her chest in an exaggerated gesture. "My dear, I'm touched. I have errands to do, but stay and use my office as long as you like." She was about to rest her other hand on his injured shoulder, and Jen struggled against the urge to jump up and drag the other woman backwards over the arm of the sofa. *Is she blind?*

No, you're definitely not jealous.

But Michelle stopped herself in time and didn't touch him, withdrawing her hand.

"Thanks, we really appreciate it," Will said.

Before she left, however, the older woman took a trip down memory lane, babbling on about Will and his ex for several minutes before she seemed to realize that he might not want to be reminded. She stopped talking abruptly, saying she had to get going. Insincere goodbyes were exchanged, and finally the coffee-shop owner was out the door.

As soon as they were alone, Will shook his head at Jen in embarrassment. "Sorry about her, Steph. She's always been both a shameless flirt and kind of a snob. But this place is perfect, so dealing with her was worth the hassle."

The kindness in his smile was reassuring. He sank back into the couch with a tired sigh, and Jen, similarly hit by a wave of exhaustion, fell back into the chair. The lack of sleep followed by the endless cycle of adrenaline and fatigue she'd been stuck in all day was taking its toll.

"So, what do we do now? We can stay here for a few hours, but after that?" She didn't expect him to have an answer. Leaning forward, she rested her elbows on her knees and hung her head, her hands tugging through her hair in frustration.

"Steph, are you okay?" His voice had a new urgency.

"What? Of course. Why?" She sat back up and saw that he was focused off to one side of her. She turned over her shoulder in confusion.

"Because you're bleeding."

"What? Where? No, I'm not. Nothing even hurts."

He'd gotten to his feet and was already approaching her. "Stand up."

"Will, I'm fine! I—"

Jen stopped midsentence as she stood, because Will was right. The left side of her shirt was ripped above her hip, and streaked with blood. When her hand skimmed over the area, she winced. He stopped inches from her, his right hand moving carefully to the hem of her shirt and tugging it up just enough to expose a small wound on her side. She winced again when his fingers brushed her skin beside it.

"Sorry."

His voice seemed gentler than she'd heard it before, and he held the fabric away from the sensitive area. He peered at her in disbelief, as if, after everything that had happened, this was the part he couldn't quite believe. "You got shot, and you had no idea?"

She examined her injury as well as she could from her angle, shaking her head. "I didn't get shot. It's nothing." *I'm broken. Otherwise I would have felt this.*

His voice remained firm. "Steph, a bullet did this. It's a graze, but it's a gunshot wound. So yes, you got shot and you didn't notice."

"Well, I was a little distracted by trying to save our lives." The words had come out far more harshly than she'd ever spoken to him before.

Unruffled, he was careful not to catch her off guard as he moved his hand to her left arm, just above her elbow. "It's not a criticism, okay? I'm in awe that you got shot and kept on going. As you may recall, I was also shot today." He lifted his injured arm in its sling, wincing slightly before lowering it again. "Firsthand experience tells me it hurts like hell. I can't imagine not feeling it."

"It's not the same thing. This was a graze, if that. You were actually shot."

It should hurt. It just . . . doesn't. Despair finally overwhelmed her. Her face was beginning to crumple when light-headedness took over. "Will, I—" Everything went black.

When she opened her eyes, she was sitting propped up against him on the couch. He was talking to her in a low voice, though at first she couldn't make out the words. She lifted her head to find him, understanding only afterwards that she'd been leaning on his shoulder.

"Steph, are you okay?"

She answered without thinking. "I'm fine."

"You're not fine. You fainted."

Frustration flared up all over again. "Of course I'm not fine!" The words came out louder than she'd intended, and she dialed down the volume but kept the same intensity in her voice. "People are trying to kill us. They already shot you—er, us—and I have no idea how to stop them. How could I possibly be—?"

The bells at the front entrance chimed, and she fell silent. They both got to their feet without a word, and when she wavered, still light-headed, he put his good arm around her waist to steady her. Frozen in place, they strained to listen.

"Hello, Nora." Jen's face fell at the sound of the menacing male voice.

No! She took deliberate breaths, trying to think. *I have to do something!* Her attempts to flip the switch, to channel Stephanie and her calm, were in vain. Nothing happened.

"But how did they . . . ?"

Will was tugging at her. "It doesn't matter how. We have to hide." He spoke directly into her ear. "Right now. Come on." Still she didn't move. Now not one but two surly male voices were talking to the poor young girl at the counter.

"Dammit, Steph." Even his urgent whisper didn't convince her to move, so he tightened his good arm around her, careful not to bump her injured left side, and dragged her toward the window on the back wall.

He settled them behind one of the thick white curtains, balancing her in front of him and wrapping the curtain around them both. The bunched-up bundles of fabric wouldn't protect them, but they would buy them a few seconds.

Once the curtain was in place, he wrapped his right arm securely around her so her back leaned on his chest, and he set his cheek gently against the back of her head, tightening his grip.

"You still with me, Steph?"

"Yeah. Thanks," she breathed,

As they waited behind the curtain in the agonizing quiet, Stephanie's cool certainty and detachment finally descended over Jen again. *I can do this.*

In her left hand, she pulled one of the guns she'd taken off the men in the infirmary out of the waistband of her jeans. "Here," she said over her shoulder. His arm still around her, she placed her right hand over his, lacing her fingers into the spaces between his and tugging gently to loosen his grip. Her left hand pressed the gun into his hand. "Take this. I'm not sure how many bullets are left, but hopefully it's more than none."

She helped Will adjust his grip on the gun, and he carefully replaced his hand against her, keeping the weapon tilted away. He spoke near her ear. "What about you? Don't you need it?"

She pulled the other gun out of the waistband of her jeans. "I told you, you don't have to worry about me."

"I probably don't have to, but I will anyway." The side of his head leaned harder against hers as he spoke. She was thankful he couldn't see her face as her eyes closed involuntarily. After that they fell quiet, listening and waiting.

The eerie silence gave way to a loud creak. Jen and Will both held their guns down but ready as heavy footsteps approached.

She wished she could turn to look him in the eye. Since that wasn't an option, she shifted to lean more of her weight against him. His arm tightened around her in response, and she did everything she could to memorize this feeling of falling and being held securely all at once. When he shifted so he could plant a kiss in her hair, inhaling before lifting his head, the sharpest pain yet exploded inside her chest.

I wish . . .

The list of things she wished for was long, but there was no time to worry about any of them, so she packed those feelings into the box with the others. She'd do what she had to do to save him. If she was lucky, maybe she'd survive, too.

As they'd entered the room, Jen had noted three long windows— the one they were standing beside and one on each side of the room, closer to the door. Assuming the men checked the side windows, their backs would be exposed, and she would have a few seconds to catch them by surprise. It was the best chance they had.

Behind the curtain, she carefully slipped her gun back into her waistband, then moved to Will's hand resting on her stomach. She tapped the back of it with the tip of her index finger, then, at eye level, she pointed to the right. Turning her hand to point to herself, she then pointed to the left.

Hoping he'd understood, she took her gun back out of the front of her jeans, peering over her right shoulder at him just as he leaned into her. His nose brushed the side of her head, giving her chills, and his words were so quiet she only heard them because his mouth sat a hair's breadth from her ear. "Got it."

As the two men moved into the room, it was immediately obvious to Jen that they were not Delta Force level, even on their best day. She guessed maybe mall-security level.

"That stupid kid said they're back here. So where the hell are they?"

"You take that side, I'll take this side. Maybe they went out one of the windows." The floorboards creaked to both sides of the room at once as the men moved.

Thankful that one small thing had gone right, Jen held up her left hand over her shoulder and counted down on her fingers.

Three.

Two.

One.

In one fluid movement, she threw off the curtain with her left hand and stepped forward, her gun already trained on the man peering out the window on the left. Will did the same on the right.

The man in Jen's sights turned first, his eyes widening in alarm. "Holy shit!" At that, the other man spun around, and they both stood frozen in place. She mentally promoted them to club bouncers, but the job of hitman was an unrealistic stretch for them.

Apparently not believing she'd fire, the man on the left put his hand on the gun at his side and pulled it partway out of its holster.

"Drop the gun," Jen said.

I've never gotten to say that before. It was kind of fun. And then, because the man didn't drop his gun as instructed, she got to say it again.

"I said, drop the gun."

The man didn't follow instructions. Instead, he tightened his hold on his gun and raised it by an inch, as if testing her. Before he could lift it any farther, she shot him in the chest. On TV, this would've been when someone rushed into the room to investigate the noise, but no one did.

Jen's victim hadn't even hit the ground yet when she had her gun trained on his partner. She couldn't help but note that Will had been aiming slightly to the left of the man, and that the safety on his gun was still on. He wouldn't be much help in this situation, but it wasn't a surprise. He'd never had to fire real bullets at anyone on the show, so it wouldn't have mattered if his aim was off. He was probably nervous, too.

She stopped herself from imagining how she could help him improve his technique.

Luckily, the second gunman hadn't caught on to Will's lack of firearms experience, revealing his own ignorance. Having watched Jen shoot his partner, he did not hesitate to drop his gun and kick it toward them, then fell to his knees with his hands behind his head.

Will now stood one step behind her right shoulder, his good arm back at his side. She crouched to pick up the gun at her feet, stuffing it in the back of her jeans, but instead of lowering her own gun, she shot the unarmed stranger in the chest. As he fell, the sleeve of his T-shirt pulled upward to reveal the lower portion of a skull tattoo—midway between his elbow and his shoulder, exactly as Will had described. If not for this man opening a closet door as Will came out of the adjacent one, none of this would have happened.

A quiet gasp from Will reminded her that she'd just executed an unarmed man. The other three had been in self-defense, but not this one. It had been necessary, but she couldn't explain that to the man standing behind her.

Just add that guy to the list of people you've murdered. Again, Will's better off disappointed in you than dead.

"Couldn't he have given us information?" His voice was different. Quieter. She closed her eyes and took a breath. *This is where he sees the monster.*

I had no choice. He could've IDed me.

She opened her eyes but didn't look away from the man on the ground. Trying her best to keep her voice from shaking, she spoke slowly. "He was a hired gun. The only information he had was that he was assigned to kill us." This may or may not have been true, but she needed Will to believe it. If he began to doubt her and ran, she couldn't save him.

As he considered this idea, Jen turned toward him, bracing herself for his judgment once again. She couldn't justify what she'd done without telling him everything. Their eyes locked for what she swore was the longest minute of her life, during which his warring emotions were written across his face.

Please, Will. Trust me.

Finally, a spark of the mischievous glint in his eyes returned. He nodded slowly, and the muscles in his face relaxed the slightest bit. "You're accumulating quite a firearms collection today." The words were forced, but it was better than nothing.

I do not deserve his faith in me.

The knot inside her eased, and she moved to retrieve the gun from near the first man, handing it to Will. "Just in case."

"Do I really need two?" For someone who handled prop guns as part of his job, he looked adorably uncomfortable holding a real one.

"You never know. Probably not, but I'm hoping I don't need three." She pointed out that she was turning the safety on before she handed it to him, and he tucked it into his pocket with the handle facing out.

"That's the understatement of the day. Or the year. And it's not the right time, but I'm dying to ask . . ." His expression was as charming as always, without an ounce of suspicion, but she stiffened all the same.

"We should check the rest of the place, and the perimeter, to be safe." She was grateful when he nodded, letting her change the subject.

The café had been frighteningly still since the gunshots, but now the sound of footsteps moved closer. These steps weren't the heavy gait of the hitmen; these were lighter, faster, more evenly paced. As if in slow motion, Erica entered the room, a gun raised in her hand as she walked straight toward them.

Shock washed over Jen. *It was Erica? I wasn't being paranoid?*

"Erica, what the hell?" Will yelled as Jen wiggled her way in front of him. "Steph, don't!" He tried to shove her out of the line of fire, but she'd become immovable despite her smaller size, her determination keeping her firmly planted.

This time it was Jen who didn't raise her gun in time. Erica was aiming at Will. Or more accurately, now that Jen was in front of him, Erica was aiming at her.

In that instant before Erica shot her, multiple images flickered through her mind.

She saw herself, bent over her laptop, writing *Gemini Divided* fanfiction. She saw Will, and the awkwardness she'd felt after bumping into him in the hall on her first day. Two days ago. In another lifetime. She saw the two of them sitting on the bench side by side in the darkened restaurant courtyard.

She saw thick white curtains in front of her and felt his arm wrapped around her as he kissed the back of her head. Along with it came the sensation that her heart was going to explode from exhilaration, guilt, and despair.

And finally, she saw Will's face. She'd shot four different men in front of him in the space of a few hours, but he was still grinning at her. He was no doubt under the impression that this was the darkest part of her—how wrong he was. He deserved so much better than any of this.

And then Erica pulled the trigger.

CHAPTER 31

IN HER LAST MOMENT, JEN'S biggest regret was that she hadn't been able to save Will.

The bullet erupted from Erica's gun with a deafening boom. Jen closed her eyes against the impact and waited. But blackness failed to claim her, and no light appeared for her to walk into. She registered glass shattering behind her, and then all at once Will grabbed her around the waist and dove to the left, pulling her down with him. They hit the wooden floor together hard, and the grunt that escaped Will told her it had hurt him badly. Even so, he held her protectively, curling around her to act as a human shield the way his character, Matt, did for Mel on TV.

Because of Will's quick thinking, they'd escaped the gunfire erupting above them through the back window. Erica fired several more shots, which were returned by someone on the deck. Only now did Jen understand that Erica hadn't been shooting at her but at someone behind her—someone who was now firing back.

Erica took shelter behind the couch in the middle of the room. She peeked out from behind it and took aim, firing again. Just when it seemed that the shooting would go on forever, the room went still.

The only movement was Erica, who crept toward the back window, stepping cautiously through the empty frame and onto the deck, her gun at the ready.

"Will, it's okay. I'm okay. You can let go," Jen whispered, laying her hand on his. Only then did he loosen his iron grip on her. Sitting up, she cringed in dismay at the blood trickling from the left sleeve of his T-shirt as he struggled to lift himself as well.

Will shook his head, wincing in pain and breathing fast as he spoke. Too fast. "She didn't shoot me. I probably just ripped some stitches. Hurts like hell, though."

"Dammit, Bryant. I didn't work this hard to save you to have something happen to you now. You need to make better decisions. You could've pushed us the other way."

"So I fell on you? I wouldn't do that to you. I'd much rather have you fall on me." His mischievous smile was strained.

Is he seriously flirting right now?

"We need to stop the bleeding in your shoulder." She whipped her green tank top over her head, thankful she'd layered it over a black one that morning. His eyebrows went up, as did the corners of his mouth. She made a face, pressing her balled-up shirt against his shoulder. His attention strayed to the tear in the left side of her black shirt where the bullet had grazed her.

"Hey, do me a favor and don't get any blood on my shirt." She held the fabric firmly against his shoulder. "Can you hold it?"

He reached his right arm across his chest, brushing his fingers over hers as he took the cloth. "Yeah. I got it."

"Good. I'm going to go find out what the hell's going on here. It's way too quiet." In the absence of gunfire, the silence was ominous. Still, she was torn about leaving him alone. "You still have the guns I gave you?"

Will's one good hand was busy holding her shirt against his shoulder. "Yeah. I just . . . Could you hold this for a second?"

She tentatively rested her hand on his, trying to ignore the sparks of excitement at the contact before he slid his hand out from under hers.

"Thanks." Moving slowly, he pulled one of the guns out of his waistband. "I'm a painfully bad shot though. You, on the other hand..."

A pain in her chest that she didn't have time for flared at the admiration in his voice. She held her shirt against his shoulder with her left hand and took the gun from him with her right, checking that it was loaded and turning the safety off, then returned it to him and slid her hand out from under his.

"Here. I'm not going far. Now scoot over there, by the wall." He did as instructed. "Where's the other gun?"

"In my pocket."

After an awkward moment in which he shifted several times, she extracted the weapon from his pocket.

"I turned the safety off on both, in case you need to use them. They're both loaded, so please don't shoot yourself." She set the second gun on the floor beside him and covered the hand holding the ruined green shirt against his shoulder with hers. "Keep pressure on your shoulder, unless you need your right hand to shoot someone."

"You make shooting someone sound like no big deal." Yet again, the intensity in his eyes was more than she was comfortable with. His words were as much a question as a statement.

I wish I could tell you everything, Will. I really do. In all the time she'd done this job, she'd never wanted to tell anyone about it. Until now.

All at once, the faces of the people she'd shot and never given a second thought to crowded into her mind, closing in around her. She had to force herself to look at him. "Of course it's a big deal. But do what you have to do. That's what I've always done."

He stared at her as if trying to read her thoughts. "Steph, please be careful."

She lifted her hand off his. They weren't safe yet. Glancing back at him as she stood, she couldn't help but smile sadly. As imperfect as the moment was, she wished she could freeze time and stay in it.

"You too. Stay against the wall, keep pressure on your shoulder, and stay low. I'll be back as soon as I can." Then she walked away.

She opened the office door a crack and spotted Nora, the young woman who'd greeted them at the counter, lying facedown in front of the counter in a pool of blood. Further inside the room, a man with dark hair held a gun on a group of customers. She recognized the back of his head; it was the same man who'd been talking to the crowd behind the warehouse the night before. Erica stood in front of the group with her gun pointed right back at him.

"It's over, Sal."

Sal, as in Sal Arrington, producer of Gemini Divided*? He hired me to kill Will?*

A hysterical voice screamed in reply, "It's not over until I say it's over! And it's not over!"

"It is over. And we're letting these people go now." Erica's voice was even, and her attention was fixed on him. "This isn't about them."

How is Erica so calm and articulate?

"Things have gotten out of control, but you're not a murderer."

Sal considered this for a few long seconds. "Fine. Get them the hell out of here."

At Erica's signal, the small group of patrons moved as one unit, their hands in the air, along the wall and out the door.

Amid the shuffle, Jen crept into the room, her gun trained on the back of Sal's head. Erica's eyes were on Sal, but they wavered in Jen's direction for a split second, and he caught the movement. In a flash he wheeled around, his gun now pointed at Jen as his rage boiled over.

Staring at Sal, she recalled him as the man with the distinctive laugh from Monday night's dinner. She'd shaken hands with him when Will dragged her over to meet the execs.

"You!" He came unglued in front of them, shrieking at the top of his lungs and vibrating with anger. "This is all your fault! If you'd done your goddamned job, none of this would've happened!"

The two of them stood with their guns pointed at each other.

Erica inched around Sal toward Jen, keeping her gun on him and speaking confidently, trying to draw his attention away. "Now, now, Sal, you don't need to yell. She has nothing to do with this. You've made your own bad choices."

Erica had apparently assumed he was spewing nonsense. Jen hoped he wouldn't elaborate.

Without warning, the front door opened, the noise announcing someone's arrival. Jen, Sal, and Erica all dove for cover, and there was a moment of chaos. "Hey, boss, sorry we're late," a loud male voice said. "This place is really hard to find. Boss?"

Peering up from where she'd landed on the floor, Jen took in the situation. She recognized one of the two large men who'd just arrived as the sniper she'd fought at the warehouse—obviously more of Sal's "associates." In the right situation, she could've disarmed at least one of them, but not three.

In the confusion, she crawled behind the far end of the counter, closer to the office.

"Dammit! Where'd she go?" Sal was irate. "She was standing right there, and you morons distracted me! And where's that other b—"

As if to keep him from calling her a rude name, Erica popped out from around the opposite end of the counter where she'd taken shelter, firing two shots at their boss. Neither shot hit him; they just made him even angrier.

"Goddammit! I'm going to really enjoy killing all three of you!"

The two newly arrived thugs glanced at each other, clueless. From where they stood, they couldn't see anyone else there. The men peered around the room warily. "Who you talking to, boss?" one of them asked.

"Well, I'm not talking to myself, you moron! And I'm not shooting at myself, either."

Jen popped up and shot twice, narrowly missing one of Sal's goons and ducking again as the men returned fire. *I need to improve our odds.*

A commotion came from the other side of the room, and something crashed to the floor, followed by more swearing. Erica and Jen had moved to the middle of the counter near the register, only a few feet apart, and they nodded at each other.

"One, two, three." Erica mouthed the words, and they both twisted around, lifting themselves high enough to fire several shots each at the men while they were distracted. Jen's two shots hit one of the thugs in the chest and brought him down, while one of Erica's hit the other one in the arm. Her second shot missed him by less than an inch.

Meanwhile, a new crisis had developed. A glass votive holder had been knocked off a table and shattered on the floor, igniting a small fire that was already growing into a larger one.

"Get me something to put this out!" Sal yelled at the remaining man, who cradled the arm Erica had shot.

Sensing a now-or-never opportunity, Jen stood again, took aim at Sal, and pulled the trigger just as he began to move. He fell to the ground with an agonized scream, inches from the rapidly growing fire. She hadn't been fast enough to hit him in the chest. Now he turned his head and sneered up at her from the ground, twisting onto his back and raising his gun.

That was when the ear-splitting fire alarm came to life, muting the sound of the men's cursing. In a flash, Jen dropped back down, Sal's return shot whizzing above her head.

"Stephanie." Erica's words were now barely audible, even from a few feet away. "Where's Will?"

"In the office. He's hurt, so I told him to stay there."

"I'll take care of dumb and dumber. You go get him. We need to get out of here. Go out the back."

Jen risked another peek over the counter. The fire had spread, and the room was filling with smoke. She did not need more convincing; saving Will was her priority, and Erica could apparently hold her own. Moving toward the end of the counter closer to the office door, Jen crouched low and waited a few beats. Then, under the cover of the rapidly spreading fire, Erica's gunshots, and the shrill droning of the fire alarm, she dashed out of the room.

Even with the extra ventilation of the missing window, the room was dense with smoke. Her heart nearly stopped when she saw Will slumped against the back wall, his eyes closed.

No!

Blood was escaping from his left shoulder much faster now, and fear jolted her into action. In a flash she was kneeling in front of him, her face inches from his and a hand on his cheek. "Will, you have to wake up now." She spoke loudly to compete with the fire alarm. Her fingers tapped his cheek firmly, her panic skyrocketing when he didn't respond. Carrying him out of there on her own was out of the question, no matter how badly she wanted to, but so was leaving him behind.

Just as desperation threatened to overcome her, his eyelids fluttered open. For at least the second time that day, Jen almost cried with relief. His face fell against her hand, and she smiled, ignoring the dampness in her eyes, unable to gulp in air fast enough.

"Hey," she said, unable to manage more. She was only inches from him, and yet she felt farther away than ever.

Confusion was written all over his face. "What's wrong?"

So many things.

"It's time to get out of here." Her hand dropped from his cheek as she attempted to get her weight under his right side to help him up. "The building is on fire, and Sal Arrington was the one behind the plot to kill you. He's here. Erica was trying to shoot him, not you. Two more of his guys showed up. I shot one of them, and Erica's taking care of Sal and the other one."

It wasn't easy, but they got him upright. He leaned against her heavily, his right hand once again attempting to keep pressure on his left shoulder. He dropped his head close to hers to speak over the blare of the alarm. "You were busy while you were gone. Wait, Erica can shoot?"

"Apparently she can. This day is full of surprises."

"Again with the understatements, Steph." He was getting heavier and heavier on her shoulder, and she worried about how much blood he'd lost.

"Where's the back exit?"

Will coughed from the smoke filling the room. "On the deck, around the corner to the right."

It was hard to breathe at standing level, but he wouldn't be able to crawl. Jen had scanned the walls of the office and knew the answer, but she asked anyway. "This room doesn't have a door to the deck, does it?"

"Oh, come on, we need some kind of challenge, don't we?" He spoke with effort, and his grin was forced. "It does have the next best thing though." He tilted his head toward the large window that'd been shot out earlier.

They'd made it halfway when two gunshots rang out from the front room, and they froze, Jen's head whipping over her shoulder just in time to be nearly blinded by a flare of bright light as they were knocked down by a wall of heat. Will let out another grunt of pain as they hit the floor again, his right side landing hard against Jen.

The fire now reached the office, the flames lapping at the doorframe and the ceiling above it.

"Hey, you got your wish," Will said after they'd caught their breath. "I fell on you this time. See? Not as good, right?"

How can he make jokes at a time like this?

She was afraid for Erica, but she had to keep moving with Will.

Once they were back on their feet, she grabbed a small statue from Michelle's desk, knocked the remaining glass away from the bottom of the window, and dropped the trinket. She climbed out through the opening while still holding on to Will, then helped him through it as well. Determined not to worry about the blood running down his arm even with her shirt pressed against his wound, she kept the two of them moving step by slow step.

They were both breathing heavily, coughing from the smoke they'd inhaled as they neared the corner of the wraparound deck. Jen saw a gate that opened to a set of stairs leading to the ground far below.

The ear-splitting fire alarm was still almost as loud as inside, and yet the click of the gun cocking behind them cut through the rest of the noise. They stopped, her arm pulling tighter around his waist as her stomach dropped. After everything they'd been through, they were going to die here.

"That's far enough." Sal was even more hysterical than before. "Bryant, I've thought of nothing but killing you for the past week, so this will really be a pleasure. And you . . ."

Jen squeezed her eyes closed, tensing all over and pressing against Will's side with all her might, as if that would protect them both. He was becoming heavier and heavier on her shoulder. She took deep breaths, wondering whether Arrington would expose her true purpose or kill them both.

"Stephanie, or whatever the hell your—"
BANG.

A gunshot rang out, stopping Sal midsentence. He stiffened for a beat before falling against the deck railing. Jen and Will peered cautiously over their shoulders to find Erica standing inside the broken window, her gun still raised at Arrington in case another shot was necessary.

Jen, Will, and Erica stared at each other, catching their breath.

"You didn't want to hear his supervillain speech, did you?" Erica asked with a crooked grin. Jen shook her head, still speechless after narrowly avoiding being outed as a villain herself, and possibly killed. Again she could not understand how Erica was so calm.

"Ready to get out of here?" The brunette stepped through the window as she spoke, avoiding the broken glass.

"So ready," Jen said, and they moved toward the back exit again. The fire drew ever closer, so they didn't have long.

As they approached the back stairs, everything around her moved in slow motion. *Arrington is dead, so Will won't be in danger anymore. With some medical attention, he'll be fine. And I get to go home after all.* While she was relieved that he would be safe, the knowledge that she had to leave him behind was already eating a hole inside her.

Erica opened the gate to the wooden stairway. She'd taken two steps down when a loud crack behind them made them spin around once more. The fire had reached the deck, and they watched as the railing collapsed and the man who'd threatened to kill them fell over the edge and into the steep abyss below.

With the flames licking toward them, they turned and moved as quickly as they could. Erica led the way, her gun drawn just in case. The stairs weren't wide enough for them to walk side by side, so Will stood behind Jen and clamped his good arm around her from shoulder to shoulder for support, and they stepped down together.

"Guess I should've worn those tall shoes today; this might have gone better," she said when their height difference made him stoop lower to hold on.

"I loved those shoes. Put you right at my eye level," Will said.

The strain in his voice concerned her.

"I wanted to kiss you that night," he added, like he was thinking out loud. His possibly delirious admission made her lose focus on her feet for a second, long enough to miss the step she had been narrowly aiming for. She felt herself falling and started to scream just as Will's arm clamped around her tighter.

"Where do you think you're going, huh?" Every time he spoke, it was with greater effort, and Jen gasped for breath, her hands clamped on the railings until she convinced herself she wasn't going to land in a heap.

"Okay?" Will asked, his face against her neck.

She nodded hard, very much not okay. Gripping the railings for dear life, she did her best not to fall down the stairs. She slipped several more times, pushed off the edge of the steps because they were not deep enough for two people, but managed to right herself.

"I got you," Will kept murmuring.

Jen couldn't tell if he really was delirious or trying to be funny as she held him up. Still, her heart squeezed at the sweetness of the sentiment.

Finally they made it to the ground, where they faced a new challenge—a rough stairway cut into the hill and lined with long, flat stones. Even with a metal railing, it was a steep climb, especially with an injured Will. Thankfully, this stairway was wide enough for two people side by side. They proceeded slowly, Will's arm around Jen's shoulders and hers around his waist, and her free hand gripping the railing.

After witnessing Erica shoot him in the head and fire take him over the edge of a steep drop, they were fairly certain that Sal Arrington was dead. Still, Will and Jen fought their way up the steep incline first while Erica scaled the hill backwards behind them, watching their backs. There was no trace of their former boss.

It was a brutal climb up the hill to the concrete parking lot. As soon as they made it, Jen's knees buckled under her, and she landed hard on the cement, Will falling ungracefully on top of her.

"See, I told you . . . it was better if . . . you fell on me," he said through clenched teeth.

"Will! Are you okay?" Despite the physical and emotional strain, hearing Will so obviously in pain made her instantly alert.

"I'm . . . good."

"Bullshit, Bryant," said Erica, who'd come up the steps behind them. "Come on, we're too close to the fire, and to that drop we just climbed. I'd rather not do it again. Can you stand?"

"Of course." He couldn't, though, at least not on his own. Jen pushed herself under one side of him, then carefully helped Erica lift him. Will hooked his good arm around Jen's shoulders and leaned in close, breathing fast and muttering curses in her ear from the pain of standing up.

Finally on his feet, he winced as Jen and Erica helped him across the parking lot to Jen's car. Once there, he refused to sit, insisting that he'd lean against the car so he didn't have to get up again. Unable to convince him otherwise, the women gave in and helped him balance against Jen's car.

Sirens wailed up the road behind them, slowly coming closer. With nothing to do but wait, Erica and Will stood watching the building burn. Jen couldn't watch. Instead, she stood facing Will, pressing her balled-up shirt against his injured left shoulder while leaning her forehead gently on his right. Her free arm wrapped around him, and his good one was draped around her—maybe for support, or maybe to keep her close. The moment when she would disappear was approaching fast, and she held on while she could.

The firefighters arrived in time to prevent the fire from spreading into the trees around it, but the building was a total loss. More sirens were heading their way, and Jen tried her best to ignore reality, her eyes squeezed shut as she leaned into Will.

He shifted to whisper beside her ear. "You saved my life again, I'm not even sure how many times. I told you, you're my good luck charm."

The pain in her chest became unbearable, and she focused on breathing in as much of her surroundings—of him—as she could.

When the EMTs saw Will's shoulder and heard his account of what had happened, they insisted he go to the hospital. Reluctantly, he and Jen shifted away from each other.

"I'll call you later, Steph," he said.

Her head bobbed slightly, but her voice refused to cooperate. Nothing she said or did could change any of it. This was the end, but only she knew it.

Just in time, she managed a quiet, "Bye, Will."

And then the medics were leading him away, across the parking lot to a waiting ambulance. She wanted to scream at the top of her lungs—to make him stop. To make him turn back.

And do what? Don't be stupid. This moment has always been

coming—the end. It would have been so much simpler if you'd just killed him, but this was what you wanted. You're both lucky it ended this way, so suck it up.

What she had not counted on was that watching him walk away would cause such intense pain.

As soon as she could get away, she would destroy her burner phone and vanish, so this was the last time they would lay eyes on each other. She had no choice but to force her face into her best semblance of relief as her heart shattered into a million pieces.

This was your best-case scenario. You should be grateful.

I am, but . . .

So stop dwelling on it and move on. You did your damn good deed. It'd better be worth it.

After that it all became a blur. The EMTs took over, and hands pulled her to sit on the back step of an ambulance. Voices fired questions at her and fussed over the graze in her side and the welt on her cheek. Somehow she'd forgotten about both injuries. When she failed to respond, the young woman in front of her asked if she was okay.

"No" was all she could manage. She was breathing, but she was numb all over, and definitely not okay. She was never going to be okay. The worst part was that it was all her own fault.

The EMTs had more questions, but she couldn't process them. "I don't know." She swore she'd said it a hundred times, and she closed her eyes until the voices left her alone. Or maybe she'd tuned them out. They treated her wounds and then gave her space.

Eventually she opened her eyes again. The fire alarm had stopped blaring at some point, replaced by the crackling of police radios and the chatter of voices. The police officers around her faded in, going about their work as if this were any other day. The EMTs packed up, but law enforcement wouldn't be finished anytime soon. The FBI had shown up as well, but Jen was too tired to worry about any of it. It was over. If they arrested her, so be it.

Overwhelmed by everything going on around her, she peered up at the tops of the tall trees ringing the parking lot. A few deep breaths helped, and she returned her attention to watching for the right moment to slip away.

A pair of police officers approached. "Stephanie Murray?" the taller one asked.

"Yes." Her voice was subdued, but not by choice.

"We need to ask you some questions."

She nodded as they studied her critically. "Miss Murray, if you were so concerned about Mr. Bryant's injuries, why did you bring him to a coffee shop instead of a hospital?"

This was the question she had dreaded. *But what answer would be the wisest? I knew the danger we were in? Could I have known that?* She hadn't yet begun to choke out an answer when the men's radios crackled simultaneously.

"Ma'am, thank you for your cooperation. We have a situation to attend to. We'll be in touch. Don't leave town." They strode away quickly, and she let herself breathe again. That had been close.

Alone on the back step of the ambulance, she surveyed the scene. Fewer people were around now. Both the gawkers and law enforcement had dwindled in numbers. It wouldn't be much longer.

Her mind was blank, except for one thing—a desperate need to find out if Will was okay.

You're so stupid.

Jen was staring at the ground as footsteps approached, and she didn't move as Erica sat beside her. "Are you okay?"

"I guess so. Nothing hurts, I'm just . . . numb." They sat in silence for another minute, at which point Jen's curiosity got the best of her, and she looked up. "How did you end up here, anyway? I'm grateful, of course. If not for you, Arrington would've shot Will. And me, too. But how did you find us?"

"I guess I can tell you now," Erica began after a moment's hesitation. "I'm with the FBI. I've been undercover at *Gemini Divided* since last year. We had suspicions of what was going on, but never enough evidence to make an arrest. Sal and his people were much more careful up until this week. My investigation had narrowed it down to a few suspects, and their chatter this afternoon made it easier to track him here. Also, did you know they had a GPS tracker on you?"

Jen sat up straight, her eyes wide. "No. But how?"

"Do you recognize this man?" Erica clicked the screen of her phone, and Jen was startled to see a face she recognized.

"Yes. I met him on the plane on my way here. Adam Lewis."

"That's not his real name, but yes. He planted it on you at LAX. That's how they found you here. It may not be on you, but it's likely to be in something you always carry, like a purse."

But when would he have gotten close enough to . . . oh.

She flashed back to the day she'd arrived in LA, naïve and determined. It had been a little strange that he'd given her that half hug after knowing her only a few hours—now she knew why.

Her heart beat fast as she removed her purse from inside her go bag. Thankfully, the former didn't contain anything incriminating.

"Do you mind if I have a look?"

Erica was already pulling on latex gloves she'd produced from a pocket. Jen handed her purse over for inspection without a word and held her breath. Erica rummaged through it, smiling triumphantly as she pulled out a tiny piece of metal clasped between her thumb and index finger. She set the flat circle in her palm and held her hand out to show Jen.

Jen shook her head, overwhelmed. It had been there all this time, and she'd never known. *How could I have let this happen?*

Erica dropped it into a plastic evidence bag and sealed it.

Dread multiplied and spread through Jen's system. *What else does she know about me? Am I about to be arrested?* Her pulse spiked.

"Did you arrest Adam Lewis?" asked Jen.

"We're working on it."

Jen stared ahead of her, taking in this new information. *No wonder he seemed "off." I should've known.*

Erica continued after a short pause, "Our preference would've been to bring Arrington in alive, but not if it meant letting him shoot you and Will. They just recovered his body, so that should give you some peace of mind. You and Will are safe now."

"That's great news," said Jen. *All this time, I was planning to kill Will with the FBI right in front of me.* She gave Erica a watery smile, trying to quiet the turmoil in her head. "And you answered my next couple questions, like why you happened to have a gun on you, and how you're such a good shot."

"I could ask you the same things," said Erica. "I assume the guns you had were from Sal's guys, since they didn't find any on them. But you're a damn good shot yourself."

This wasn't something Jen could deny, but at least she had a plausible reason. "In another lifetime, I was in the Army." While it was vague, those eight words were more of a discussion about her past than she'd had with anyone in many years. Guilt flared inside her—not because of what she'd left out, but over the fact that she'd shared it with Erica and not Will.

"Well, Will was lucky you started this week. Thanks for saving him. I'm going to miss that guy." Erica smiled fondly into the distance.

Me too. Jen tried her best to keep her face neutral despite the urge to fall apart. *Just be grateful the FBI doesn't seem to suspect you. At least not yet.*

Silence fell between them, both lost in their own thoughts. Erica was the first to speak. "Let me give you a ride home. You're not in any shape to drive, and the police are going to be combing through everything here for a while. Including your car." The parking lot was roped off, and officers were indeed examining the cars.

Thank goodness my go bag is strapped to my back. Part of her hated that she would be losing the dress and shoes that Will had bought her, along with the items in her duffle bag, but it was probably for the best. A clean break.

"Okay, thanks."

"Did they clear you yet? The EMTs? The police?"

"The EMTs did, but I'm not sure about the police. They were called away to something else."

The brunette's head bobbed sympathetically. "I'll go find out for you." As soon as she walked away, Jen scanned the area. The crowd by the road had dispersed, and at that moment no one was patrolling the perimeter of the parking lot. The few police officers and other agents nearby each had a particular task, and none were concerned with her. This was her chance.

She stood and jogged to the edge of the concrete, ducked under the police tape that roped it off, and hopped down to the slanted ground. One more look over her shoulder brought the bite of heartbreak back, and she squared her shoulders and darted toward the trees. More than anything, she needed to get away from there. She'd fly home under one of her other aliases, and as soon as she got there, she'd destroy all traces of Stephanie Murray, physical and electronic.

If only she could also erase both Stephanie and Will from her mind.

After moving steadily through the trees for thirty minutes, she stopped and took out her burner phone, holding the button impatiently until the screen lit up. She typed hurriedly: *This project did not go as planned, but thanks to a third-party vendor, your client has no complaints. I understand that the balance of my commission will be forfeited. Not ready for any new projects at the moment. Will advise if this changes.*

Once the message had been sent, she smashed the phone as hard as she could against a tree, picking up the remains and smashing them against the tree again with her foot. She'd never used quite so much force to destroy a burner phone before. She'd never found tears on her cheeks when she'd finished before, either.

She picked up the mangled pieces of her lifeline to Will and put them in her bag for disposal later, far away from there. A light rain fell as she moved farther from this life that had never been hers, back to the one in which she no longer belonged. Maybe she never had. She'd met Will three days ago, but she would have sworn she'd known him for most of her adult life.

Forget him. How many times had she said it now?

If only it were that simple.

CHAPTER 32

JEN LAY ON HER STOMACH on a blanket she'd spread out in the grass. Small children chased each other nearby, shrieking with delight. Past them, a group of teenaged boys had started an impromptu game of football. People strolled by on the gravel path not far away, while others sat on benches in the shade. It was an unseasonably cool day in early summer, and life was happening all around her.

Behind her sunglasses, she was oblivious to it all.

In the week since arriving home from California, she hadn't been able to face going to Jane's even once, and in her apartment, the walls closed in on her. Instead, she spent her time outdoors in locations that held no connection to Will. Too bad that didn't stop her from thinking about him.

In the end, I did the right thing. She clung to those words desperately, even as she fought them. *But if that's true, why am I so destroyed?*

She had discarded every physical reminder of the past month, so a brand-new purse and her own personal phone sat on the blanket in front of her. Gone were the pictures of Will and Rachel from *Gemini Divided* on both her home screen and her lock screen, plus the thousands of them stored in the phone's memory.

It wasn't only the phone that had been wiped clean. She'd taken everything she owned that had anything to do with the show and shoved it in boxes that now lived under her bed. It didn't occur to her that she had so little besides *Gemini Divided* in her life until she'd purged it all. Her fanfic? Also a thing of the past, though she couldn't bring herself to delete it. All she wanted was to forget it—all of it.

A few days after she'd arrived back home, FBI agents tracked her down, and Erica was not among them to give her a sympathetic smile. They had more questions, along with evidence of her past crimes. It all came back to bite her at once. She'd been sure she was going to end up in jail for the rest of her life, but after sitting in a cell for most of one long miserable day, she was led to an interrogation room. A new face awaited her there—a man in a suit. For a split second she saw herself as a character on *Gemini Divided*. But this was not fiction. In the nightmare reality her life had become, she was offered a plea deal. If she told them everything she knew about Brett Kingston, her former mentor, friend, and commanding officer, she would get immunity from prosecution.

A clean slate, in every way except the one that mattered most.

Before all this, she had never imagined turning on someone she trusted so completely. Then again, she'd also never imagined anyone she trusted pulling her into the deep, dark pit that she'd ended up in, either.

She told them everything, and then she was free. Now all she had to do was find a way to defeat the demons that haunted her. They were more difficult to appease than the FBI.

Jen was jolted back to the present by a squeal erupting from the children nearby. A tiny boy had fallen to his knees in the grass, and an even tinier girl ran over to help him up. The corners of Jen's lips twitched, despite the emptiness inside her, but a squeeze in her chest told her that even that small bit of happiness was too much.

She glared at her phone accusingly. It had quickly become apparent that Will's phone number was seared into her memory, even though it had been at least ten years since she'd remembered anyone's but her own. The harder she tried to forget, the brighter the numbers flared behind her eyelids.

Her eyes remained glued to her phone. Eventually, she unlocked the screen and swiped at it idly, pulling up the keypad. Over the past week she'd done this so many times she'd lost count. It was always the same: she'd stare at her phone for a while, then pull up the keypad and imagine calling him, even dial the number sometimes. Playing this game was bittersweet. While she missed talking to him more than made logical sense, she could not give in.

You need to forget him, she thought at least five hundred times a day. It wasn't Stephanie's heartless brand of "honesty" telling her this. Stephanie had been left behind in California. But whichever voice was in her head, it didn't change the fact that her only options were to forget Will, or to torment herself indefinitely with thoughts of him.

I'm trying.

She always minimized the keypad before it could get her into trouble, but this time she scowled at the numbers she'd typed until the digits spun in circles.

I can't call him.

Or I could call and tell him everything. The question is whether it would help or make it worse.

She was supposed to stay silent about everything until after Brett's trial, but she wasn't sure she could hold it all in that long. The date hadn't even been set.

I betrayed Will in the worst way.

But he deserves the truth, doesn't he?

The more Jen thought about it, the more she became convinced that she owed him an explanation. After working so hard to keep it all from him, now she needed to confess. Maybe it had been the exercise of confessing to the FBI, but she needed to tell Will, too.

Am I being selfish? What will hurt him more? Knowing, or not knowing? He might eventually hear something about me in the news, when Brett goes to trial. Would that be better?

Staring at his phone number, she deliberated. And then, sick of overthinking it, she touched her finger to the green circle, put the phone to her ear, and held her breath.

He's going to hate me, but maybe after this, I can finally let him go.

The ring tone was shrill in her ear, and all at once she was nauseous with anticipation.

"Hello?"

For a second she was elated by the sound of his voice, so full of hope, only to remind herself that she was about to crush him.

"Hi, Will."

"Steph? Is that you?" The happiness in his voice made it worse.

"Yeah. It's me."

"I've been calling you, but it always goes straight to voicemail. I've answered every unknown call I've gotten for the past week, hoping you would call. I've talked to some real characters, let me tell you." He paused for a breath, then spoke more slowly. "Are you okay? What happened? Where are you?"

She kept her voice as even as she could. "I have something I need to tell you, and after that we . . . probably won't talk again."

"Why? What's wrong?" She'd thought her chest couldn't hurt more, but the worry in his voice proved her wrong.

Jen willed herself to remain composed. *Breathe. Say it out loud.* "I called to tell you that . . ." She filled her lungs, then let the air out before continuing. "When I came to work for you, it was because I was hired to kill you." She was relieved that she didn't have to watch his face change as her words sank in.

"You . . . what? No. You saved me. Again and again."

Keep going. She tried to go on, but the words choked her.

"Hello?"

"I know. I was supposed to make it look like an accident. That's all they told me. I'm not sure how you got on their list, but my guess is that after you ran into the guy with the skull tattoo that day in the warehouse, Sal must have contacted my handler. Even though you didn't think anything of it, I assume he was afraid you'd figure out what they were doing."

The silence on the other end of the line was agonizing. When Will finally spoke, it came out as more of a growl. "And what about you? You kill people for a living? That makes you, what? A mercenary? An assassin?"

The truth was the truth, after all. "Yes."

"So Sal got you the job as my assistant so you could kill me and make it look like an accident." He sounded every bit as horrified as she'd been when she got the assignment.

"Yes," she whispered. "And when I got home, the FBI tracked me down. They gave me immunity in exchange for everything I knew about the man Sal contacted. That part of my life is over."

"Oh, let me guess. You're a changed woman now!" He was yelling, and she didn't blame him. She flinched at the rage in his voice.

At that moment, a family walked by her. "Do they really have rockets that went into space, Dad?" one of the young children shouted, and the others joined in. Jen only perceived the commotion, not the words, and let them to pass before continuing.

"I don't expect you to believe me."

"Believe you?" She winced at the hostility in his voice, hunching her shoulders as if he could reach through the phone and grab her. "I did believe you! I never questioned a single thing you said! Even though apparently every goddamn thing was a lie!"

She wished the ground would swallow her.

"So, I guess you weren't really a 'superfan' of the show?" His sarcasm cut through her.

"No, I was! I am—the biggest fan of the show, ever since the first episode." Her voice broke on the last few words.

"You have quite a fucked-up way of showing it."

Her head bobbed in agreement, even though he couldn't see her. "You're right." Exhaling a ragged breath, she kept going. "For years I'd been hired to kill very bad people, at least as far as I knew. When I found out you were my target..." She trailed off and closed her eyes.

Keep going.

"I— I didn't know what to do. I thought you were hiding a dark secret, or something, because why else would they...? I didn't want it to be true, and I had to find out for myself. I wanted to refuse, but I'd never refused an assignment before. I figured they'd kill me if I did. That's not an excuse, but it's the truth."

Even silent, his anger radiated through the phone, making her tremble.

Of course he's furious. I just told him I was hired to kill him, after letting him believe I was his friend. I betrayed him.

"So why didn't you kill me?" Will sounded angrier with every word. "You came all the way out here to do it. What stopped you?"

"It was never something I wanted to do. I was desperate to find a reason not to. And I did." She stared straight ahead at the beautiful summer day, only now aware that tears were streaming down her cheeks. "At first, I assumed I'd been wrong about you, because why else would they have given me this assignment?"

"Wrong about me how?"

"That you were secretly a monster or something, which seemed impossible, because everything I knew about you showed that you were a genuinely nice person. But this assignment made me doubt my instincts, so I—"

"So you would've killed me if you thought I was a bad person? How ironic. That's for you to judge, is it?"

Conscious of her surroundings, she kept her voice low, though her desperation to explain overflowed. "I never wanted to. Not for a second. And I know none of this makes it any better."

I am the absolute scum of the earth.

"You're right. It doesn't."

He would never understand, but she was determined to say what she needed to say anyway. "When I figured out what was happening at the studio, and you confirmed that you'd stumbled into it by mistake, it turned out I'd been right about you in the beginning. I couldn't kill you, no matter how badly I needed the money. I didn't care that it put me in danger. I had to save you, even if I couldn't save myself. And—"

"I've heard enough. I get it now," he said, cutting her off abruptly. "You're the monster. Not me. You."

His words took her breath away. She'd always known it, but coming from him the words cut deeper than ever before.

"I am." Her words were so quiet she barely heard them herself.

They were interrupted by a loud ruckus in the distance. A stage had been set up at the far end of the long strip of grass where she'd plopped down that morning, and someone was standing with a microphone. "Hello, everyone. We'll be doing a sound check for the jazz festival in a few minutes," a voice boomed, and then fell silent.

"Your name's not even Stephanie, is it?" It was more an accusation than a question.

"No. It's Jen."

"Well, Jen," Will spat as if her name had a vile taste, "we're done."

Desperate for something to say, she blurted out the only thing she could come up with. "I'm sorry, Will."

"You should be." His words were hard and angry, and she deserved them.

When he didn't say another word, she pulled the phone back from her ear and confirmed that the call had ended. She was lucky, really. If she'd been in his place, she'd have hung up much sooner.

She told herself to be grateful she'd gotten to say what she wanted to say.

Contrary to her expectation, her confession hadn't lightened her burden at all. Even emptier now than before, she lay in the grass, floating alone on her cloud of unhappiness. *I did the right thing. He deserved the truth, and now he finally has it.* As she repeated this over and over, the gaping hole inside her grew wider and deeper.

Life went on around her. Unable to find the energy to move, she watched the sun sink lower in the sky. Evening fell and the air cooled as sounds of the jazz festival floated on the breeze, but she was barely conscious of any of it. She shoved every bit of frantic emotion into the box in her mind, leaving her with a gaping void and the knowledge that she had created it.

Finally, hours after the crowds dispersed, she stumbled home in the dark.

CHAPTER 33

THE RELENTLESS BEEPING OF THE monitor on the far side of her mother's hospital bed was slowly getting to Jen. She had no idea how long she'd been hunched over in a plastic chair, her elbows balanced against her knees and her head in her hands. After a few minutes of semiconsciousness earlier, some highly effective pain medication had helped her mother drop off to sleep. Jen knew from experience that she wouldn't shake the fear that gripped her until her mother woke up again.

Sitting and waiting went against her nature. She dealt with situations by making a plan and acting on it. Her inability to do anything now but watch her mother sleep made her stir crazy, and helplessness gnawed at her insides.

"Does it help if I tell you that you're the least helpless person I've ever met?" Will's voice echoed in her head, accompanied by the nausea she knew all too well. She pushed both away with all her energy.

In the past month, her whole life had been turned upside down and shaken violently, and the pieces no longer fit together. The worst part was that she had done this to herself. Brett Kingston had influenced her, but her choices had been her own. Adding insult to injury, there was still the issue of how to afford the relentless medical bills. Even if her mother went into remission, the invoices for past treatments would continue to arrive in Jen's mailbox with alarming frequency.

She gritted her teeth hard and fought a rising wave of dread. She couldn't go back to the life she'd finally escaped even if she wanted to, so she had to find another way to deal with the mounting debt. So far, she had yet to come up with a single option.

In the hall, voices rose and fell. A nurse bustled in behind her, but Jen did not turn around, her hands tugging at her hair and her eyes squeezed shut.

"Honey," the woman said softly, placing a gentle hand on her shoulder.

For a split second she saw Will lying on his back that morning after she'd flipped him to the ground. The stab of pain in her heart was intense, but she pulled the spear cleanly through, then shoved the memory away. She'd been doing a lot of that lately, but had yet to discuss this tendency with the therapist she'd been seeing.

Jen slowly turned into the gaze of the kind-faced stranger, who looked about her mother's age. Her mostly gray hair was pulled back tightly, and her nametag read *Hope.* If she'd had any energy to spare, Jen might have laughed at the irony of that.

"You've been sitting there for hours. Chances are that your mom's not going to wake up for a while yet. Why don't you go get yourself something to eat? Just take a few minutes." When Jen started to shake her head, Hope added sternly, "I know your mom wouldn't want you sitting here stewing, would she?" She dropped her hand and moved to check the machine by the bed.

Hope's motherly tone penetrated Jen's numbness, and she had to admit that the nurse was right. Rising from her chair, she saw the older woman's nod of approval from the corner of her eye.

"I'll see you in a little while," Jen whispered to her mother, patting her hand before turning to go. She slipped out of the room, exhaling a sigh at the door latch's soft click.

Glancing up, she was suddenly frozen in place. A familiar gaze stared straight into her eyes from across the hall. As nurses and doctors walked past, interrupting her view, she wondered if she was imagining him.

It can't be.

Her breathing was suddenly the only thing she heard. Standing just as still on the far wall, with the same baseball cap he'd worn at the Griffith Observatory pulled down low, was Will. As she stared, he moved toward her in slow motion, their eyes never leaving each other.

She swallowed hard, trying to calm her thundering heart and pressing her damp palms against her jeans to stop them from shaking. She couldn't tell if the butterfly wings beating wildly in her stomach were caused by excitement or fear, or maybe both.

"You're here," she said, barely loud enough to be heard over the din around them.

He said nothing, just continued to stare at her.

"I was on my way to the cafeteria."

Though he still didn't respond, she grew a little braver with every second that passed without an angry outburst. "Can I buy you a coffee?"

He nodded once, his face serious.

They walked side by side toward the elevator, the tension thick and the questions already beating against the inside of her head.

How? What? Why? But none of them came out.

By the time they'd taken their coffees to a table at the back corner of the cafeteria, he still hadn't said a word to her. The butterflies in her stomach had become angry bees. As they regarded each other warily, Jen was reminded of a place and time not too long ago when they'd sat across from each other with coffees in hand and she'd laughed until her sides hurt. She pushed that memory back into the box, wishing she could forget it permanently.

When he finally spoke, she was unsettled by the iciness of his tone. "I'm really angry with you."

She clenched her teeth and nodded. Of course he was.

"I trusted you, and you lied to me."

She nodded again. Painful as they were, those were the facts.

"Worse than lied. So much worse. You . . ." He shook his head, his face clouding over.

"Yes." Her voice was small, and she took shallow breaths.

"You wanted to kill me."

Her head moved back and forth, the words tumbling out awkwardly. "No. That was why I was there, yes. But I didn't want to."

His arched eyebrow told her than he didn't see a big distinction between the two.

"Then why, if you didn't want to?"

She focused on her coffee, which wasn't any more help with finding the right words than it had been in California. "My mom had cancer. Has cancer. Two years ago, her insurance was about to run out. If I was going to help her, I needed money. A guy I knew— my commanding officer when I was in the Army—had started this . . . business after he got out. He talked about his noble cause, but basically, he was a vigilante. He asked me to work with him. I said no, but then I couldn't find another way to make a lot of money, fast, to pay for her treatments—"

"You said on the phone that you're not still working for him?"

"No. Like I said, I got home and the FBI found me. I told them everything about Brett, and they gave me immunity."

His face gave away nothing. "Let me guess. You said you didn't know better when you started?"

"No, I knew better from the beginning. But for my mom there was almost nothing I wouldn't do. Brett had been a father figure to me. He was my mentor, and I trusted him. For two years, the targets he sent me were the worst of the worst. Terrorists. Monsters. The kind of people—"

She stopped abruptly and hung her head, tears leaking from her eyes. "Yes, I knew it was wrong, but I forced myself to do it anyway.

When they were terrible people, I could pretend I was doing the world a favor. How could I not save my mom's life?"

His face softened just a little.

"Seeing your face as my target, I wanted to believe you weren't one of them. That assignment made me question everything I'd been doing. It turned out that you were right, before, when you said . . ." Emotion overtook her, and her throat closed. Finally she choked out, "You said I was the monster."

Lifting her eyes from the table, she hazarded a glance at his face, which remained stony. "I started therapy. It was one of the conditions of my deal with the FBI."

"Why didn't you kill me?"

The question caught her off guard. "I promised myself that if I could prove you were innocent, I wouldn't do it—even though it was my job. I'm just glad I figured it out."

Something flickered in his eyes. It lasted only a second, and she decided she'd imagined it—until he spoke again. His words weren't warm, but his hostility had diminished.

"That bruise on your cheek is gone."

"What?"

"The last time I saw you, you had a nasty bruise forming on your cheek, right here." His hand moved to his cheek. "That was the first time you saved my life."

She nodded slowly, remembering and flinching when she saw herself hit the ground face-first.

"Did you know they were going to do it? That sniper in the rafters who you"—he made air quotes with his fingers, sarcasm spitting from each word—"'stopped' from shooting me?" More than a hint of accusation hung in the air.

"No! By then I was fairly sure they knew I'd turned against them, and I had a feeling they were going to try something, but I didn't know what. I was trying to watch every direction at once. I couldn't tell you that your life was in danger without telling you how I knew, so—"

"So you chose yourself over me."

A split second of anger flared inside her. *I risked everything to save him!* But he wasn't wrong. At that moment, she had put her well-being before his. Nothing she said would change the past, or the fact that they both knew it. One of the things she was working on in therapy was being honest with herself about her part in what had happened, the good and the bad.

"Yes. I did."

Perhaps he'd expected her to deny it; his face creased as if he was sorely disappointed.

"Usually for work I can lie without a second thought, but lying to you was agony. I told you as much of the truth as I could. Like when I said I'd never been so scared as that night in the closet at the warehouse—that was the truth."

"I wish you'd trusted me enough to tell me all of the truth. When it mattered." His anger had been bad, but the hurt in his voice now was even worse.

Translation: I will never forgive you.

"Yeah. I wish a lot of things."

"When you shot those guys in the infirmary . . . to save me . . ."

His voice seemed to have lost its edge.

"To save us."

"And then you shot the ones at the coffee shop. I'm not even sure how many. To save me again."

When she opened her mouth to correct him, he interrupted her before she could begin.

"You could have run and left me to die. It would've been easier to lose them if you'd been alone, right? I was injured."

She shrugged. "Maybe."

"But you didn't."

"No. How could I?"

He stared at her as if seeing her for the first time. "You got me out of the fire, too. You could've left me there and saved yourself. Either

I would've burned to death or Sal would've shot me."

"Probably."

They stared at each other again, both burdened by the weight of their thoughts.

"I'm really mad at you," he said again, but the anger was gone. This time his voice trembled, and it sounded like he was reminding himself.

She nodded, hoping he'd be done soon so she could escape. There was nothing she could say or do to fix this, and looking at him ate away at her insides. Staring into her coffee cup, she willed the tears behind her eyes to evaporate.

"Why did you save me?" The genuine confusion on his face was yet another stab of heartache.

He sees me as such a monster that he can't understand why I would save his life.

Her chair scraped backwards as she stood. "I'm sorry. I can't." She had to get away. "I'm sorry," she muttered again as she stumbled away from the table, needing to be anywhere but there before she fell apart. Though it didn't make sense, the straw that had broken the camel's back was when the hostility faded from his eyes.

Outside her mother's door, she took a deep breath, swiping at the wetness under her eyes and attempting to paint a smile on her face. She opened the door to find her mother awake, propped up against several pillows and gazing at the TV mounted near the ceiling.

"There's my favorite person," she said as Jen faced away from her to close the door, her composure already slipping. It was pointless, she knew, to pretend with her mother, the one person who could read her best.

As Jen feared, Marilyn Calley's adoring smile disappeared. "What's wrong, Jellybean?"

Lowering herself into the uncomfortable plastic chair by the bed and pulling it closer, Jen sat as far forward as she could, her knees against the metal rail, and took her mom's outstretched hand. Her mother's squeeze gave her the strength to form the words, though her voice shook.

"Will's here."

The older woman's eyebrows shot up. "Did you talk to him?"

"Yeah, he was waiting in the hall when I left a little while ago."

"And?"

"We went downstairs and got some coffee, and he told me how angry he is at me."

"Well, that's understandable, considering the circumstances."

Jen nodded, feeling the dam breaking inside her as her face crumpled.

"Oh, Jellybean, come here." Marilyn pulled Jen onto the bed beside her, into a tight hug, slowly stroking her hair like she used to long ago.

"I know. I just can't—" Jen broke off, unable to speak with free-flowing tears.

Once the flood had subsided, her mother spoke again, gently. "So? What happened?"

Jen sat back far enough to look at her. "I could handle him telling me he was mad at me. But then he started talking about how I saved his life, and he asked me why I did it." Her breathing faltered, but she pushed on. "I know I didn't deserve the way he looked at me before—like I was someone he liked and respected. But he looks at me now and sees a monster, so the fact that I saved his life doesn't make sense to him. I can't stand it."

"And when someone you love sees you that way, it hurts," her mother said in a soothing voice.

Jen went rigid, her eyes widening. "What? Why would you . . . ?" She digested her mother's words slowly, her head shaking as her face crumpled. Marilyn pulled her close, which released the floodgates of her tears again, and she melted against the older woman's shoulder.

"Okay, Jellybean, okay," she murmured. After that, neither spoke again until after Jen's sobs had subsided. "Maybe he's angry and grateful. I imagine he's probably confused. But it says something that he's here, doesn't it?"

"That he wanted to yell at me in person?" Jen's voice was thick with self-pity, which Marilyn ignored.

"Did he yell at you?"

"No. He should have, though."

Her mother sighed. "I'm sorry you're so deep in this because of me." Jen tried to shake her off to correct her, but Marilyn held firm to her daughter's shoulders and looked her in the eyes. "Don't you dare tell me you'd have joined up with a hitman, no matter how noble his cause or who he was to you, for any other reason. Because I'm still mad that you did it for me. You'd be in even more trouble if you did it for anything else."

Jen stifled a laugh, even as she cried. "No, of course not. But—"

"So that means you're in this because of me." Her *don't argue with me* tone told Jen that protesting wouldn't do any good, so she stopped trying. "You shouldn't have done it, of course, but I understand. If I had your skills, and something threatened you that way, I'd have done the same thing. But you have to promise me that you're out for good."

"I am. I swear," she whispered. "And it helps that the FBI are watching me now, of course."

"Good. Now, I want you to go home and get some rest. You look like something ran you over."

Jen was too emotionally exhausted to react to her mother using the same words that Brett had, back at the beginning. She took deep breaths until the pain in her chest subsided. Though she didn't want to leave, she was exhausted. "Okay. I'll be back tomorrow. I love you, Mom."

"I love you, too, Jellybean."

She kept an eye out for Will on the way to her car, disappointed but not surprised when he was nowhere to be seen. *He's probably on his way home already.*

It couldn't be any other way, of course, but it was painful to think that he'd been right in front of her and there was nothing she could do to fix things with him. She allowed herself a heavy sigh as the elevator doors creaked shut, then told herself to get over it. Some things in life weren't meant to work out.

The fact that Will had said that once upon a time only hurt for a second, before she stuffed the thought into the box with the rest of them. She had embraced enough of her feelings for one day.

CHAPTER 34

THE NEXT MORNING, THE SUNSHINE was extra blinding as she climbed into her car for the drive back to the hospital. Despite her best efforts, she searched for Will everywhere she looked, resulting in a constant sense of disappointment. The hard truth was that he was gone, and she was back to post-Will, day one. This time it was a hundred times worse.

At the hospital, Marilyn was in an especially cheerful mood, and she chatted on and on. A large vase of pink and white lilies had appeared beside her bed since Jen's departure the day before. "Beautiful, aren't they?" Marilyn asked when she caught Jen looking at them.

"Who are they from?"

"There was no card. I thought maybe there were from you." Her devilish grin suggested that she thought no such thing.

Somehow Jen kept a smile plastered on her face and held up her end of the conversation, though her mother did most of the talking. Doctors and nurses came and went, and Jen sat back and let them work, taking the interludes as short vacations from the strain of pretending to be okay.

As one of the nurses left, Marilyn reminded her of her promise to send in the "hot doctor" who was on shift that day, and Jen once again pulled her chair toward the bed, shaking her head in amusement. Her energy was fading, and she had a feeling her mother was going to send her home to rest soon, as she had the day before. As much as she wanted to be at her mother's bedside, she looked forward to crawling under the covers and blocking out the world.

"Jellybean, don't take this the wrong way, but you don't look like you slept last night. I'd send you home, but I have a feeling that the young man behind you would probably like to speak to you before you go."

Jen's head whipped around to find Will standing only a few feet behind her, shifting awkwardly from foot to foot by the door.

Now that his presence was known, he stepped toward the bed. "I'm sorry to intrude, ma'am. My name is Will Bryant." He extended a hand, which Jen's mother shook with a smile.

"Well, Mr. Bryant, I've heard a lot about you. I'm Marilyn Calley. Recent events notwithstanding, you should know that to say that my daughter is a big fan of yours would be like saying the Grand Canyon is a hole in the ground."

"*Mom*," Jen squeaked out, her face turning bright pink. Will's soft chuckle only made her color deepen. She was acutely aware of how close he was. Fixing her mother with a wide-eyed stare, she willed her not to say anything else that would embarrass her, unsure whether to laugh with delight or cry in despair.

Marilyn's laughter echoed through the room, and she leaned forward to kiss Jen on the forehead. "I'm sure it wasn't a secret, Jellybean. You've never been good at hiding your feelings."

She'd hidden many things from Will, but her true feelings were not among them, no matter how she'd tried.

Apparently finished torturing her daughter, Marilyn looked back up at Will. "Do I have you to thank for these flowers, Will? They're beautiful."

"Yes, ma'am. I'm glad you like them."

"Well, thank you very much. They've brightened things up around here." Looking down at Jen, she whispered, "Turn around, already."

Jen turned slowly and met his gaze again. This time neither of them looked away, sparks of emotion flaring between them.

"Jen, could I talk to you when you have a second?"

He seemed different today. Lighter. Her muscles tightened in anticipation.

"I come in peace, I promise." Raising both hands in surrender, he gave her an embarrassed half smile.

Looking back and forth between them in amusement, Marilyn gave her daughter a playful shove. "Go on, talk to Will. I'm fine here. And then go home and get some sleep. Just text me when you get home, if you remember."

Jen turned back to her mother and nodded, less panicked but more confused than the day before. In her mother's expression there was serenity—and maybe joy?

How can she possibly be enjoying this?

Except, Will had just given her half a smile. *But that doesn't mean anything. Or does it?*

"Okay. I'll see you tomorrow."

When she kissed her mother on the cheek, she caught her quiet instructions: "Hear him out." With a nod, Jen sat back and allowed a look of understanding to pass between them, giving her answer without a word: *Only for you.*

Standing stiffly and attempting a smile for her mother, Jen followed Will out of the room, her insides churning. The waves of anger that had flowed out of him the day before were gone, replaced by a hint of the familiarity that had existed between them in California. Still, she could not relax.

He kept his head down, the same baseball cap pulled low, but even so, she heard a few whispers as they walked down the hall.

"Was that Will Bryant? I heard he was here yesterday."

Jen could only hope that people would leave them alone.

They settled on a bench in the far corner of a garden on the hospital grounds. The buildings were blocked by greenery, and Will faced away from anyone who might happen by. Jen sat angled toward him, her back stiff, with a generous amount of space between them.

Will Bryant was the most handsome man she'd ever laid eyes on, but as she studied him now, all she saw were her own mistakes. Her insides twisted, winding tighter and tighter as she waited for him to say whatever he'd come to say. But the silence stretched on, the two of them watching each other and taking turns looking away. Finally, she couldn't stand it any longer.

"So, what are we doing here?" she blurted out. "You already made it crystal clear that you're angry at me. And with very good reason." Before he could reply, she added, in a tone more pleading than defiant, "Before you disappear again, at least tell me how you found me."

"Okay," he said slowly. "But I want to point out that you're the one who got up and left—both times, actually."

She blinked in surprise, having forgotten that detail. "Oh. Right."

A look of amusement crossed his face. "As far as how I found you? Believe it or not, you gave me almost everything I needed to find you when you called me."

Frantically trying to rewind her hazy memory of that day, she couldn't think of anything she'd said that might have given her away.

"First of all, you didn't block your phone number. Granted, a DC number doesn't necessarily mean you're calling from DC, but it was something. The rest I got from the background noise. Kids yelling about the Air and Space Museum, an announcement for the Jazz Festival. Don't forget, I know DC. Those things added up."

"I . . . It didn't even occur to me to block my number or go somewhere quiet. I wasn't planning to call you. All of a sudden I'd dialed, and I told myself not to press call, but I did it anyway. Afterwards, I realized how stupid that was, and I thought about changing my number, but it wasn't as though you were going to call me back. And I'd already gotten in trouble with the FBI by that point, so if you'd called the police on me, it wouldn't have mattered much." Her eyes bobbed down to her lap, then back up to meet his.

The muscles in his face twitched slightly. "You were sitting on the Mall, weren't you? When you called me?"

"Yeah. Bad idea, apparently." It hadn't been a joke, exactly, but his mouth tilted upwards ever so slightly, making her heart squeeze in a way that was both more and less painful than before.

She closed her eyes and plowed forward. "I hadn't memorized a phone number in ten years, maybe more, but apparently I couldn't forget yours. I dialed it a thousand times but never pressed call. Until then." Her eyes opened slowly to gauge his reaction.

His expression had softened, and his voice held an unexpected surge of emotion. "Do you know how badly I wanted to talk to you?"

Her lip trembled. "Maybe you've forgotten what I said when I called?"

He frowned but said nothing.

"I tried to stop myself because it was selfish of me, wanting to confess. I knew you would hate me. It sounds ridiculous, after going there to kill you, but the last thing I wanted was to hurt you. So I told myself it was best to let you go without explaining." She sighed, forcing the words out and wincing when her voice cracked. "I tried. I just couldn't."

"I'm glad."

She shook her head, fighting a stinging sensation around her eyes as her voice wavered. "You weren't."

"No. But I am now."

She ignored the kindness in his voice. It only made things more complicated. "So, that's how you got to DC. How did you end up here? DC is two hours away."

"Remember that keychain you have with a coffee logo on it? The one with just the picture? I searched for it online. Combined with

DC, it came up in a search. Going to Jane's was a long shot, but it turned out that there are a few waitresses there who were possibly even more concerned about your whereabouts than I was."

She grimaced, imagining the young waitresses' confusion at her unexpected absence.

"One of them mentioned that your mom had been treated for cancer at a hospital out this way in the past. This was the biggest hospital in the area, so I started here. It was an even longer shot, but once those waitresses gave me your full name, I spent some time online and found your mom's name."

Her thoughts must have showed on her face, because his voice was suddenly full of concern. "What's wrong?"

"It seems like nothing compared to everything else, but I just hate that you had to ask them my name."

He gave her a sad smile of understanding, nodded, and kept talking. "And then I got lucky again, because after I signed a few autographs, one of the nurses let me in." Will grinned hesitantly. "I just hope I didn't get her in trouble."

Jen stared at her hands, which clasped and unclasped on her lap, her mouth drawn into a tight line. As backwards as it sounded, his kindness was making this harder.

"But why go to all that trouble just to tell me that you're angry with me? You didn't think I felt bad enough? Because trust me, I do." One tear managed to escape down her cheek before she swiped her fingers under both eyes.

He slid closer to her on the bench and caught her fidgeting hands in his, pulling them together and forming a protective outer layer around them. Remembering his temper all too well from the day he'd pushed her out of the way, she went still.

He must have seen the fear in her face. "It's okay," he said under his breath.

His grip on her hands was gentle, and he was looking at her more like the old Will had looked at her, the one she'd known in California.

The urge to run retreated. She would listen to whatever he'd come to say, no matter how horrible it was.

"When I left home, part of me did still want to scream at you. But I had a lot of time to think on the way here. I admit that when I saw you yesterday, the anger came out first. After we talked, I had to decompress a little, and process everything you said. But I was never just angry. The fact that you saved my life more than once was difficult to reconcile with . . . the rest of it. I'd already repaid you for that by being as cruel as I could on the phone. Looking back . . ."

He shook his head. "I thought about it a lot. Justified or not, that's not a person I want to be. I hated myself for the way I treated the people around me after Ryan died, and I thought I'd learned my lesson. But I guess I still have some work to do on myself." He paused. "I wish I could take back the things I said when you called."

"No, I—"

But he didn't let her go on. "Please listen. It's important to me that you hear this. And I'm not good at this—being emotional without a script."

She smiled a little, her face twitching with emotion. Will didn't usually lack confidence, and it made her feel a little better to see that she wasn't the only vulnerable one.

"I've been trying to imagine what I would've done in your shoes. What you were doing was horrible, but . . . it came from a good place. I had to get past the way it started."

Again she opened her mouth to speak, but he lifted an eyebrow at her and she closed it again. "I wouldn't have been anywhere near as brave as you were. You risked your life for me, again and again, when you didn't have to. You deserve to hear me say it in person. I'm sorry. I was an asshole."

Her head was already shaking back and forth, and fresh tears welled up, a few of them spilling over and rolling down her cheeks. She focused on his hands, which tightened around hers. "No." It came out in a whisper the first time, and then more forcefully. "No. That's ridiculous. I don't deserve an apology from you. I'm a monster."

"Don't say that!" Appearing surprised at the vehemence of his own tone, he took a breath, and his next words came out calmly but firmly. "I'm sorry. I didn't mean to snap at you." He shook his head. "You're not a monster. A monster would never have had second thoughts about killing me. A monster wouldn't have saved me, even once. When I called you that, I was being cruel on purpose because I was angry. That's on me, not you. There's no excuse for my behavior."

Her head shook hard enough to make her dizzy, and the tears fell faster, blurring her vision. "No! You were the victim! You were right. And I'm sorry. For all of it. I never should've—"

"Jen, stop. Please." The urgency in his voice had never been there before, and his hands squeezed hers harder. He waited for her to catch her breath before going on, slowly and deliberately. "We never know for sure what we'd do in someone else's shoes. We all like to believe that we'd never do something like . . ."

"Like what I did."

He nodded. "But that's easy to say when you're not the one in that situation. Desperation can make us do things we hate. All this, it happened, and there's no changing it. But that's the thing. I wouldn't change it." He let his words sink in for a few beats. "Because if not for you, I'd be dead. Sal would have hired someone to kill me no matter what. But no one else he hired would've thought twice. No one except you. You are the only reason I'm alive today. I'm sorry I couldn't see that before."

She opened her mouth again, but he kept talking.

"I know you're sorry. It's all kind of a mess, and I didn't think I could get past it, but I thought about it a lot since I was here yesterday. No, it was all I thought about. I barely slept last night. Seeing you again—the real you—I thought I'd say all the bitter things I wanted to say and walk away, and that would be that. I thought it would make me feel better. But I didn't feel better; I felt worse. I realized that I didn't want that to be the end. I guess a big reason why I was so angry was that . . ."

He paused, inhaling slowly before continuing. "Being around you was so easy. I know you were pretending to be Stephanie, but at the same time, you were Jen. Your reasons for being there were a lie, but what was between us . . . I could be wrong, but I think that was real." His voice shook.

"That was what scared me the most," she whispered.

"When you disappeared, there was a hole in my life where you should have been, even though we hadn't known each other long. I guess it hurt more to find out that you hadn't been who I thought you were because I liked you so much."

Liked. Past tense.

She bit down hard on her lip, trying to dull the new pain. She tried to pull her hands back from his, but he kept hold of them.

"Wait! Let me finish." She stilled, the urge to fight against his words getting weaker every moment. "I obviously don't love the reason you were there, but what you did was very brave. You should feel good about that."

She lifted her gaze hesitantly toward him, and neither looked away. "I don't feel good about anything anymore." They watched each other, and he kept hold of her hands, his thumbs barely moving back and forth over her knuckles. She hated that the sensation was relaxing, and she told herself she didn't like it—which was just another lie.

As if he knew she had reached her breaking point, he changed the subject. "How is your mom doing now?"

"She had been doing much better until right before, uh, before I left for California. And then she ended up back here. She's been in and out. They've done more tests, and I don't know. Some days are good, some not so good. You never know with experimental treatments."

"And her insurance ran out?"

"Yeah, she hit her insurance's lifetime maximum almost two years ago, so it's been all out of pocket since then. Even if she goes back into remission, I still have to finish paying for the treatments she's already had. And if it ever comes back . . ." Her pulse accelerated, and to her dismay, she felt herself shaking. "Anyway, she's not great, but for now she's okay."

"Let me help you."

Even the vague suggestion made her tense. "There's nothing you can—"

"Let me pay for it."

Her breathing faltered. "What? No, I'm making a plan for that."

He looked at her evenly, even as she now avoided his eyes. "What are your other options?"

For a moment she considered making something up, but she had lied to him too much already. "I don't have any yet."

"Jen, you saved my life. Let me do something for you."

She stared up at him, wide eyed, desperate to make him understand. "No! Saving you was the only decent thing I could do after getting myself mixed up in all that. I owed you that much, and so much more. I don't deserve a reward. And it's too expensive. I couldn't ask that of you."

"You didn't ask; I offered. And not to brag, but I can afford it."

"You don't even know how much it is."

"How much is it?"

The numbers swam behind her eyes, and she flinched. He'd called her bluff. She didn't actually know the total, only that it was huge. "Too much," she murmured.

He spoke softly, leaning into her again. "Please let me do this for you. I want to help. It doesn't have to be you against the world."

She stared at him in confusion. A few stray tears slid down her cheeks, but this time she let them fall. Her resolve was weakening.

"Wow, and I thought you buying me a dress and shoes were a big deal."

When his exhale sounded like a second of laughter, lightness bloomed in her chest. His eyes crinkled the way they always had when he used to smile at her. Before.

Her eyes squeezed together tightly, releasing more tears. She tuned out everything but the sensation of his thumbs moving lightly across her knuckles until, little by little, she could breathe normally.

"Will you think about it at least?"

She nodded, her energy suddenly depleted.

He inched closer to her on the bench until their knees touched, then leaned forward until he could whisper in her ear. "Please don't cry anymore. You don't have to keep punishing yourself. And you don't have to do this alone."

She lifted her eyes just far enough to focus on his hands, which were still clasped around hers. Without stopping to think, she dropped her head forward, closing the distance between them until her temple rested against the side of his face. Slowly, he shifted just enough to brush a soft kiss on her cheek.

"Hey." He sat back a few inches, waiting until he had her attention before continuing. "I don't know everything about you, but I know you're a good person. I've seen you at your best."

"You mean my worst."

"No, I mean your best. Maybe not your happiest, but I like to think I'll get to see that, too."

Will's words rolled around in her head. She'd been stumbling down a dark tunnel alone for so long that she was afraid to believe it could be any different, or that anyone could help her. Having hope was a wonderful, terrifying thing.

His expression was sincere. "Do you think we could start over? It would be nice to get to know the real you without anyone trying to kill us. Although running for our lives did give me a lot of reasons to end up close to you, so it wasn't all bad."

His mischievous grin resurfaced, and she blushed at the flashes of memory: teetering on her tiptoes to help an injured and bare-chested Will put his T-shirt back on in the exam room at the studio infirmary, his steadying hand on her waist; kneeling in front of him in a burning building, her hand on his cheek as she yelled his name, and a rush of adrenaline shooting through her veins as he opened his eyes; and then standing in front of him and holding pressure on the gunshot wound in his upper arm, her forehead against his good shoulder, each of them with an arm around the other as sirens screamed in the background. The heartbreak she'd felt at that moment, knowing it was their last, was just beginning to overwhelm her again when his voice snapped her back to the present.

"Seriously, though, I mean it. Give us another chance?"

"But I don't deserve—"

His index finger landed across her lips, stopping her from finishing her sentence and sending a charge through her as he said simply, "Yes, you do."

His hand returned to hers, and Jen watched the tiny specks of green within the brown of his eyes as they danced around his pupils. Slowly, her muscles began to unclench.

She couldn't form a coherent thought to explain her hesitation.

"You know you can trust me, right?"

She nodded, the words sticking in her throat, emerging only with great effort. "You're the only one I trust. I mean, besides my mom. But why . . . why would you trust me?"

"Because I know you. The real you. That's all I need."

She exhaled slowly, still trying to wrap her head around it all.

Maybe . . .

During the past few confusing weeks, she had rejected the possibility that she could rebound from this. Even her therapist couldn't get her to believe it. But now, looking into Will's eyes, the thought formed all on its own.

Maybe I can be okay.

"Maybe" wasn't certainty, but it was a first step.

It was all too good to be true, except Will was there in front of her, holding her hands. If he could forgive her, shouldn't she be able to forgive herself?

I want to be the person Will sees in me. Maybe I can.

"I have to tell you one more thing. It's important."

She steeled herself. "What's that?"

"Before, you said that when you called me to confess, you knew I'd hate you. I hope you've already figured out that I don't hate you."

"But you did," she said stubbornly.

"It was never that simple, and you know it. I wouldn't be here if it was."

Her mother's words echoed in her head. *And when someone you love sees you that way, it hurts.* The opposite was also true—if he could see good in her, maybe she could find it in herself, too.

Oh God, that's so cheesy. Please don't say that out loud.

As she stared up at him, her mouth curved into a genuine smile for the first time in two weeks. "Okay."

"Okay what?" The kindness in his eyes was too good to be true.

"Okay, I would really like for us to start over."

"Good."

His forehead creased when she pried her hands out of his and sat back just far enough so she had space to extend her right hand toward him. "Okay then. Hi, I'm Jen. It's nice to meet you. I feel like I've seen you somewhere before. What was your name again?"

Will's confusion gave way to a smile, and laughter danced in his eyes as he took her hand, encircling it in familiar warmth. "It's a pleasure to meet you too, Jen. I'm Will."

ACKNOWLEDGMENTS

GEMINI DIVIDED **WOULD PROBABLY NOT** have come into existence if I hadn't spent years obsessed with USA Network's *Covert Affairs* (2010–2014) and NBC's *Blindspot* (2015–2020). Those two TV shows and a few others like them hooked me with their dramatic storylines that still had room for strong emotional connections between the characters and just enough romance. So thank you, Matt Corman, Chris Ord, and everyone who worked on *Covert Affairs*, as well as Martin Gero and the team who created *Blindspot*. My obsession with these shows led me to reading all the fanfic I could get my hands on, which led me to writing—first fanfic of my own, then original stories. I am where I am today because of the TV shows I watched over the past ten years.

A special thank-you to Denise Eckert Bled for reading every single draft of this book she could get her hands on, each time with the enthusiasm of the most devoted fangirl, and giving me round after round of comments—both constructive and just plain enthusiastic. All those hours of international texting helped make Jen and Will their best selves.

I would also like to thank Heather Dixon and LN Russell for

being fantastic critique partners, and the Spun Yarn for an immensely detailed feedback report. This book would never have gotten this far without you.

And of course, thank you to John Koehler, Miranda Dillon, Hannah Woodlan, Joe Coccaro, and the whole team at Koehler Books for being wonderful to work with.

ABOUT THE AUTHOR

LAUREN ROBERTS IS A RECOVERING elementary school teacher. She writes books about stubbornly independent women whose lives have spun out of their control, helping them land safely on their feet. After moving from city to city all her life, she settled in Northern Virginia with her husband, three kids, and their rescue dog, Thor—who is, ironically, afraid of thunder. *Gemini Divided* is her debut novel.

Find Lauren online at
www.laurenkristenroberts.com
Twitter: @LaurenKRoberts
Instagram: laurenkrobertsauthor
Facebook: @LaurenKristenRoberts